Graveyard Love

Graveyard Love

T. C. Littles

www.urbanbooks.net

Urban Books, LLC
300 Farmingdale Road, NY-Route 109
Farmingdale, NY 11735

ISBN 13: 978-1-64556-143-9
ISBN 10: 1-64556-143-7

First Mass Market Printing January 2021
First Trade Paperback Printing July 2019
Printed in the United States of America

10 9 8 7 6 5 4 3 2 1

Distributed by Kensington Publishing Corp.
Submit Orders to:
Customer Service
400 Hahn Road
Westminster, MD 21157-4627
Phone: 1-800-733-3000
Fax: 1-800-659-2436

Graveyard Love

by

T. C. Littles

The Voice of a Battered Woman

I wasn't born a bitch; I was made into a bitch. And because of the power of his fist, I'll probably die being a bitch. To the woman who can truly say—"he made me do it," I believe that shit and rock with you to the end. To the woman who can't cry, has cried her last tear, or who is crying right now . . . Dry your tears and tell yourself you're beautiful underneath the scars. Sometimes, all we need is a power-up partner. Sometimes, all we need is real love and a free space to receive and give love. That's all I needed. Be a warrior for your soul, your peace, and all the women who have been silenced.

—Jakia

1

Jakia

My eyes popped open to Spade giving me early-morning head. It felt like he was writing his name into my soul with his tongue. Part of me wanted to enjoy the sexual moment because it was taking me to the clouds that laced heaven, but I was scared to get comfortable with him. His Gemini split-personality wasn't one to fuck with. I don't think I've ever witnessed Spade be a cuddly, warm-hearted Negro.

Spencer "Spade" Johnson was a mean son of a bitch with rigid rules and a hard hand to dish out swift and severe consequences if the rules were broken. His temper is worse than any savage I've seen or known. I've endured more lumps and knots, bites and bruises, and scars of low self-esteem with him than I did growing up with my abusive mother. She's the one who taught me how to take a beating and keep it moving. The only reason I wasn't numb to Spade's ass whoopings was that he was a male. I often wished he'd keep it on his mental that I was his girl.

I never left the house without rocking huge, framed shades to mask my swollen, red eyes. No matter how hard I tried to warm his iced heart, Spade took advantage of my young and fragile mind and manipulated me into thinking I couldn't survive without him. He knew how I grew up and how much I relied on my brother, so it was easy for him to slide in and use me for what he needed me for. He knew that my mother was so strung out on drugs and more concerned with chasing a scheme so she could get high that she wouldn't see me slipping me through the cracks or be strong enough to save me from a savage like him. Some days, it felt like he got off on tormenting my mind, body, and soul. Matter of fact, I'm sure he did. All I could do was pray his cruel behavior wouldn't last forever.

"Oh my God, Spade . . . Why can't you love on me like this all the time?" I moaned and squirmed uncontrollably.

Although Spade's been having a problem with keeping me emotionally happy, he's never had a problem stroking my body into pure pleasure. Spade trained me how to please him sexually as soon as we got together, but it got hella intense when I moved in. He had me watching pornos and imitating his favorite stars, plus maneuvering my young body into positions that had me sore for days. I kind of miss those days because that's when shit was simple between us.

"'Cause you don't be acting right," he said between licks. "Now shut up and enjoy gettin' ya pussy ate before I get out of the mood and stop." Then he dove back between my legs.

The last thing I wanted to do was piss him off during sex. Spade wasn't the type of nigga you could withhold your goodies from. I hurried up and arched my back, then grinded my vagina into his mouth like I was riding his dick. If he wanted me to explode in his mouth, I would. I was submissive to everything Spencer Spade Johnson wanted.

Somebody once told me that if you controlled a bitch's mind, the body would follow; and they ain't never lied. Spade had stroked me out both mentally and physically. The more I fell in love with him, the more he gassed me up in preparation for what his ultimate plan was.

"It's yours. I'm yours. Oh my God, I'm about to come." I lost control over my senses and my limbs.

"Are you feelin' good, ma?" He came up from between my thighs with a mouth full of come.

"Hell yeah. I'm *better* than good." I cuddled up to my pillow and smiled at him. "That was amazing." I was drained from the earth-shattering orgasm he'd just brought me to. "That was one helluva way to say good morning."

"I know, so get that mouth ready to service your man. I only went first 'cause a nigga felt a li'l bad for last night." He didn't give me time to enjoy the apology before he whipped his dick out and dipped into my mouth.

My throat was sore from his aggression as my saliva mixed with his precome fell from the corners of my mouth. I struggled not to gag from his humongous mushroom as I felt it swelling up.

Giving him on-demand head should've been something I was used to. I've lost control of being able to say when I want it and how I want it. Spade cupped my chin and jaws tightly with his right hand as he slow-guided his meat in and out of my mouth with his left hand. I was a pro at pleasing him, just as he was at pleasing me, and it only took a few seconds for me to feel him tensing up.

"Let it go," I hummed and tickled his shaft with my tongue.

"Then suck it harder." Spade plunged himself into my mouth like he was trying to find my tonsils.

I felt his thighs lock up and his booty cheeks clench together right before his bitter nut hit the insides of my cheeks.

"Don't stop until you suck all that nut up outta this monster." He bit his lip like a girl as his body shook like an earthquake. I almost suffocated from the weight of him being on top of me. This was the only time I could ever get Spade at a disadvantage. After shooting a long stream of warm semen down my throat, he pulled out and sprayed the rest all over my face. "That's right, you pretty-ass bitch. Let me coat this shit on yo' face like you do that clown-ass makeup." He mushed and rubbed the tip of his penis all over my face, then fell back on the bed gasping for air. "You be having a nigga acting sissy soft with your dick-sucking skills, girl," he half-joked.

I rolled over and wiped his come from my face as he rolled over to grab his ever-ringing phone. I stayed irked by him being in love with the streets, but that was what got me here in the first place, so I played my position with the best of 'em.

Spade stroked me slow, mind-fucked me hard, and manipulated me into believing I couldn't survive without him. But in reality, he'd groomed me into being his number one moneymaker.

It was easy because he was my only lifeline. I didn't have anyone else to turn to or nowhere else to go. We were in a relationship, but it felt like I was the only one against the world.

He had me strung out on having the finer things in life, not the ragamuffin hand-me-downs I had all while growing up. I was hella grateful that he'd upgraded me from having nothing but scraps. My closet was filled with designer labels, my house was decked out with plush furniture and flat-screen smart televisions, and I wore diamonds because they were my only best friends. Spade didn't allow me to have friends.

"Hey, babe, you might wanna rest up for a minute while I hop in the shower and make a few calls." Spade climbed out of bed, then slid on his boxers. "I gotta see whose money is up for the taking."

"Yeah, whatever. You're probably going in there to cake with that trick, Tiff," I scowled, bringing up his ex-girlfriend. Ever since I stepped in and took her position, she'd been doing double backs with Spade as a payback to me for stealing him.

"Don't start on no bullshit, Jakia. I'm about to holla at these streets. Ain't nobody thinking about ole girl but you. You're acting way too pressed."

I knew he was lying by the smirk on his face. "Whatever, Spade. I might let you play me like I'm dumb, but I ain't no damn fool. I know you still mess around with Tiff."

"I'm gonna bring her into this muthafuckin' bedroom if you keep bringing her up," he threatened me with a devilish smirk on his face, then slammed the bathroom door.

A second later, I heard the shower turn on and Spade's voice mumbling. Knowing his trifling ass, he was taking a dump and talking to Tiff. I dare not say another word because I wasn't down to have a threesome with his ex. If he'd spoken it out loud, then he'd already thought about doing it. Tiff could have him back if it came down to me having to get down with her.

"You've gotta find a way to uncross your heart, Jakia," I told myself, then dozed off.

Eighteen Months Ago . . .

"Whatchu doing, baby sis?"

"Nothing much. Bored. Momma didn't pay the cable bill with the money you gave her, so I've been forced to watch these old sitcoms that have been out of syndication since you were born." I rolled my eyes, wishing I had some fresh clothes to go outside in. I was tired of getting talked about. Even though I wasn't having sex, many of the girls my age were and getting broke off by the dope boys who loved young twat. They always came at me sideways because I wasn't rocking fly clothes and kicks that cost a grip.

"Well, I'll give you the money tomorrow to go pay the bill. Me and the crew are about to go out and hit up a few stash houses." My brother Juan was a stick-up kid.

I was happy that he was going to get some money to pay the bill but didn't want him risking his life. "I hope your crew ain't Spencer and Rashad. Ma said them niggas are always in trouble and that you're gonna end up in trouble too if you keep runnin' up behind them." I didn't always listen to our mother, but I had a weird feeling in my stomach that she was right this time.

"Fuck what Momma talking about. She was probably high when she told you that. I ain't never been caught slipping, and I sho' ain't about to start getting caught up now that I'm getting put on to some real money. Spencer and Rashad be getting inside info on muthafuckas that be having that bread, sis," my brother spoke confidently about the two street thugs I had no trust in.

"I know Momma be off them rocks, bro; but that might be even more reason why you might want to listen to her. She be hittin' up the same stash houses you be creepin' into, which doesn't necessarily sound like the smartest plan."

"Says the same person who always has their hand out for some money," he snapped. "Keep ya nose up outta my business and don't wait up." He walked out of the house.

Neither of us knew that was the last time we'd stand in our mother's house together, or that we'd have a word-for-word disagreement between us without a thick piece of security glass separating us. Juan ended up getting caught up in a case that sat him down for a few years.

I still remember how my heart crumbled into a million pieces when I first heard his voice on the collect call.

"What, Juan? You ain't killed nobody, so why are you facing so many years? It doesn't make any sense," I helplessly cried into the phone because there was nothing else I could do.

"I know it, sis. But they are trying to make an example out of me. I might gotta take one for the team. Holla at my manz Spade, though. He'll look out for you while I do this bid. I made him promise me that you wouldn't want for nothing."

"Ain't nobody thinking about his creep-foul behind. He's the one who got you in this mess." I copped an attitude at Juan for even suggesting I link up with the one responsible for his demise. "What about a lawyer? Maybe they can get you out since this is your first offense." I tried coming up with solutions.

"Naw, baby sis. Don't waste your time with a fantasy. We barely had money to eat daily, so you know there ain't no money for an attorney," he killed my faith. "There's a stash in my room, though. Go cop that; then sell everything else in there. You should at least be able to get a few grand off all the Jordans and shit. Don't let nobody get off on you with no lowball prices either."

"Okay," was all I could say because my voice was caught in my throat. I couldn't believe I was making plans on how to survive without my big brother.

"Make sure your stubborn ass goes to holla at Spade for whatever you need, sis. I'll call again when I can. Hold yo' head up and don't get caught up in Mom's bullshit," Juan blurted out across the jail's hotline before the line went dead.

Tears were streaming down my face like a faucet. I couldn't believe he was willing to take a case for some dumb-ass hot boys that barely made him an afterthought. Juan hadn't been down twenty-four hours before ole Phoebe was on to something more than little white rocks.

"Ma, where are you? Juan's been locked up," I erratically screamed throughout our tiny run-down house. When she didn't answer, I pulled the spare key I had for Juan's dead bolt, unlocked the door, and went in. I had to follow through on my brother's orders so I could be prepared when he called back.

"Wow, wow, wow," was all I could mutter as I hung my head low. "This right here is truly the low point of today."

Juan's room was trashed and emptied. His fifty-inch plasma television was no longer mounted on the wall, the dresser drawers were bare and tossed across the room, all of his gold jewelry was gone, and, of course—every sneaker box was empty. Phoebe's petty ass even took the sheets off his bed.

I knew it was a waste of time searching for his stash because that was probably the first thing she pocketed, so

I scrapped his room as valueless and came out more deflated than I was when I went in it. Come to find out, ole Phoebe caught wind of the news through the hood grapevine during late-night hours while she ran in the back alleys. And with the help of her crackhead comrades, they came through Juan's window so they wouldn't wake me and cleaned him out completely.

When it was all said and done, my brother ended up getting stuck with a whack-ass public defender and only a few dollars from Spade and Rocko for a suit. His chances started as slim but ended up being severely bleak.

With just my moms and me in the house, there was no filter to the bullshit. For one month straight, which seemed like an eternity of hell, I watched Phoebe run guys through our front door like it was a legal-running brothel. She didn't bother taking them to her bedroom as she sucked, slobbed, and took it in the ass in the kitchen, living room, or even the front porch if our house was too hot for rocks. Phoebe got down raw. I was lucky she didn't try tricking me out.

When it was time for Juan's trial, I sat in the tiny, cold courtroom staring at the blue and gold State of Michigan seal positioned behind the judge's bench and prayed that my brother would walk out a free man. The butterflies in my stomach tripled with the sight of his deteriorated appearance and had me fearing the absolute worst.

All I heard was the judge saying was, "Blah, blah, blah."

I was in a zombie-subdued trance, and the hum of the fluorescent lighting made it worse. I kept watching the slow-moving hands of the wall clock and the facial expressions of my brother as he sat shivering angrily and stone-faced, unwilling to blink or give the judge and everyone else the satisfaction of knowing he was sick to his stomach and terrified of his future.

My fam was gonna keep it gangsta all the way to the end and not snitch, no matter how hard they tried to cut him a deal if he gave the names of Rocko and Spade. Juan denied the leniency and road with loyalty.

I twitched and fidgeted on the hard, wooden bench, wishing he would change his mind. I'd take a snitch for a brother over a caged one anytime.

Surprised that she could even see straight after stealing and selling everything in my brother's room and getting high for days, Phoebe stumbled into the courtroom clothed in the poorest Salvation Army dingy red dress she could find, her hair slicked back in a dirty, greasy ponytail, and reeking of alcohol. The odor poured into the room as she did and got worse as the door swung closed and shifted the air.

"Excuse me," she pushed past a few people that were sitting down the bench from me. She didn't even notice them twisting their faces up, or them covering their noses to block her smell. I was completely nauseated and disgusted by her decrepit-looking presence. Not only did it look like her face had sunk in more, but it also looked like she'd lost more weight, which wasn't a good thing since she was probably only a hundred pounds with winter clothes on.

I saw the immediate expression of pure disgust on Juan's face; then the glimmer in her eye that said: "I told you so." Phoebe should have been the one on trial for failing both of us. She's never shown up to parent-teacher conferences, the school plays we were in in elementary school, or even noticed that Juan stopped going to school months before he finally dropped out. I wanted to jump up and scream at the judge that my brother shouldn't be accountable for his actions because we weren't raised right.

Juan's inexperienced, state-appointed attorney shook with nervousness as the prosecutor rambled off the charges Juan was being sentenced for. He'd barely uttered a word about his innocence, his upbringing, or how he's never been in trouble before during the trial. I started to think he was a puppet for the prosecutor at one point because he actually asked what amount of jail time would make them happy.

As Juan's inept attorney barely uttered a word on behalf of his innocence, in a true dramatic fashion, my mother got up and stumbled out of the courtroom acting as if the world was coming to an end or the dope man was giving out free samples. Before the door slammed behind her, the words *"I told you so, fool"* were blurted out.

The entire scene was almost too much to bear. Refusing to stand out of respect for the proceedings, Juan got two extra years for being a "badass," as the judge proclaimed. *Bam!* Just like that, the judge banged his gavel down.

My brother's fate was sealed. Still emotionless, Juan shifted in his seat, then leaned with the posture of a man who'd lost all hope. I couldn't break my stare because I knew deep down the days of me having him at my side were over.

Damn! No more late-night walks to Coney Island for chili-cheese fries, me being able to call him to beat down some cocky boy, or having him to throw a few dollars in my pocket. It was over. I was on my own.

Hearing the judge read his order for time confinement had still set the record for the saddest thing I've witnessed in my entire young life. As the brown-uniformed Wayne County Sheriff placed him in handcuffs, Juan found my stare, and we spoke volumes.

I jumped up and ran over to him, tripping over those waiting on trials, hoping they didn't receive a verdict like my family. I hugged my brother around his neck tightly, crying and screaming.

"What am I going to do without you?" I trembled as he stood strong in stature.

"Get at Spade, sis. He'll look out for you while I'm locked down," he whispered. "Look at me, Jakia. I'm more serious than a heart attack."

"All right, break it up. Let's go, prisoner," one of the sheriffs laughed, and then pulled Juan back.

Like a baby, unsure of what to do next, I cried and stood helpless as they led him away. I yelled for them to have mercy and let him come home. My unfit, drug-crazed mother was gone in the wind.

No one was there to help or comfort me as I sobbed, watching the small windowed steel door, hoping the judge would have mercy on me at least. But he was foul, rude, and cutthroat, and asked that I be immediately escorted out as well or face contempt of court charges.

Why? Why? Why? I felt my knees buckle as the anxiety started to become too overwhelming. There was nothing else in the courtroom left for me. Truth be told, the next time I wanted to stand in a courtroom would be for the murder trial of putting a stiff, cold bullet in the judge's ass for the over-the-top harsh sentence.

As a gray-haired sheriff arrogantly held the door open for me to exit, I caught a glimpse of Spade sitting quietly off in the corner. *You shady coward!*

His cool demeanor accompanied by his hard-pressed professional clothes made him a chameleon. He was a criminal in borrowed attire and should've been shaken nervous being in this fate-dealing room.

He and his creep-ass cousin should've been under the jailhouse for recruiting my brother in the first place. But, naw, he wasn't sharing the time. Here he sat styling and low-key profiling as he watched my brother go away for ten years like it was nothing.

I kept my eyes glued to him until the heavy wooden door closed me all the way out. When it slammed loudly, it sealed the deal to my loneliness and my brother's future. This game I was witnessing was confusing, and I didn't understand it. Truth be told, I didn't know if I wanted to!

For weeks and months, I tried contacting my brother with no luck. Without him, a major void was left dangling. And as for our mother, she was doing worse than usual. Seeing her bent over some abandoned car in a vacant lot or giving some stranger head for a hit had me desperate to detach from her.

Some nights, I even prayed for God to send me in with Juan. The nonpayment of rent notices were stacking up, and the landlord was not in the mood for many more excuses or sad luck stories.

He wouldn't even take her crack-infected slob as an extension. Nine outta ten, we'd be staying in a homeless shelter somewhere or squatting in one of the many abandoned homes around the hood in no time.

Until going up, my brother kept the bills paid and our house looking somewhat decent. True enough, our furniture did not match and was worn when we got it secondhand, but it was ours and all we had.

By now, Phoebe had sold it all, pillows included, and had gone on a weeklong binge. She would've stolen his dirty drawers if she hadn't had to wash them first before selling them. I knew it was only a matter of time before my room was going to get hit for the little stuff I had. It wasn't much, but Juan made sure she never stole from us.

Finally, my brother was able to communicate with me:

> *Jakia, baby sis,*
>
> *It's important for you to know that Momma is a lost case, and if you stay around there, she'll suck you dry. You've gotta pray on that, let it go, and get out the very first chance you have.*
>
> *I know by now y'all sitting on shit row, and she's smoked up everything I've worked so hard to get up in that hellhole. Real talk—don't be out there feeling sorry for me, either, baby sis, 'cause you've got a life to live.*
>
> *Oh, and damn, I heard you grimed my nigga Spade in court that day. No matter what you think, that's my dude, and he got me. That's the code of the street, baby, something you'll have to learn on ya own cuz I can't protect you no more.*
>
> *The boys done took me, and it ain't shit I can do. You gonna have to be grown before your time, baby, but hold it down and be strong. Hit my manz up when you get a chance and get right.*
>
> *Don't let your hard head end up being your soft behind. You'll live, baby sis 'cause Coleman blood is thick like that. Please don't forget to write me, fam; you're all I got.*
>
> *Juan*

Holding a stuffed animal my brother won for me at Cedar Point, I balled up crying, resenting my momma 'cause she wasn't shit for letting her habit hold her back from raising us and doing what she needed to do for us to have a normal home life. That bitch!

If I could trade her life for his freedom, checkmate—her time would be up on this earth, and I'd have no regrets. But outside of the tears and wishful thinking, my brother was right. I had to start living and get up and away from her junkie ass.

As much as I despised Spade, I was gonna have to cross the line to get a come-up. There weren't very many options in the hood, and Juan wanted me to cuff a nigga with security, so I didn't have to struggle out on these streets alone.

Juan was naive in feeling Spade was loyal. The first giveaway should've been Spade leaving him out to dry on the lawyer tip. I didn't agree, but I went along with his plan to have me with whom he thought was a real boss to protect me.

What man doesn't want their baby sister with twenty-four-seven security? His information about Spade and stories shared in letters made me go from being confused about the game to being intrigued, wanting to wife the life.

It didn't take me long to catch his drift and get my mind wrapped around the idea of it actually being my reality.

My young mentality wasn't truly ready for the manipulation and pain street life presented on the back end. But I cared more about getting away from trife-life Phoebe than anything else. I guess it was a family trait.

2

Jakia

"Wake yo' ass up, Jakia," Spade yelled and shook me awake.

"I'm up, bae. What's wrong?" I jumped up, startled, not knowing if he was coming for me already. It wouldn't be the first time Spade had beat me up out of a slumber.

"Ain't shit wrong, Kia. Chill out," he calmly responded like his reputation didn't proceed him. "Get that fat ass up and cook me something to eat. I got that pussy together for you, so do your job and feed me. Your man is hungry." He propped his pillow up on the headboard and grabbed his phone to call and pillow-talk with Tiff probably.

At first, it pissed me off that he still kicked it with her, but I soon learned she was the distraction Spade needed to keep his hands off me.

Every night that Spade stayed home, he demanded a feast for breakfast the next morning. Today was no different. I stood in the kitchen wearing a pair of hot-pink booty shorts, a tight, yellow, wife beater, and shiny, hot-pink pumps while Spade watched me be the perfect homemaker he'd trained me to be.

Thirty minutes later, I had the kitchen smelling like a Coney Island restaurant on a Sunday morning. I'd cooked pork sausage links and bacon, grits with butter and cheese, scrambled eggs, and hash browns that had bell peppers and onions chopped up in them.

"Damn, it smells good in here." Spade walked in slapping his stomach. "It got a nigga's stomach churning in a good type of way."

I set two plates down in front of him. "Dig in. I hope you like it." I then hurried up and fixed me a plate so that I could start grubbing too.

"This shit is good as hell, Kia," he said, smacking like a horse and shoving forkfuls of food into his mouth. "Bring me a glass of cranberry juice so I can wash this goodness down."

And here comes the bullshit. My appetite was ruined instantly because I knew there was not any cranberry juice in the fridge. We'd been having a peaceful morning, but I knew Spade was about to overreact behind me not being able to fill his request. I was supposed to go to the grocery store yesterday but ended up getting caught up binge watching my favorite show. It wasn't worth me being out of Spade's favorite juice, though.

"Here's a tall glass of cold orange juice to get you started." I set the beverage down in front of him with a shaky hand. "I'm about to run to the corner store right now for your cranberry juice. I didn't make it to the market yesterday." I backed up, trying to quickly put some space between us because I saw his nose starting to flare.

"What the fuck you mean you didn't have time? Me and this house is all that you should be making time for, bitch!" He slammed his hand onto the counter and almost shook his plate off it. "What were you doing that you couldn't get yo' ditzy ass to carry out yo' duties?"

"I'm sorry, babe, I swear. I got overly tired from scrubbing the house clean yesterday and passed out. Like I said, though, I'll be back before you take another bite." I tried backing away from the breakfast bar again but was snatched back.

"You know I ain't trying to hear no sorry-ass excuses." He wiped the corners of his mouth with a napkin, then slid off the bar stool. "You'd think I would've knocked some sense into your head by now. You claim you're tired of gettin' ya ass beat, yet you keep fuckin' up. Why do you keep disobeying me?"

I didn't have to pee, but I did now. I was so scared of getting hit that I didn't want to say the wrong thing. "I'm sorry, Spade. I swear it won't happen again," I whimpered.

"Shut up. That crying shit don't mean nothing to me. I've heard you say that same line over and over again." He threw the cold glass of orange juice in my face, then knocked my plate of food to the floor. "Hardheaded hoes don't deserve to eat. Now get your dumb ass to the store for my juice and be back here before I count to one hundred."

I grabbed the dishrag from the sink and wiped the juice from my eyes while putting some clothes on at the same time. I damn near tripped on my own two feet rushing out the side door. From the menacing look in Spade's eyes, I knew I only had until he got to ninety-nine.

Spade

"What up, cuz? You up?" Rocko and I have been getting down in the streets since crib size. Today was just another day in our grimy worlds.

"You already know it. I just finished digging ole girl's guts out and put her ass to sleep. I was able to swipe that clown's whole itinerary—so we on. Holla at li'l momma to put us down with that room."

I shot Tiff a quick text message while I listened to Rocko run down everything about the man we'd be using Jakia as bait to set up. It was more than important that I got everything right so that I could give her more than everything she needed to know on how to play her cards right.

The one thing I had to be certain to leave out was my ex-girlfriend's involvement.

"Bet. What time should me and Jakia fall through? I'm ready to get this shit popping." It was only slightly after 8:00 a.m., but I was up and hungry for this money.

While cats were rolling over and getting their second wind of sleep on, I was bright eyed and bushy tailed setting up a master plan to murk they ass.

"The sooner, the better. His window closes at two p.m., and your wifey has to have time to do her thang. So get at me when you're ready."

"With a ticket this big on the table, I'm about to make sure her ass knows she needs to be efficient, plus in and out."

I took a big swallow of the cheese grits Kia made and couldn't wait for her to return with my cranberry juice. I wasn't gonna bash her head in as promised, but I had to keep her shook up and on her toes.

"You do you. It ain't even gotta be said that you keep Kia moving to yo' music. Holla at me when you on the way."

"A'ight, fam, peace."

This setup was about to bring some heavy racks home. Rocko was banging a basic chick he'd met off Facebook who was connected to this heavy moneybag's dude in Chicago.

He'd just Olivia Pope'd her ass for all the information we needed to hit a lick on him. Leave it to my cuz— pimpin' chicks must've run thick in our bloodline.

My phone went off on cue with a text alert from Tiff. On her end, things were in motion. I might've dissed her consistently for Jakia, but my ex never failed to look out for me.

She was my "Bonnie" back in the day when Juan got mixed up in our robbery. As suspected, she sent a few more texts asking if I was gonna hit it later on. Of course, I told her yeah, then got back to grubbing until my live-in pussy returned. If all went well today, I'd celebrate my stroke inside her all night long.

Jakia

My hand trembled as I twisted the doorknob and opened the door. I knew when I ran out of it that I wasn't going to be up the block and back by the time he counted to a hundred, so I'd grabbed a bag of ice that I could prop up on my eye after he finished blacking it. I don't know how many bruised parts of my body I've iced.

"Here you go." I handed him a red plastic cup that was already full of juice. I didn't want to waste any more time coming in and having to fix him a cold glass of juice when the store had cups, ice, and, of course, the juice. The store owner thought I was a fool for staying loyal to Spade, but he always helped me out when he could. Like today . . . I hadn't left the house with a dollar.

"See, this is why you be gettin' smacked around," Spade acknowledged what I did. "You oughta use yo' big-ass head all the time to think things through. Are you still hungry?"

I nodded. "Yeah."

"Okay, well . . . I'll do you a favor and let you eat the food off the floor. You still fucked up by not going to the store yesterday, so you still don't deserve to eat like no civilized muthafucka. After you fill my plates back up and throw them in the microwave, I'll let you get to business." He smirked, knowing good and damn well that he was Lucifer himself.

"Hey, clean this shit up and sit down. I just got done yapping with Rocko, and the lick for this afternoon is on."

Spade pulled out his phone and started scrolling through a gang of pictures showing me the target for today. I made sure to pay close attention because, in a few hours, I'd have to pick him out of a crowded casino.

The target was a dark-skinned man who had a plump face accompanied by glasses and was sporting a clean, bald head. There wasn't one thing I could say was attractive about the guy. He was simply dressed in khaki slacks, a polo shirt, and boat shoes. His pictures were really boring and real bland, so I automatically assumed his personality would be too. I was happy about that, though. Most of our targets lately have been thugs, savages, and dope boys from other parts of the city since Spade didn't squat and shit where he lay his head; so, it would be a breath of fresh air and a breeze to scam an average Joe Schmo. Ole boy looked like he was rolling in legit money.

"So, what's his story, and what do I need to do?"

Spade clasped his hands together and rubbed them like he was a professor getting ready to school me. "A'ight, listen up 'cause this hit is important. Rocko said this corny nigga is an investor from Chicago that's here looking to invest in some real estate. He's staying down at the casino's hotel until his meeting, but he won't make it there because you're gonna cut him off in the lobby and make sure me and Rock can rob him in the room.

"This one's important, babe, so I need you to work his ass all the way over. Wear something to have him drooling 'cause this one can't be missed. He's an investor from Chicago who's here to capitalize in this upcoming real estate company. Rocko got the one-up on the job, so we cutting the stack a few ways."

I knew he didn't include me in the cut, but I listened anyway. I didn't have any other choice.

"He's staying down at Motor City, room 1253. His addiction is gambling. That's why he came in so early and has plans to hit the dice table hard. He's got about fifty Gs that Rocko knows of."

"Wow, Motor City? They've got heavy security down there."

We'd never done a hit so large and definitely not in a public place of this magnitude. My mind was racing fast, trying to come up with an outfit and what wig I'd wear.

I had pounds of foundation in all different shades of brown to cover my light-colored skin, so I knew disguising my face a little wasn't going to be too much of a problem.

"When have I ever been froggish about security? Them slow-moving cocksuckers better be on alert for me and Rocko. We tryin'a step into the big leagues and eat off this nigga's pockets for a minute, ya feel me? So, if you take care of this, we can sit down for a minute."

The first thought to cross my mind was how he left my brother hanging, but I was overly thrilled about this being quite possibly our last lick. I wasn't trying to be Spade's setup girl forever, or even viler, in some women's penitentiary rotting away.

I kept staring at the pictures trying to get my mind right.

"Spade, that cat looks funny to me. I'm feeling the money, don't get me wrong, but there's something about his look that makes me nervous."

"Don't get intimidated. I don't know much about him, but me and Rocko will be trailing you with the device. Plus, he's connected to my cuz through some chick he's banging—we good on this 'cause it's an inside job. All you've gotta do is play your part and play it well. Please don't tell me you need some *motivation*."

He took another bite of his food, then rubbed his hands together like he was preparing to get me together. I could sense him getting heated. His posture got tense as his shoulders and brows lifted.

"Naw, baby, I'm good. As always, you already know I'm going to work my magic so you can get some money.

Let me go get myself together for the job." I couldn't win for losing. Everything I did rubbed him the wrong way.

"That's more like it. I'll bring you a li'l something to get your mind right while you soak in the hot tub. Then we've gotta be out. Now go." He shooed me out of the kitchen.

3

Jakia

I walked into our bathroom to start my hustle day. Popping a Motrin 800 to relax my muscles along with a Valium to calm my nerves, I stared into the mirror and didn't like what was staring back. I was tired, and without makeup, you could easily notice the dark bags underneath my eyes.

Every dollar Spade rationed to me from the setups were used to purchase Mac Pro Longwear concealer to cover the stress marks, battle wounds, and enhance the beauty he was helping to wither away.

Spade has added ten years to my body in just the short while of us kicking it. I was only 19 and damn near looked 30. The youthful appearance I was supposed to have was buried by the life I was living with him.

The more he said he loved me, the more I felt like his property. Not only was he treating me less and less like his lover and more like a hooker, but he was also putting me in danger by halfway tricking me out to set unsuspecting men up.

Every ounce of self-worth, respect, and strength I had was stripped from me each time Spade put my life and safety on the line. And to make matters worse, he was going upside my head in private.

It was hard to believe Spade truly had any love for me because all signs pointed toward me only being the perfect pawn in his scummy street lifestyle. It was nothing I could dwell on. This was the life I chose—or the life that chose me, I wasn't sure.

After making sure my long Brazilian wavy hair was secured underneath a few stocking caps, I picked out a long, blond, curly lace front wig that I'd wear as mine today.

It was going to go perfect with the catsuit I'd just ordered online. Since I spent so much time nursing my battle wounds, I seldom went to public places like the mall. So I used setups or date nights to model my wardrobe.

I slid into the hot bubble bath and allowed the lavender smell to soothe my overwhelmed body. Today was gonna be a long day with a lot of money on the line, and I couldn't be the one to mess up.

Like always, it was crucial every move I made on this unsuspecting cat was perfect 'cause if anything went wrong, Spade would be on my head in a heavy sort of way.

It was my job in the trio to sexually seduce men and put them into a position where Spade and Rocko could successfully rob them. Even though it was damn near impossible, Spade expected me to control the situation and prevent as much touching as possible.

Sex with them was definitely out of the question. If I failed to keep these men off of me, Spade punished me afterward and was upside my head by the time we got alone. It was never a win-win situation. I was always in a catch-22.

"Here's some fruit, a Mimosa, and a fat cigarillo to get you right." Spade made good on his word, cutting into my time in the bathroom.

I guess this tray was some weak-ass apology for knocking my food on the floor earlier. I popped a few grapes in my mouth, not daring to speak one ill word. It wouldn't have killed him to utter the words "I'm sorry" once in a while, though.

"Are you good on ole boy, or do you need another rundown?" he questioned, leaning back against the sink and lighting the blunt. Spade always liked to be prepared. He lived off the wealth of other men in the streets, so it was vital his moves were always quicker and well thought out.

"I listened just like you told me earlier, but I'll feel better if you tell me again."

I reached for the blunt and inhaled deeply while he started running down everything once again. As much as I tried to stay focused on every word coming out of his mouth, I was lost up in the physical attraction.

Don't get me wrong. Spade was a monster. But his dick game was mad crazy, and our physical attraction to each other couldn't be denied! My pussy was starting to want seconds. There wasn't a time his big, black, 250-pound body didn't make me orgasm.

"A'ight, you've got it?"

"Most definitely, but can this be the last time, though? Since it's at least twelve and a half Gs waiting for us today, can we try to milk that for a while until you find a replacement?"

"I see you do math good," he chuckled. "We'll see. You do such a damn good job, and if I bring another bitch in, I'll have to split our cut more ways. Just stay focused on today."

"You've got it, daddy," I replied, knowing I didn't have a choice to deny him of what he truly wanted—which was to use me.

"That's my girl." He leaned in, kissing me on the forehead. "Don't be all day in here, Kia. You've got one hour tops to be dressed and downstairs so we can get out of here." Just as quickly as he'd entered, he was gone.

I blew through the rest of the blunt and zoned out remembering a little over a year ago when I first made my deal with the devil.

Twelve Months Ago . . .

When Juan's visitation list first opened up in prison, Spade volunteered to be my transportation for the two-hour ride. The prison chaplin knew my mother was a drug addict, and I was the only family my brother had.

He, along with the inmates' shrink, felt it was best to have me visit as much as possible for my youthful brother's initial adjustment to the long prison term he was facing. Spade driving made that happen.

He put it on being loyal to my brother, but it was the least he could do since my bloodline was doing time for a crime Spade committed. I didn't complain, though, 'cause it guaranteed me the time Juan said I needed to get on the inside.

It was hard being around him at first, knowing if it weren't for his gutter ways rubbing off on my brother, I'd still have my comfort zone, but I couldn't jeopardize my ride with a sharp tongue and bitter feelings. So, I guess you could say I was slowly learning how to play my position.

As the days went by on our many road trips, I tried everything time and time again to show him my availability; laughing at his jokes that weren't funny, frying him chicken for the ride, and sometimes bending over in the rear seat acting like I was getting something so he could see my ass in the air.

Initially, he was playing that role acting like he wasn't about hitting off his man's li'l sister and that his chick Tiff would flip out. But my attempts were far from subtle, and I ain't never been friendly with females.

In other words—fuck how Tiff was feeling. I had a game plan to execute. No matter how hard he tried to deny me, I continuously threw my stacked body into his face.

I was relentless when it came to pressing him hard with my pursuit. Once he found out my pussy juice was virgin fresh, I didn't have to press much longer.

When Spade hit my cell up on my eighteenth birthday talkin' about getting a room at the Atheneum, I didn't wait five minutes before writing Juan a letter to tell him the game was on.

I couldn't wait for him to break the seal on the envelope and read I was close to on my way up out of Phoebe's house. This had been all we'd written about since he'd been locked up. What I didn't expect was to be part of a threesome that included me, Spade, and his girlfriend Tiff.

Her face was ice-cold pissed when she saw me walk through the room with my hand interlocked with Spade's. I thought I was about to be in for a birthday catfight, but, instead, she welcomed me to the bed just like he was doing.

Already, my young mind was turned out, but Spade was aiming to do much more damage. That night, Tiff threw it on him like I'd seen Phoebe do many nights—but wasn't nothing competing with my show.

He might've been jerking from her sloppy head job, but his eyes were fixated on me. And when it was my time to shine, I threw it on him hard, young-girl-gone-wild style.

Even Tiff had to fall back and give my young-ass props. The longer she watched me, though, the more ripped her mug became.

Juan would be proud. He told me dudes liked chicks to get scummy in the bedroom, so you better believe I was doing just that. Within the year it took to get here, I'd watched every freak-nasty, no-moral porn on Xnx I could find and practiced moving my body seductively in the mirror for hours.

All my crunches and squats had paid off. Spade was going wild crazy while Tiff watched sourly. *Yeah, chick, you've just been replaced.* Little did I know, I should've stayed in my own lane from back when I first said he was no good.

Our first night together had us both gone. Not sure of the outcome, I pulled out all the punches. The more twirls I did on the internet-ordered travel pole Tiff bought, the more his eyes bulged, and his manhood sprang out of his pants.

All my training and hard work paid off quickly, placing me deep into his pockets, but even deeper into his deceiving world. Tiff worked like a beast in the bedroom that night and several days following our weeklong hiatus of a three-person couple.

When he dropped her off at home after the fourth night, I hopped in the front seat kicking the little gum from the bottom of my shoe off at her. I didn't know how Spade paid her back for throwing a tire rod at his car, 'cause I was too busy writing to Juan that his li'l sis was winning.

Please believe that after Spade realized he could get winning head and sex on-demand, I was packing up my most prized cheap possessions and leaving the rat-infested scum-hole Phoebe called a home.

Without remorse, I walked out of the bedroom I'd been barricading myself in and dropped the bolted lock and key onto the warped wooden floor in front of her. Departing ways with my mom wasn't hard, emotional, or even a tear-jerking Twitter tweet.

"Here, maybe you can sell this lock for a dollar!"

"Aw, you li'l bitch, I see you feelin' yo'self. That nigga gonna get you caught up just like he did yo' stupid-ass brother," she spoke and shook.

"As long as I don't end up like my stupid-ass mother, then I'm good," I hissed, then turned my back on her.

She didn't dare bark back 'cause I was stacked tight enough to drop her with one punch. I walked out the door with the few green garbage bags of belongings I'd managed to keep from her stealing hands with my head held high.

Graduating high school was an afterthought at this moment in time. I glanced over my shoulder seeing Phoebe leap off the couch. Did she rush over to me? Naw, that witch sprinted into my bedroom scavenging for whatever I left behind.

Grabbing the change bank off my now-old dresser, she beat me down the front porch stairs, then shattered the pink porcelain ballerina bank she'd gotten me for my fourth birthday on the hot concrete walkway.

When old, tiny, colorful buttons I'd collected and filled it with went flying everywhere instead of coins, Phoebe looked at me with pure hate.

"So, you're just gonna leave me broke down and with nothing? You don't care if I die?" She didn't give me a chance to answer, but I wasn't going to anyway. "Well, fuck you too, Jakia. The same grave you want me in, you'll fall in before I will," she bitterly spoke as I hopped in Spade's car. "Karma is a bitch, and knowledge costs."

"Gon' and kiss my ass, Momma," I spat. "You ain't got no kids now. Let's just consider this our final good-bye."

Jakia

Standing at the top of the stairs, I heard the surround sound speakers playing an episode of "Breaking Bad." In a perfect world, I'd be able to cuddle up on the couch with my man and a blanket, completely caught up in the melodrama that was Walter White. But our dynamic was everything *but* simple.

Finally, at the end of the stairwell, I saw Spade stretched out on the leather sectional with his phone nestled in his hand. Day in and out, he stayed lurking on cats' Facebook, Instagram, and Twitter pages scoping for a come-up.

The more they flashed and celebrated their riches on social networks, the wealthier our crew became. Spade and Rocko stayed snatching niggas down from their pedestals. Unfortunately, that also included me.

I watched Spade's tattooed chest rise up and down as he slept deep and without fear. His dreads hung around his smoke-black skin as his tight jawline signified deep thought and anticipation of the lick we were hours away from walking in on. I wished the pain in my eyes could penetrate through his soul and kill him. I was too scared to even attempt it for real.

My Red Bottom six-inch heels clicked on the marble floor as I made my way across the foyer into the living room. Spade jerked out of his sleep at the sound, startled by my introduction.

"Damn, a nigga was sleeping good." He rubbed his temples before stretching and yawning. "Thank you for not making me come up there." He sat up, looking me up and down. From the nod and smirk on his face, he seemed to be pleased.

"Well, do you like what you see?" I modeled for him, walking back and forth across the room. I even had to admire my own reflection in the full-length mirrors that covered one of our walls.

Spade watched my body intently as I worked the hell out of the black, one-piece catsuit that suffocated every curve and proportion of my stacked frame. From the slight bulge in his pants, I'd chosen the right "get money outfit" and was off to a good start.

But with all the shots he constantly took at my ego, I needed to hear the words. Spade judged me hard, and if I would've come down here looking broken down and off the clearance rack, he'd roast me rough or smack me up. With Tiff lurking in the background, I kept my presence up on a regular.

"Without a doubt, baby girl, that ass is getting thick." He licked his lips, then pushed his dreads from off his forehead. "Come over here, ma. Let me get a close-up of you." He slid back comfortably and opened his legs wide. "You sure are looking like money." He grinned devilishly, showing his filthy intentions.

"Well, you did say it was big money for us on the line. I want to make sure I catch his eye."

"Good job. I would say you're ready for work. You've got the girls sitting high and looking delicious." Saliva was forming at the corners of his mouth as he rubbed his hands all over my frame.

My face might've aged, but my body was still on point. I was a bad bitch, and he knew it. That's why he used my looks to make us money. He snuggled his head into my chest, then leaned up for a kiss.

"Come on, babe, don't mess up the package," I smiled teasingly as he continued to kiss my lipstick off.

"Oh, I like it when you're ready to make that chedda. But this right here is all mine," he said, grabbing the gap between my legs.

The jumpsuit cuffed my imprint perfectly, letting everyone know I was working with something great.

"Don't be in a rush to flaunt it, though," he scorned. "You know a nigga gets mad jealous."

"Then you should let me up out of the game. I'm supposed to be your girl, not the number one worker on your roster. I know you've got hoes in the streets. Why don't you put one of them at risk?"

"Okay, I've heard that shit enough, Jakia. Don't have me slap you up real quick." He flipped from touching me sexually to aggressively grabbing me. "I'm gonna bust yo' head to the white meat if you throw me off my square, so you better get your emotions in check real quick. I might have a plethora of bitches, but you're the best out of all of 'em for the job."

I bit my lip and nodded, bottling up a ton of anger and bitterness. If this man had love for me, he had a way of making it seem like hate.

"Now, get your shit and let's get ready to rock and roll. I've had enough of trying to baby you, Jakia. You already know the deal. It's hustle time, baby."

With that, he snatched my wrist and flung me to the door. I tripped over the rug with my stilettos, almost falling but managed to keep my composure and stand tall. Ain't no telling what swift blows I would suffer on the ground beneath him.

He collared me up by the back of my jacket and force-walked me to the car. Smacking the back of my head real quick, he shoved me into the backseat of the truck, then made his way to the driver's side. I wanted to jump out of the car and run up the block screaming that he was abusing me, but I knew he'd catch me and kill me if he didn't lock me away for punishment. Spade spoke so much ill will against me that he mentally controlled me. He slid in to smack me another three quick times from the front.

"That's so you'd have a reminder that I don't play no games."

"I've got it. Trust me, I do." Chill bumps ran up and down my spine.

"Make sure you do, Jakia. My word is bond. I will put you six feet under."

One day, you probably will. I sat still and scared, praying that I would one day get strong enough to make a break for it.

Spade

Don't judge me—flat-out, period. A nigga gotta do exactly what a nigga gotta do to survive. It wasn't a sunrise or sunset that I, Spencer Spade Johnson, wasn't about making money.

If you were a hustler and my first cousin Rocko, or I knew about it, we'd rob your pockets dry and leave you digging for lint. Jakia, my beautiful woman and companion, was the pawn in my game, and I used her whenever necessary.

She'd replaced Tiff in my tricks 'cause her pussy was better, and her bloodline already proved to be of a loyal-type pedigree. A nigga of my caliber never thought twice when it came to doing dirt. I wanted everything the next man had, and, yes, I felt entitled to it.

I wasn't from money, so I hated those who had it and flossed it. I didn't have the luxury of being a spoiled brat, rocking Jordans on the release date or official store-purchased name brand fits.

People didn't jock me or want to copycat my style 'cause everything about me represented the gutter. Low breed and never the popular kid, I was nicknamed "Doodie" as my mother graciously accepted all of the old clothes, shoes, pantry items, and freezer-burned food as a means of our survival from our surrounding neighbors.

Rocko stayed fighting for me when he and auntie came over. They had a pot to piss in, but still just as bottom level as us.

Being a grown man looking back on it, I couldn't blame my moms for being crippled and welfare bound, but, damn, she could've gotten on her back a few times for her only son to jump fresh.

I hated being poor and every person that reminded me of my moms and my pitiful situation. You could trust that I saw what dinero could do at a young age; it was then I developed an insatiable love and desire for it.

My first targets were those same bullies I watched get new bikes, Chuck-E-Cheese trips, and always had a dollar for the ice-cream truck.

Working for minimum wage and paying Uncle Sam was only beneficial during income tax refund time, and that petty change was nothing compared to the number of stacks my cousin and I were bringing in.

We'd clock major hours searching for cats with low security, flashy behavior, and deep pockets. Easy targets were easy money, but I used young Jakia to my full advantage to reach the more untouchable marked hits.

Her body was irresistible, and the downfall of many hustlers. My rare breed wasn't weak to be her prey.

Juan was right for wanting to protect his baby sister. She proved early on to be young, dumb, and naïve—allowing me to use her so dangerously. But I'd notice the same glint of hunger in her eyes on more than one occasion, making me question her loyalty to our team and my right hand for being her saving grace from Phoebe.

I'd created a monster within her, making her hungry for the better things in life. The more setups we executed, the more courage she attained. The thought of my moneymaker leaving me caused me to erupt with rage.

Leaving me wasn't going to be an easy feat, even if it was an easy thought to her. Every time she made hints to wanting out of the game, I went in extra hard to make sure my point was proven clear—biding out wasn't an option until I made it one.

She sat in the backseat quiet as a church mouse, and that was how I liked it. Pulling up to Rocko's crib, I barely stopped the truck before he hopped in and was talking business.

He and I were blood family and partners in the game. Our mothers were twin sisters, which made us genetically inclined to fuck shit all the way up.

"What up, baby girl?" Rocko turned around to acknowledge her. "You looking salty enough to give a nigga high blood pressure." He called himself cracking a joke that made me take notice of Jakia through the rearview mirror.

"Naw, I'm good." She rushed to fix her tore up mug once she peeped my menacing grime.

"Y'all two always on some back and forth love-and-hate shit." He shook his head, looking from her to me while low-key laughing. "I ain't never getting serious with no broad!"

"Yeah, whatever, nigga. You know what's up if you do. By any means necessary—keep these hoes in check."

4

Robert

"Yeah, I'll take those too," I graciously accepted the double stacks of one hundred-dollar-valued chips from the dealer as she nodded and smiled. I was tearing this table up each time I blazed the dice, and my winnings were stacking high.

The late-night crowd and party scene had died down. I loved the early-late-morning vibe.

"Bets are open." She stood back from the table but watched our every move.

Each hand I played was worth a stack. I had money to blow, and there was more in the room if I bet too big for my pockets. But it would be a cold day in hell to have that happen. Each bet doubled me up, and the Patrón drinks the house kept sending made my blood hot with my tempo even higher.

"Bets are now closed." The dealer waved her hand across the table, signaling us gamblers to stop.

I blew on the dice, rolling them around in my hands, waiting until I felt like it was my lucky moment to throw them. I needed to hit the jackpot. I gripped them like a pair of perky nipples, then tossed them across the table so they'd pop off the backside and land back on the felt table, hopefully on the numbers four and five, or six and three, or whichever combination as long as it was nine. Shooting dice was a skill, and I was the nerdy brother in a Brooks Brothers suit whose pockets were fat off the addicting habit.

"Yeah, pass my money over, sweet lady. I'll take those," I winked, smiling widely. By now, I'd hung my suit jacket over a chair and loosened up my silk tie. My business meeting wasn't for a few more hours, and I was ready to hit Motor City Casino deeply.

"Yes, sir, of course. But we have to shut the table down momentarily for shift change. It's been a pleasure being your dealer tonight. Good luck," she smiled.

"Oh, I hate that you have to go. You've been so kind." I winked again. It wasn't a flirt, but I considered myself a ladies' man. Women loved when men put that extra touch into a conversation.

"Please enjoy a round on the house," the dealer smiled and winked, referencing for me to turn around as her replacement and banker arrived to break her table and bank down.

"Anything you like, sir. What will you have?" The waitress's innocent doe eyes were adorable and cute.

"I'll take a Patrón, straight up."

"Okay. If you are hungry, I can take you over to the restaurant. Specials are going, not like you need them," she suggested, looking over toward my winnings.

"That you are right. But whatever the case, I am starved and could use a refill. Besides, my flow just got rudely interrupted." I was ready to get into something dirty. "Cash me out," I told them, turning my attention back to the waitress.

"I don't mean to interrupt your flow." She looked down, unsure of her presence.

"No apologies necessary and look up when we're talking. You're too pretty to look down." I tried to build her ego. This young girl was cute and young, and legal. "Lead the way." I smiled and pointed for her to walk ahead as I grabbed my coat and cashed out chips following behind closely.

Her uniform was skimpy and left little to the imagination. Mixing the Patrón shots I'd taken in the last few hours on the gaming floor had me looking at her like a mad dog in heat. I was starting to feel a thump in my Ralph Lauren boxers.

"Do you want to dine in with me as your waitress or bill your order to sit down in that section? Either way, the Patrón is still on the house, boss's orders."

"I'm just trying to grab something quick and head back to the money," I replied, rubbing at my stomach. "I'm starving for food, but I'm hungry for money, ya understand?"

"I guess I understand," she innocently replied, leaning over to one side. She was now casually holding her serving tray to the side, relaxed and taken aback by my question. "I'm at work on a paper chase, waiting on people and all that. I guess I do."

My cell phone vibrated, and I pulled it out of my pants pocket, noticing it was my assistant. I couldn't send the call to voicemail even if I wanted to. There was too much on my itinerary, meaning money was on the floor to be made.

"Hold on. I've gotta take this call. Here, take this," I said, pulling out a wad of cash and peeling off five one hundred-dollar bills.

"Really? Damn, this is very nice of you," she smiled, reaching to accept my generosity. It was nothing for me and obviously, everything for her. "Well, thanks a lot. Trust and believe it's appreciated. Let me get that drink." She excused herself.

I watched her as she glided away. Damn, she was a fine young piece of ass that I wouldn't mind hitting before this trip was over. Hopefully, those bills could help her troubles or help my nut out later on.

"Hey, how's it going, Lezlee?" I spoke into my head-set.

"Good afternoon, Mr. Taylor. I'm sorry if I'm interrupting you, but I was just calling to inform you that the driver will be in front of the hotel's entrance in exactly two hours. I can accompany you to today's meetings if you'd like."

My assistant always made sure my day was efficiently planned, especially when I was traveling. She was truly a gem, and had I not been giving her an allowance for sticking my rod in her from time to time, a raise would've been in order.

"Sure, sweetheart. I'm certain you'll be more than helpful. You've never steered me wrong in the past, so I trust you with business decisions," I spoke, giving her the upmost respect.

"Thank you, sir. I aim to please. That is my job," she replied, showing her sincerity.

"Okay, look, I'm grabbing a bite to eat, throwing a few rounds at the craps table, and having a shot or two. Make sure you've glanced at the paperwork and are prepared. See you in a few hours."

I hung up the phone relaxed, knowing I had a longer time to play now. Since I was a married man, these business trips were more than a breath of fresh air, but it was my time to dangle my meat in whatever clean-looking trick made herself available.

The waitress was taking a little longer than anticipated, so I found my way to the buffet, loading my plate up. All the gambling and drinking I'd been doing all morning was starting to catch up quickly. After smashing this, I'd bypass going back to the table to catch a catnap in my room.

"Here's your drink, sir. Is there anything else I can do?"

"Yes, baby girl. As a matter of fact, you can meet me in my room around eight p.m. for drinks. Is that possible?" I couldn't help myself. I was like a kid in a candy store when it came to women.

"How about nine thirty? I don't get off till eight, and I want to go home first to get cute for you," she shyly spoke to me but looked at me dead-on.

"Nine thirty it is. I can't wait to see your pretty face." I knew she was hooked. Every girl I smiled at was hooked once my hazel eyes connected with theirs, and they thought my kind words and sweet-nothings were genuine. Naw, never that. I gambled women like I gambled money—high and frequently.

"Is there anything else I can do for you, sir?" She slid the bill over which had her name and number scribbled on the back.

I paid her with an additional twenty and shook my head no. Her managers were watching from afar, so she had to play it cool. It was no problem for me as long as I got to have my way with her and that cat later tonight.

"You've been more than helpful, Iesha." I looked down at the receipt noting her name. "There's no need for me to call you this evening. Just show up once your shift is over. I'm staying in room 1253."

"Okay, I'll be there. And I plan to be even more helpful once I arrive," she flirted.

She just didn't know—I'll tear that li'l kitty cat out of the frame.

"Damn, I'm glad her pesky ass is gone. I've been watching and waiting on my chance to introduce myself."

"Is that so? Well, who might you be?" I sipped my drink and traced the curves of the inviting body that seemed to appear out of thin air. The slight hard-on I felt from the waitress was starting to pulsate even more at the sight of *this* bombshell.

"Jakia. And, yes, I'd like a drink."

"Well, nice meeting you, Jakia, I'm Robert," I said, extending my hand. Her soft fingers massaged it softly before shaking it back. I was turned all the way on from her sexiness and boldness. Tossing the Patrón down my throat, feeling the instant burn, my confidence increased even more.

"It's so very nice to meet you, Robert." Her voice was soft and seductive as she stared into my eyes. My grip on her hand was starting to loosen, but she didn't move away. "How about drinks?"

"The private pleasure would be all mine, sweet lady. But you'd have to accompany me to my room because that's where I was on my way to. The room service here is impeccable." I held my arm out for her to lock in. Since she was straight forward, I didn't see the need for me not to be. Jakia approached me like a trick, and I had money to burn. I liked a woman that wasn't about games.

"Lead the way," her words reassured my every thought.

The waitress watched with an evil eye as I disappeared from her view. I made sure to wink and nod—There was enough dick in my drawers to stroke her too.

Rocko

"Don't be on no slow-moving shit tonight, fam. Take it easy on them pills," I preached to Spade as he got down with his usual prescription pill popping.

You couldn't pay me not to believe he didn't pick that habit up from my strung-out auntie. The arthritis pains that shot throughout her body daily kept her doped up on the strongest opiates the rheumatologist could prescribe.

He used to sneak some back in the day to nod out from getting bullied . . . and must've never stopped.

"Ole dude's assistant said he is a straight perv, so we gotta be on our toes."

"Yeah, cuz, but cool it with all that preaching. I ain't trying to hear that right about now," Spade slurred, and then swallowed his drug followed by a large gulp of Red Bull. "Besides, that's my moneymaker in there. If something happens to her, all three of us suffer big time. I wouldn't jeopardize that for nothing in the world."

"A'ight, nigga, whatever."

I swigged on a bottle of water, then pushed my earbuds back in. I didn't want to miss one word of the conversation being exchanged between Jakia and this mark buster. Spade might not have treated her like fam all the time, but I tried to.

"I love the way your ass looks right now. It's got my dick getting hard. Can you tell, pretty girl?" Robert's

voice over the headphones was snaky and made my skin crawl.

"As a matter of fact, I can." Jakia's voice was sexy and seductive. "It looks quite big."

"Come over here. Would you like to touch it, pretty girl? Aaah, yea, you just keep your hand right there. Feels big too, right?"

I wanted to go in and shoot the mark buster in between his eyes myself for having her like that, but if Spade allowed his woman to be degraded, then who was I to call otherwise?

He and I might've been blood cousins, but I swear to God he must've had his daddy's genes of psychotic crazy.

"I can't wait until you get me up to this room and show me just how big it actually is," Jakia whispered, right before I heard her gasp.

"Sweet, pretty girl, I've got so much money I can let my dick out to hang."

"Hey, I think it's about that time we start putting this plan into motion. And from how Kia's playing it, this nigga has more cash than we anticipated."

"A'ight, I'm on it," Spade replied, replacing his Red Bull for water. "I'm about to scope out downstairs and security. Gotta make sure we can get up out of here with no problems."

"Bet." I continued listening to the conversation while loading my pistols in preparation for killing a nigga. I knew it would be inevitable. And when Spade got back to hear the way this ole nasty nigga was on his girl—shit was really gonna turn south.

After concealing my weapons on each side of my hip, I pulled out the cleaning supplies Spade's little girl-friend brought in her "luggage" when she checked in. Tiff

looked out big-time with Lysol, bleach, and disinfect-
ant. That nigga was taking a huge risk by involving his
ex, but for some reason, chicks loved staying loyal to
his nutty ass.

I wiped the entire room down for prints, then gathered
any empty water bottles or paraphernalia that was lying
around. I didn't care what plans Spade might've had
of coming back with Tiff later on, but my fingerprints
weren't going to be swiped by forensics.

5

Jakia

"Damn, you are so sexy, pretty girl. Take your clothes off. Let me see more of you. Let me feel your skin."

His hazel eyes locked into mine as I stepped out of my heels, then dropped my Chanel purse and walked toward him. I was in rare form working my role tonight, but I'm sure Spade was going to find something wrong with my performance.

"You should take off yours first. Show me more of that big dick you had me feeling in the elevator," I slurred, feeling a head rush from the shots we'd just taken at the wet bar.

Everything was moving so fast. I started to feel the urge to act on the words coming from my mouth, which was different for me when in character.

"Humph, I like it when pretty girls get nasty. Can I call you names? Like 'my little slut,' 'my nasty little tramp,' or 'a filthy come whore'?" He was more of a pervert than I thought he'd be.

"If that's what turns you on," I devilishly smiled, unbuckling his pants so he could whip his hardness all the way out. His suit pants fell to his ankles; then he casually stepped out of them with no effort.

"I'm about to give you exactly what you came looking for." He smacked my ass roughly and pulled me in for a longing kiss.

His tongue explored my mouth as he slid his hands down the backside of my pants. Even though I was putting up a helluva fight, my resistance wasn't strong enough. He grabbed my neck gently with one hand while cupping my camel toe aggressively.

"That's it, you li'l freak. Yeah, you like it. I can tell you like it. Your nipples are erect and puffy from this roughness. How much do you want me to pay you so that I can taste that sweet, fat pussy?"

I pushed back from him, sliding my cat suit down. I needed to hit a lick on any extra money unaccounted for 'cause, for real, I was in the most dangerous position.

There wasn't any time to waste if I wanted to catch this nut. By now, I'm sure they knew we'd left the gaming room and were in the hotel.

Pulling out a wad of cash and placing it in my purse, Robert didn't waste any time kneeling in front of me, sucking on my stomach, then licking up to my breasts. My head fell back as I focused on the green light of the smoke detector.

Hurry up, nigga; you ain't got all day.

"You taste delicious," he said, and then went back down to licking my clit like a hungry beast.

For a moment, I closed my eyes and got lost in the feeling. The rush of knowing Spade was only a few floors away had my adrenaline pumping, but I'd die if he caught me, literally.

My eyes flew back open as I checked my watch, coming to reality with my last thoughts. Time was running crucially short, and Robert wouldn't be the only dead body left here tonight if Spade caught me enjoying any minute of this.

"Do you have somewhere you should be?" He caught me checking the time. The expression on his face made it apparent that he felt disrespected.

"As good as you are at licking this cat, baby, not by a long shot. I'm here for the night." I winked, trying to sugar him up and buy me some time to regain my composure and control of the situation.

"Money makes the world go around, and with me, pretty lady, there's no concern about traveling." He was a corny-ass big spender. I held in my laughter.

"Good, 'cause I have a lot of places I'd like to see. Find your way back between my legs, please."

"Naw, I'm trying to see how tight you can grab this meat with your pussy lips." He pulled out his ten-inch cock and rubbed the tip around my slit. "I've got your juice all over my mouth and none over my dick, bitch. Buck those hips up and give me more than a taste."

His face turned cold, one too similar to Spade's. He was serious, and I was in trouble. Me wanting to get a quick sneak nut had gotten me into some shit I wasn't about to get out of.

Robert was controlling the game now. As he rammed his dick inside of my warmth, I squealed loudly to let Rocko and Spade know I was in trouble. He was terrorizing my vagina way worse than Spade had ever done. I was more thankful now than ever that I'd left a pen in the crack of the door so they'd have easy entry.

"Oh, you are a filthy little whore. I see you like it rough."

My eyes flickered to the back of my head when he started biting my nipples and sucking hickeys all over my neck trying to break through my skin. The louder I screamed and scratched at his back, the harder he attacked my body.

"Get the hell up off me, you crazy-ass nigga," I shrieked, not caring if I blew our cover. At this point, the setup was feeling more like rape.

"Naw, pretty baby. You were watching me, and you came to me willing to do a few tricks for a little cash. Don't back down now. This is *exactly* what you wanted. I plan on giving it to you good, though, so relax and don't fight. And don't worry; you'll get your money." He aggressively grabbed my thighs and shoved them up in the air and slammed into me harder.

"I'm not fighting. I'm trying to save your life. Don't make this the last pussy your manhood crawls up in." I pressed my lips together and swallowed hard. "Now, get up off of me." *Where the hell are Spade and Rocko?*

He continued to hold me down, this time with his hand cupped over my mouth.

"Shhh, pretty girl. There's no reason to waste your voice or make me angry at you for talking so recklessly. Either it's going in your mouth or in that delicious wet box between your legs. You can pick, but I will have you, for a fee, of course."

My pussy was dry as sandpaper, and my body was as tense as a board. I should've never let my purse leave my side, and I was gonna catch hell on the flipside with Spade behind that.

It was taking so long for them to get here that I panicked the device had failed me. At least if I had my purse, I could've used my blade to slit this man's throat. That earlier adrenaline rush for a quick nut was causing me severe humiliation and pain now. And it was too late to turn back the hands of time.

The room was starting to spin. Part of my air supply was cut off, and the other half was strained because all of his weight was lying on top me. Sweat was pouring from his face and hairy chest as he continued to ravish my now-limp body.

"If I take my hand from off your mouth and you scream, I *will* kill you." He locked his eyes with mine.

Little did he know I wasn't afraid to die at the hands of an abusive man—Spade made sure of that. I nodded to him, blinking my eyes to signal that he was well understood.

He removed his hand slowly while still slow stroking me. I fought the urge to regurgitate in my own mouth at his version of lovemaking.

"Please let me get up and get myself together. I get it, no turning back. I'm all in," I gasped for air as he continued to rub his stiffness on me.

"I'm not a fool, sweetheart. There's no leaving this bed until this nut spits up out of here."

And he meant just that. I watched the digital clock beside the bed as I tried to make up in my mind if this was rape. But I'd gotten myself into this position—with the guidance of Spade, of course.

Robert used all his force to grind, plow, and dig my guts deep for what seemed like an hour 'cause it was so vile, but in reality, it was only two minutes. When I thought the worst was over, I felt his hot semen shoot up my coochie and instantly started praying for it not to marinate. The missed birth control pill I didn't take this morning suddenly seemed really important.

"Climb out from under the pussy, bitch. It's payout time!" Rocko and Spade rushed into the room with their guns drawn, ready to ripple Robert's body up.

"Whoa! What the fuck is going on? Bitch, I know you didn't set me up." Before I could answer, Spade snatched me up, tossed me to the floor, and was stomping my naked body with his fresh pair of Cole Haan loafers.

While Rocko steadily held his pistol to the dome of Robert's head, they couldn't help but watch Spade beat me black and blue.

"Please, stop! I'm sorry. Oh my God, help me," I cried out, begging and pleading for Spade to have mercy on me. The haymakers he was throwing my way were coming too fast.

"What type of crazy hood nigga shit is this?" Robert had the nerve to utter.

Whap!

"Shut the fuck up, nigga." Rocko pistol-whipped Robert, then leaned over to pull Spade from off top of me. "Back to business, yo. Handle that domestic shit at the crib. There's money on the floor."

"Get your nasty ass up and get dressed." Spade yoked me up by the throat. "I'm not done with you."

Rocko

I collared the perverted business professional up and dragged him over to the safe his assistant, the one we were both probably sleeping with, swore his cash was in. Spade and Jakia might've been on that dumb shit, but I wasn't veering from the plan.

"Please just take what you came for and go," Robert pleaded for his life.

"I ain't here for no fuckin' compromises, perv. And since you were diggin' ole girl over there—any mercy

we was gonna have on ya ass is dead and gone. Damn—
kinda like you." There was no need for me to sugarcoat
his fate—this was it whether or not he liked it.

"I can't believe I'm about to die behind a tricky-ass
whore." Robert hung his head low.

Whap!

Like a bat out of hell, cuzzo rushed Robert and pistol-whipped him square in the center of his eyes. The
surprising off-guard blow caused his head to snap back
as blood was drawn instantly and running down his face.
He'd just split this nigga's shit to the white meat.

"Nigga, ain't you realized you're about to die behind
this whore?" Spade was foaming at the mouth as he
continuously pistol-whipped the rich, black man as blood
flew and splattered across the walls. "Where's the cash at,
nigga? You know what we came for, you ole get-pussy-
ass nigga."

Jakia sat in the corner with her knees close to her
chest, crying her tears out over a red, swollen face. I only
pitied her for a few seconds. She knew the consequences
of going too far with a mark. But had it been my woman,
she wouldn't have been here in the first place.

Tonight, Spade had played Russian roulette with his
woman and got the bullet gutted to his ego. I mean, real
talk, all shit aside, sometimes you make the bitch that
hurts you the most.

"Hey, man, let's get what we came here for and be
out."

Spade didn't follow my suit immediately as he taunted
the now-half-dead man. But he was the one with a
personal vendetta at this point, not me, so I let him alone
to do him. I rushed to the safe, pushed in the code I got
from Lezlee, and then tore the room up to make it seem
like more of a random attack.

I tossed everything he owned—including high-priced slacks, shirts, shoes, cuff links, and a few wads of cash I stuffed in my pocket for my own come-up. Had Spade been attending to stickup business, he could've been in on the extra Benjamins too.

The final thing I did was wipe everything down with Clorox so any fingerprints Jakia left while on her mission couldn't be traced back.

"You got it, dude? We straight? 'Cause I'm about to ice this nigga," Spade gritted through his teeth with a menacing stare.

"Yeah, man, we good, fa'sho," I slung the two duffel bags of stolen cash over my shoulder. "Do whatever you gotta do so we can get up outta here. Time is wasting, and it ain't on our side."

"Time is always on our side, nigga. Believe that," Spade responded, putting one in the chamber of his Smith & Wesson. "We the muthafuckin' bosses out here, chief. *We* run this city!"

Spade

The room reeked of open ass and my woman's pussy. I could smell Jakia's scent from a mile away.

"Hey, baby, get over here and so I can show you the stroke of a real man."

I dropped my pistol to my side, then grabbed my balls, feeling the need to throw my weight. The more I watched her half-nude, freshly fucked body scramble to get up from the floor, the more enraged I got.

"I'm sorry, baby. Please, can we just go home? I don't want to do this anymore."

"Yeah, when I'm done. So, hurry yo' busted ass up! Don't make me skull drag you over this way. I ain't trying to hear but two words—'Yes, daddy.'" It was taking everything in me not to leave her creep foul behind right next to this mark buster.

"So, what this nigga do to you before I got here? And don't lie." I stood over her with one hand itching to lay her out and the other aiming my pistol at ole boy. Either situation, I was prepped to come out the winner.

"Please," she sobbed, taking a few steps back, and throwing her arm up as a shield of protection. "He made me. I said stop, but he kept going."

Her cries meant nothing. They were the fuel to my insanity. "What the fuck did he do to you?"

"He ate my pussy and what you walked in on." She spoke low with her head held lower.

"Well, I tell you what," I leaned down, now talking to the mark buster. "Since you did all that, got robbed of your cash, and took one helluva ass whopping—the least I can give you is a nut before you die. Drop to your knees, boo."

I now pointed my pistol at Jakia. How dare she lie there and let all this shit go down? I'm about to teach her an unforgettable lesson.

She took two steps toward the mark while keeping her eyes fixated on me. I looked down at him and saw his eyes moving from left to right in bewilderment. Neither one of them spoke a word, but their fear could be sensed without effort. Yeah, I was on some ill-bred grime ball shit, but I had a point to prove.

"Look, chief, I've sat on chill too long." Rocko intervened, then snatched the Smith & Wesson from my hand and pointed it directly at Robert.

Pop!

Without hesitation, Rocko sent ole boy straight back to his Maker without an ounce of remorse. Robert died with his eyes wide open with one bullet lodged in the center of his skull. The attached silencer made the gunshot ring off at almost a whisper.

"Like I said, time ain't man's best friend. Let's be out!"

"You better be happy Rock saved your ass." I grabbed a handful of Jakia's hair and slung her to the door. "Grab one of those washcloths and slide those Chanel shades down on yo' face."

It was easy getting out of the casino. No one suspected us three of just committing a heinous crime. Rocko and I were dressed down in denim jeans, button-ups, and loafers—carrying duffel bags that could've very well been our luggage for our short stay.

With our fitted caps low, we kept our heads down, acting like we were engrossed in our phones—like most people do nowadays anyhow. We kept it plain and simple while blending in with the crowd.

No one would've assumed we were two street thugs from the most notorious part of Detroit. Jakia, even though I'd rammed her head into the floor plenty of times, sashayed in front of us in her usual oversized fashion shades like nothing happened . . . or was about to.

Since I didn't get done proving my point up in the room, I fa'sho was gonna pick up where I left off once we got home.

"Have a good evening." One of the security guards nodded our way as we exited the casino/hotel in the parking structure.

"You do the same," Jakia's voice cracked as she broke the barrier setting us free.

And just like that, I was flying down the ramp from the rooftop back onto the dangerous Detroit streets.

6

Jakia

There was a bone-chilling silence in the truck. No one spoke a word, even though there was a celebration to be had. All of us were at least twelve grand richer, including the silent partner Rocko didn't speak about to me; but my fate, on the flipside, was doomed.

Spade made it clear back at the room I was due for an ass whopping once we made it home. So the disaster I was in for was felt deep in the air and had my stomach twisted. I couldn't stop my mind from replaying the flashbacks of Spade coming at me as he tried to beat me into the carpet of that hotel room.

I trembled in my seat and fidgeted with my phone, wishing I could be carefree and peruse Instagram for the latest online boutiques to order from. If only my life could be so simple.

"Put that shit back up to your eye before I black the other one," Spade barked loudly at me, making even Rocko twitch.

"Hey, yo, dude, cut it out with all that Tourette's-syndrome-ass shit. Real talk and I ain't speaking for ya girl—but I almost went for my piece with that sudden spaz out." Rocko looked back and forth between the backseat and Spade just as he'd done earlier with a look of disbelief, then continued. "I swear to G—y'all be on some straight Ike & Tina new-school-type shit. Hurry up and get me to the crib."

I couldn't blame him. He spoke the truth. I hurried to place the hotel washcloth of ice back over my eye in hopes the swelling would go down. Even being short one eye, I still managed through a squint to see Spade mean mugging me from the driver's seat.

I guess he figured his grim silence meant just as much as a bellowed command. The rest of the ride I stayed silent and unspoken to as the two men chopped it up. Damn, if I can hold out nine more years, Juan will be out to save me from the bullshit. I haven't told him what's been going on between Spade and me because I don't want my brother going crazy behind bars. The weight of his little sister being abused would be too much for him to hold on to and still do his time. I wasn't trying to be the reason Juan got into a fight, thrown into the hole, or have an outburst that could extend his time. All I wanted was for us to be together again.

Rocko

The drama Jakia and Spencer had going on wasn't about to be my downfall. In all situations from here on out, family or not, my freedom was my first and only concern. I could see the headlines pointing me as the only witness in one of their murders.

Either Spade was gonna lose his life 'cause Jakia had a *Snapped* moment, or she was going to be found overdosed on an ass kicking. Either way, they weren't about to name Rashad "Rocko" Dinwiddie responsible for shit involving a setup or hood crime.

"A'ight, bro, I'm about to hook up with ole girl in a few and get her right. What time are you coming back out?"

"I think I'm on freeze tonight, Rock." Spade glanced over his shoulder at Jakia, then at me. "But hit me up once you handle business on your end."

"No doubt, I got you."

With that, I got out of Spade's ride carrying one of the two black duffel bags and disappeared into my shack of a house. The way Spade burned rubber from my curbside let me know it was about to be one helluva night for those two, and I was on my own to hustle the block.

I stashed the money in my bedroom closet, then texted Lezlee so she could pull up. In the back of my mind, I hoped she was coming to bust a nut too. After dealing with Spade and Jakia, I needed to release some stress more than murking a nigga.

When Lezlee responded she was on her way, I grabbed a Budweiser, then sat on the porch to scope the next house Spade and I would hit before I moved. He and I got down in the grimiest of ways—but went about getting our bait differently.

He preyed on cats that used Instagram to floss. I preyed on cats who flossed in the gutter neighborhoods, then ran in when they least expected. I never lay my head in a flophouse longer than a month—maybe two—and never frequented the local spots to become a regular.

My whole MO was to stay low key, so I could creep on suckers and was in and out before they could whisper my name. I finessed fools from Detroit on a daily. They ain't never seen two menacing niggas like me and Spade—not ever. Spade was more than making up for being the bullied kid growing up.

Out of the three banging houses on the block, I picked the most popping of them all. Just in the time I was waiting for Lezlee, I watched cars of all types pull up and drive away. Saabs, Cutlass Supremes, Jeeps, and even bicycles rolled up with custos looking to get served.

People from all walks of life frequented this house—which told me the product on hand ranged from marijuana to blow, with pills in between. I'd seen some of the highest paid salaries cop a fix from this joint, so I wanted in on their profit.

Spade might've been busy getting his broad in line, who already walked a thin one, but I shot him a text as Lezlee was pulling up that our lottery ticket across the street was ready to be cashed in. Like I said, with me, money was always on the floor.

Jakia

"Why are you doing this to me? Please, stop!" The way Spade was coming for me, you would've thought he was going for the "kick Jakia's ass trophy." We'd only made it across the threshold to our house, and I'd already taken it upside the head, in the gut, and across the same face he made me ice in the car. Life for me right about now couldn't get any lower.

"I was only doing it for us—because you told me to. Don't send me back out. I swear I'll never cheat again."

"Shut up, trick! I ain't trying to hear that crap. I saw you enjoying that punk buster's stroke. Don't insult me with that whining shit 'cause you were playing for more than our come-up. You were in it for the nut too."

He strong-armed me up into the air and had me dangling like a ragdoll as I struggled to breathe and get loose. I momentarily stopped breathing on my own, not wanting his hands to be the ones to take me out of the game, but I kept fighting for the chance, hoping he'd give in.

With no such luck, he slammed me down onto the couch, then rammed my head into the wall. I saw stars like the *Looney Tunes* characters I laughed at as a child as he sat on top of me with all his weight.

"So, you ain't like his dick? Tell the truth and shame the devil," he scorned me, having some right to judge.

"I swear he forced himself on me. I couldn't stop him, Spade, and I hated every minute of it." I was being honest. The disgusting feeling of having him inside of me still lingered.

"So, you gonna keep lying, huh? Damn, you've really hurt my heart today."

He fell into me out of breath with his chest beating a mile per minute. I kept begging for him to stop, declaring my love for him, and reminding him of my track record of loyalty. But once he caught wind, he rose back up again ready to attack.

"Look, quit humoring a nigga. Be real." Spade must've felt slightly inferior 'cause no nigga should've been so pressed on the real about another dude's pipe game.

"I am," I whimpered, wiping crocodile tears from my face.

He shoved me in the chest when I leaned up to hug him. I didn't know what my last resort was, but if he was gonna kill me with his fist, I was gonna at least put up a fight.

Each time I tried to make a move, Spade either pushed me back down onto the couch by my throat or barricaded me with his weight. I felt helpless and at his mercy as the devil tried to manipulate my actions.

The more I defended myself from him, the harder he beat me. I was no competition to the thug Spade was, even with my best try. I couldn't win, so I gave in and let my body black out.

Spade

Jakia's small body lay sprawled across the floor, black and blue from taking my fists left and right. At no point did I let up or respect the struggle she was going through 'cause I felt mad disrespected.

Before my pops died, he prostituted my mom out when his pockets couldn't support his drug habit. And when she skimmed off the cash, she had to be put in line for stepping outside of boundaries.

I inherited my father's ways but had my own hustle. In setting niggas up and robbing them of their riches, I wasn't pimping Jakia's pussy out, so she wasn't getting ready to either.

Deep down inside, I loved this girl, but the only way I knew how to display that affection to a woman was with brute force and control. Her stepping out of line with ole boy totally threw me out of my square, but watching the madness unravel in front of my eyes with her being with another man was like a wake-up call.

I couldn't take it. That shit drove me in too deep of a rage. Without a doubt, Rocko and I would have to scout another girl for our setup sprees because as of now, Jakia was retired. I was gonna have the blood of every nigga out here that stepped to her—the line was officially drawn.

I leaned down beside her moving to the side the few strands of hair that were matted and sweated out across her caramel face. The features that I was once attracted to were hidden underneath the streams of makeup that were smeared across her cheeks.

She was breathing lightly and starting to make subtle movements, letting me know she was coming out of the slight blackout. I'd beaten the spirit out of her, and she didn't have any strength to move.

I ran my rough hands over her body, gripping her titties and pinching her nipples. "Damn, you feel so good." I continued trailing my fingers down her stomach until reaching her thick thighs. I wanted to indulge so badly, but they were covered in hickeys, which rekindled the rage I'd tried bottling inside.

"Why'd you have to give my pussy to another man? Why'd you go against the grain and break my rules?"

I couldn't resist the urge, so I spread her legs, then placed my head right up on her coochie. Not only did she reek of another man, but she also reeked of his spit and her cum as well. I oughta split her pussy slit open even farther. I stared at her fat cat resisting the urge. Another dude being inside of her was a direct violation to me.

I hopped up and lit a blunt, knowing I needed to take my go-hard down from a million. After a few puffs and sniffing her foul-smelling vagina again, I heard her whine and sob.

I drew her a scalding hot tub of water with her favorite lavender bubble bath. Then I poured damn near half a bottle of vinegar in with it to combat ole boy's tainted smell. She was lucky I didn't pour a bottle of bleach in the damn water too.

I took a second to get control over myself before getting her up 'cause I knew she was gonna rise up swinging. I took a sloppy sip of Hennessey straight from the bottle, not bothering to wipe the spillage, and tossed the bottle onto the floor. I didn't care about the mess. She could clean that shit up later.

"It's bath time." I swooped her up into my arms.

"Get your hands off of me, Spade! I hate you!" She swung and hit me upside the head.

"You don't hate me. And you ain't got nobody else," I had to remind her. I was trying to be nice, but she needed her memory jogged—her brother was serving a bid on my behalf, and her moms was a stone-cold junkie. "I'm the end all in your life. You better respect that."

"I know, and you don't even love me." She continued trying to fight me off. "You treat me like I ain't shit 'cause I ain't got nobody else," she screamed, crying hysterically. "I miss my brother so much. . . ." Jakia's voice trailed off.

"Fuck yo' brother. He don't run shit from the inside. Hell, even if he step foot outside of that jail, he won't be calling a shot inside of *this* house." I stopped dead in my tracks and gripped her body tightly. "And you better hope you make it that long. If you keep talking crazy, your chances are looking slim to none."

"Aaah! Oh my God!"

I didn't give her a chance to react before I dipped her body into the steaming hot tub of water. She leaped from the sweltering temperature and began blistering, but I forced her back down by her shoulders, making her take the pain.

She needed to hurt just as much physically as I was feeling emotionally. Jakia needed to be taught a lesson about fucking me over—especially if I didn't want it to happen again. I'm sure after this that I'd reclaim my throne as the king dick in her life.

"Please, can you at least turn the cold water on?" she stuttered, damn near boiling to death.

"The more you resist, the worse this will be for you. I can't make love to my woman if she's reeking of another nigga's musty balls. Bitch, be still." I turned the cold water on some, then started to wash her body roughly from top to bottom. I Brillo Pad-scrubbed her vagina until she twitched aggressively and yelled out in pain.

"Can you take me out of here?" Jakia's whispers could hardly be heard. Her head was dropping to the side as I held her up by her underarms to keep her from sliding all the way in.

I pulled her out and carried her to the bed, drying and putting lotion on her body at the same time. Then I dropped my jeans, jacked my dick, and then propped her delicious ass up to take my meat. "Whose pussy is this?"

"Yours," she screamed at me plunging into her.

"What did you say?" I dug deeper inside of her, letting her know that answer wasn't sufficient enough.

"It's yours, daddy; this pussy belongs to you."

"That's right, baby girl. And do you love your daddy?"

"Yes, you know I do." She was still talking low, but the sobs were now moans of passion. "I love you so damn much it hurts." She pushed herself back up on me, then clenched her walls down tight around my dick making me twitch.

Don't let her get control. Nah, this ain't that. It ain't never gonna be that. I abruptly pulled my dick out of her wetness and felt myself jerk from missing out on the goodness. Then I began taunting her. "You want daddy's dick? Huh, baby girl?"

I pushed her down by the arch of her back, then began flicking the tip of my dick over her clit making her booty tighten around my shaft. I was about ready to explode because it felt way too amazing.

"Yes, yes, yes!" Jakia was screaming and backing her booty up, throwing it on me just the way I wanted her to.

Whap!

I slapped her across her behind. "Are you gonna step outside of this house again?"

"No, daddy, I promise," she cried out in a mixture of pleasure and pain.

Yeah, she likes this kinky shit too.

Whap!

"Do you think you've learned your lesson?" I spread her cheeks, ran my finger down her slit, and then tickled her hole.

"I did, I swear to God I've learned my lesson." Jakia was horrified of anal sex, so I knew if at no other point in me punishing her, I had her full attention now.

Whap!

"You promise? And think before you answer because you know I hate liars, those that betray me, and disloyal bastards." I leaned down whispering into her ear in a cold tone. Every word out of my mouth was serious.

"I promise, Spade, and I'm sorry. It'll never ever happen again."

"Just one more thing." I rubbed her smooth skin with my fingertips.

"Yes, daddy," she panted.

"I made you bitch. You belong to me!" I ripped her hole open with my fat mushroom tip.

"Stop! Oh God," she screamed until I cupped her mouth shut.

I wasn't getting ready to stop or let up. She needed to feel my meat going up in her raw dog in every hole on her body. I was getting ready to set the record for the number of nuts I could bust.

I'd already taken another pill, so I was ready to go all night. When she calmed down and fell into my stroke, we both enjoyed a session of anal sex before passing out. I got to bust three fat ones, so I felt all the way satisfied.

Rocko

"Are you sure ole boy is dead? If you left that nigga blinking, he's gonna fight through it and have all our heads on a platter. He's the type of nigga who'll snitch in a heartbeat." Lezlee rolled over onto my chest with a messy head of curls.

"C'mon now, baby, you already know the answer to that." I stroked the fine baby hairs lying across her face. "Don't worry your pretty little head over that. I ain't the type of nigga that leaves clues and shit."

"I'm gonna try. At least I can go wild in the mall to keep my mind at ease."

"Hey, ma, on that note—let me school you right quick. You've gotta play the low-profile role for a while until you find a new gig. Don't tell ya friends shit. And don't make no erratic, large purchases you can't back up with real income. If that cat was as high profile as you claim he was—and I do mean *was*—you'll have some heat behind this if you stand out too much. Ya dig?" I'd just laid a heavy amount of information on Lezlee. It was crucial for her to follow the rules.

"Well, can I lie up here with you till all of this blows over?" She looked deflated not to be able to shop, then she snuggled back up to my hairy chest.

"Naw, baby girl, I can't have that. This ain't no home." It might've sounded like a blow off, but it wasn't. I'd just grilled her guts on an air mattress in an empty room that had a box-TV set on top of a milk crate.

The few run-down kicks I rocked were lined up across the wall alongside the only five outfits I put into rotation while here. Like I said earlier to these cats, I had to seem like the average run-down bum.

"Weeell," she dragged the word along, "we've both got twelve Gs apiece, so that's at least twenty-four total to disappear. That way, neither one us gotta worry about nobody on our trail." Her sweet voice sounded sincere, and truth be told, I wanted to get caught up with the fantasy she was selling herself.

"I was thinking I'd put your hot ass on a flight back to Chicago and catch up with you once everything blows over. This is serious, Lezz."

"I'm serious. We've got cash, Rocko—and I can make your wildest fantasy come true." She ran her fingers up and down my chest, down to the pubes, and all around my dick and balls. "Do you need a reminder of my magic?"

"Gon' and stroke daddy over. Let's see if him and my brain can come to an agreement on what to do."

I didn't need a reminder of how baby girl could lock her lips around my dick. Lezlee was working with the whole package—ass, titties, and a warm pussy that welcomed my manhood each and every time.

I couldn't wife her up or even play the constant side-piece nigga she might've accepted. Not only did I stay on my grind in the streets, but also Spade and Jakia's relationship taught me that it was spawned from the devil.

Until I got up out of the game, I wouldn't be locking no bitch down, and I wasn't giving no bitch the key to me—especially if they were about that life. When my day was over and my last nigga was robbed and left for dead, I'd bow out to a quiet, innocent woman who led a boring life.

7

Iesha—From the Casino

I walked down the casino hotel's hallway looking for room number 1253, ready to turn this trick out for every dollar he was willing to spend. I'd already made a night's worth not doing much but my job and flirting with him.

So, I could only imagine what type of damage I could do at the mall later off his generous tips on the late-night level. I was dressed in the skimpiest, but the most expensive-looking outfit I had in my closet—which was handed down from my last ex-best female friend.

The hot-pink spandex minidress barely went over my booty as I intentionally wore it to turn heads. Accessorizing the right way to make females hate me too, I rocked my dress with a pair of black Chuck Taylors and a denim jacket being a trendsetter.

After taking a few selfies and full-body shots, I was feeling myself, and you couldn't tell me I wasn't shit. My curves were working overtime in my favor—finally.

I tapped on the door, then waited a few seconds before knocking again. It was slightly ajar, but I suspected he left it like that for me since it was close to our scheduled meet up time.

After waiting for what I felt was too long, accompanied by the feeling of something being weirdly wrong,

I pushed the door open and screamed to the same God I just thanked for sending a moneyman into my life.

The luxury hotel room I was planning to trick in was completely ransacked. Not only did my nose instantly start burning from the reeking smell of bleach, but also my olfactory sense kicked in marking the smell of death.

Living in the D, I saw dead bodies dumped or knocked off in the abandoned buildings that were in between our houses. This might've been nothing new, but it was most certainly shocking. Murders didn't happen on state-patrolled grounds—obviously until now.

My feet finally moved—straight across the room toward the phone, and I called the front desk for security. As I waited, I took another glance around at all his clothes, personal items, and furniture within the room that was flipped over. He was robbed. I felt bad. But I felt worse I didn't get here in enough time.

"Hotel security! Ma'am—step back from the body." More than one security guard of the four-star casino-hotel screamed out as they rushed in.

I backed out of the hotel room and spoke with security about why I was here and how I'd found him. I kept making it known I'd just found him in this condition, not murdered him.

"Listen, ma'am, we must hold you until the cops get here for questioning." The security guard stayed tight-lipped as I plead my innocence.

"But I ain't did nothing. This could be my job, sir!" By this time, I was getting hysterical. The only reason I was here in the first place was that I needed the money. If I lost my job, I'd really be up shit creek without a paddle.

"Calm down, ma'am. This is just a normal procedure."

He walked away, and I was left in the hallway with another security guard to make sure I didn't leave. I slid down the wall with my heart racing, wishing with all of my might I could go back just twenty minutes ago. I would've taken my ass home to my kid instead.

When the elevator bells went off, I turned and saw my manager getting off. *Aw, shit, it's about to be hell.* It was company policy for employees not to fraternize or stay in the casino's hotel with patrons. Not only was I in violation, but also I was busted red-handed with a dead body.

"Iesha Morrison, you have some serious explaining to do."

Spade

"Let me get five dozen of these long-stemmed rainbow roses, my dude." I spread five large bills across the counter griming the small Chinese man. I swear they owned everything in the hood.

"No problem, sir. You like vases for them or just wrapped in box?" His broken English aggravated me.

"How in the fuck am I supposed to get five fuckin' vases home, chinky? Huh? Wrap them bitches up so I can be out." I was rude and disrespectful to him and his race and didn't care or show any remorse. He and his people stayed opening businesses in our communities and overcharging, so why should I care about how I spoke to them?

He scurried off to get the boxes for the roses I was purchasing for Jakia. I owed her a few peace offerings for yesterday, and this was just one of the stops on my list.

She'd been eyeing a pair of Gucci leather sandals and a matching bag that I'd surprise her with that should help ease her open wound, so I needed to hit the mall before the crowd and make it back before she woke up. And from the pounding I put on her face, pussy, and that tight, virgin asshole, she should be out cold for a few more hours.

"Would you like the vases in a separate bag, sir? They be nice for you girlfriend," he smiled, showing a rack of gray, rotten teeth.

"Yeah, man, whatever." I threw another hundred on the counter.

I hit up Rocko's cell when I got back to my truck to check in, but it went to voicemail after a few rings. Knowing my dude, he was probably still paying ole girl off with some stroke for the overcharging.

I couldn't blame him 'cause she'd come in handy, fa'sho. When we finally got a chance to speak business, I'd let him know I was ready to rock-n-roll on the lames he'd been watching.

I set the cruise control to seventy and coasted up I-75N toward Somerset Mall. It's whatever. I'm about to spend a few racks on myself too.

Somerset Mall was in the suburban city of Troy, almost thirty minutes from the city of Detroit where Rocko and I did most of our dirt. I parked in valet even though my truck reeked of green buds, then walked in ready to do some damage.

I got a mad rush when it came to spending other niggas' hard earned cash. For it to still be early, the mall was packed with big spenders eager to splurge. I might've been walking with rich white men from elite walks of life, but my pockets had bricks of cash in them ready to spend just like theirs. Today was like any other day for me. I demanded respect, and when I didn't get it—I took it.

Within thirty minutes, I'd spent over a grand on just myself, and it felt hella good. I'd copped a Louis Vuitton belt with a matching shirt and kicks, plus a few pair of denim shorts for the summer season.

My swag game was getting ready to be hella official. We'd made licks before that set us up to make moves— but never this major. For once, I wasn't worried about writing a check I couldn't cash or breaking the bank.

After setting Jakia up right with her Gucci stilettos, purse to match, and some Mac makeup to cover the bruises I'd so effortlessly beat on her face, I was on my way out the exit until the salesman at Rogers & Holland's jewelry store flagged me down.

"Excuse me, sir, I see you're taking some fine gifts home to your lady." He noticed the bags I was carrying. "Let me get a moment of your time to show you a few things that'll really have her smiling." He walked out into the hallway putting his arm over my shoulder.

"Hey, dude, I'm gonna need about five feet." I backed up, letting him know off rip I wasn't comfortable with a man touching me.

"Not a problem. My apologies." He stepped back adjusting his gray tie. "Please, if you have a moment, sir, let me show you a few pieces that you might be interested in." He took another glance down at the high-priced shopping bags in my hands and couldn't resist the urge to lay his sales pitch on thick. "And if you like what you see and are ready to buy, I'll give you a real sweet deal."

"Shit, man, yeah—whatever. Lead the way."

By the time he was done showing me displays of diamonds, including watches, rings, earrings, bracelets, and the catalogue of merchandise giving me the option to customize a piece, my pockets were three grand shorter.

"Here you go, sir," he slipped the 1-karat white gold diamond ring on my pinky finger. "And I'm sure your beautiful lady will love this gorgeous Julianna-style engagement ring. The diamonds are flawless, simply impeccable at a full carat to show just how devoted you are to her." He smiled widely as I handed him thirty crisp one hundred-dollar bills knowing his commission just went straight through the roof.

"A'ight, my dude, you can chill trying to up-sale me shit else. You've worked my pockets enough." I swooped up my bags, not being rude, but feeling my pockets take a hit.

I was glad he'd hooked me up with the jewels, but in the back of mind, I was already plotting on another hit.

"Well, here's my card if you change your mind. You'll be needing a band to go with that ring once you two set a date. Congratulations, by the way."

I threw my hand up as I strutted out the door. "Yup, yup, holla at cha', playa."

Jakia

The morning after was always the worst, but this particular sunrise was terrible. I peeked through my eyes seeing the room was pitch black but couldn't manage even opening them wide. Spade had smacked me in the face more times than I could count, and I could still hear my ears ringing from his mighty blows.

I lay there feeling miserable and alone. I missed my brother but resented him for sending me to hook up with Spade in the first place. Since the first day of being under his grip, I haven't had my own mind or another alternative for happiness.

I took a deep breath feeling my chest cave in at the excruciating pain. I was scared to take another one just in case my lung had collapsed. I couldn't even use my hands to rub my wounds 'cause even they ached.

Spade had been far from the love of my life as he bent each finger back on both of my hands like a monster. At that moment, I prayed for death.

Feeling the sensation to pee, I climbed out of bed, wishing I had a catheter. As gross as it sounded, anything would've been better than pissing from my sore coochie hole Spade slammed in and out of relentlessly last night.

I picked at his come on my thighs and around my mouth as I swallowed hard, almost gagging at the salty taste. The few minutes before I blacked out, he was tag teaming my tonsils with no remorse.

After grabbing a few crackers and a bottle of water, I checked the mail and was overjoyed to see Juan had written back. I'd taken a chance giving him my home address. Spade seldom got the mail, but if he did, I'd just suffer the consequences like I'd been doing for doing nothing at all. I ripped the envelope open to a one-page letter, front and back, that I couldn't wait to read.

Jakia, baby sis . . .
Thanks for the cash on my books, but I'm so sorry for sending u to that bitch nigga. It was hard reading the type of shit u out here doing.

My word, when I'm out, he gonna have 2 explain his beef with u. I swear to Allah I'm gonna take care of shit, sis, better than b4. I been learning shit in here no man can take away, and fuck that nigga for putting his hands on u.

I wish him death b4 I get out cuz payback gonna be a bitch. Have u seen Momma in them streets? I gotta get my whole fam right. Be strong, sis. I talk to my lawyer in a few days to give up Spade and his ho-ass cousin.

4u, I'ma let the grain hold itself down and come out like a snitch. I love u, sis. It's cool. Ain't no man worth my time. Be strong 'cause u got that Coleman blood.—1.

Juan

My legs felt like putty as I took a seat on the bottom step crying my eyes out. If Juan got out of jail early, my whole life would be fixed. I swear I couldn't take this shit anymore. Spade was turning me into something I truly hated, a wounded bitch.

8

Iesha

I sat in the corner of the hotel room in the large, plush chair biting away at my fingernails. The 710-square-foot room seemed to be the size of a thimble as Michigan State Police officers crowded in dusting for fingerprints, taking pictures of the crime scene, and what daunted me the most—their constant questioning of me.

"Ms. Morrison, how is it that you knew Mr. Taylor?"

My supervisor stood over me with a tight lip, waiting for me to give my response.

"I met him down in the gaming room this evening. So, I guess you could say I didn't really know him," I stuttered.

"Tsk tsk tsk! Iesha," she whispered through clenched teeth.

The officer put his hand up to silence her, then continued. "And what were you doing here?"

As if he couldn't tell from the skimpy, hot-pink minidress I was wearing what my intentions were, I humored him simply because I didn't have another choice. Had he been a bum from the hood, I would've cut into him rough and raw.

"He asked me to meet him here when I got off. So I went home, got dressed, and came back. That's when I found him. He was dead when I got here."

"He asked you where? You need to be very specific with me right now, because, as of now, my superior is telling me to take you to the station. I'm trying to work with you."

White people scared me, and he was no different. I broke under pressure. I went over everything from the first greeting he and I shared. I started babbling beginning with the first moment ole boy and I first flirted, the huge tip, proposition, and exchange of numbers.

I even broke down crying about the eviction notice taped to my door yesterday, which prompted all of this tricking business in the first place. I didn't care if my shabby life wasn't much to go back to—I wasn't trying to end up fighting a murder case.

"We've got the tapes," another officer announced, saving my behind from further questioning.

"Now, Ms. Morrison, I won't see anything on these tapes that are contradictory to the story you've just told me, right?"

I hopped up from the chair excited as hell. I knew my story would check out. "Hell naw, let's run that tape!" As the film began to play back tonight's events over the 42-inch television, I wiped the tears from my eyes happy that I was about to be cleared.

"Don't get all happy now, Iesha. You broke several rules, so regardless how this plays out, your continued employment with this casino is still up for termination," my manager rudely snapped, then crossed her arms while waiting on the tapes to finish.

The casino's security tapes were so vivid, meticulous, and close-up on every patron gambling at the tables and slots that it made my skin crawl. If I hadn't told the truth, my story was about to check out right about now.

I watched myself on tape serve the late-great-possible-trick, lead him to the bar, and even take the wad of cash he considered a tip. Watching him on film made me wish I would've gotten a chance to feel his stroke for real—for real. He was sexy as hell.

"Hey, stop that tape. He left with that girl!" I'd forgotten all about him dissing me for some rich, paid-looking woman. Well, here she was, and now the heat was shifting from me.

"Can we get close-up shots of this woman?" the officer standing nearest to me spoke up after hearing my claims. "From the time she enters the casino until the time she leaves, I want tapes from every camera in here. I don't understand what type of sloppy security team allows this ratchet bullshit to happen. Well, not on my watch," he yelled, turning beet red. "I want a list of everyone who was involved with this room, cleaned this room, and dealt this dead man his last card. Leave no rock unturned when it comes to solving this murder, you peons!"

As all the cops scattered around trying to appease the obvious boss, I sat quietly in my seat like a church mouse afraid of getting caught. All of this bullshit, and for what? Those few Benjies ain't even get me off of scraps.

Ring! Ring! Ring! Ring!

"Captain, it's the man's wife on the phone," another cop said, holding the phone out so someone else could deliver the grave news.

My manager used that time to snatch me into the hallway where she gave me the tongue-lashing of a lifetime. I watched her mouth move as she attempted to belittle me, but I was too caught up in trying to figure out how I was going to pay my eviction notice tomorrow.

"Iesha Morrison, you're no longer an employee of this hotel. Please remove your belongings from the locker downstairs. Security will be certain to escort you out."

"I don't give two sweet fucks, lady. You can shove this job up your tight asshole and go straight to the burning fires of hell." I hawked up a glob of spit in her face. What did it matter? As of now, I had no job and was on my way to getting sat out on my ass.

She stood in amazement as I devilishly grinned at her, knowing she wouldn't spit back. "You little degenerate," she grimed me before screaming to the cops to arrest me on assault charges.

They waved her off as there were more important things to tend to. Her petty claims were mediocre compared to an unsolved murder case.

"Bye, Felicia!" I burst out into laughter, then ran down the hall toward the staircase. I could hear her talking cash-shit to the cops in the background, but I didn't care.

Wasn't no one checking for my unemployed, broke ass with a dead body sprawled out in a casino hotel. I took the steps down two at a time until I bolted out the door, running full speed. Forget just leaving this hotel. I was about to jump fresh out of Detroit. After this night from hell, I needed a fresh start. Iesha Morrison was officially off into the wind.

Rocko

"Hey, ma, wake up. Rise and grind. It's time for you to start making moves up out the D."

I was already up watching the block and thinking over where I'd squat at next. As much as my dick wanted thirds and fourths of Lezlee's kinky sex acts, I wasn't the type of man that made decisions based upon a nut.

"Aw, are you serious? What about what we talked about earlier? You ain't trying to make moves with me?"

I wasn't trying to hurt Lezlee's feelings or send her back to Chicago scorned, but in a hot second, there wasn't about to be any other way.

"Listen, once everything blows over with your now deceased boss—we'll hook up. You've gotta play the game, baby girl." I leaned over and kissed her cheek as she looked up at me believingly.

"Say you promise." She grabbed my head and locked eyes with me.

Ring! Ring! Ring!

"Grab ya, phone, ma; you got it." I was saved by the phone and able to blow off her question.

"I ain't worried about this phone," she mumbled, then rolled over to snatch it up from the floor anyway. "Oh my God! Rocko, shit—what should I do? It's Robert's wife calling!"

"Calm your ass down and breathe," I yelled. "Answer the phone and try not to act any different."

"Hi, Mrs. Taylor. This is Lezlee." The longer she held the phone, the worst her facial expression got. Within forty-five seconds of hearing the woman's rundown, Lezlee had crumbled and was stuttering and crying into the woman's ear. "I'm so sorry, Mrs. Taylor. I'm soooo sorry. Please, fo—"

Before I knew it, I was having a Spade moment. I didn't know what her next few syllables were, but I wasn't taking a chance. With all intent of yoking Lezlee up, I snatched her up by her throat ready to choke the life out of her. "Are you fucking crazy? Keep it short and end the call," I mouthed.

"No, no, I haven't talked to him since earlier." She paused, looking at me with panic. She wore nothing but anxiety on her face. "I told him what time the car would be out front and his itinerary for the day. Then we ended the call. I haven't spoken with him since."

Unlike Spade's girl, Jakia, it was apparent Lezlee wasn't cut out for the games I was into. "Don't you say one wrong word," I spoke in a low, powerful tone.

Tears streamed down her chocolate face as she held the phone for what seemed like an eternity. After making her turn the volume up, I hovered over her, listening closely to hear whatever leads they might've had without needing Lezlee's translations.

From what I could make out through the wife's screams, Detroit police had found her husband dead and was apparently hot on the case. They were going over security footage, dusting for possible prints, checking with other guests to see if they heard or saw anything, but there were two main things his wife said that had even a gangster like me shook up.

They were planning to release a picture to the news of the woman he was last seen with to stir up leads, and they were dusting his body for prints, bodily fluids, and hair. Since it was clear her dead husband was a cheater, she at least wanted to know who the whore was who killed and robbed him.

"Please let me know how I can help. I'm so sorry for your loss," Lezlee's voice was dull and monotone. She stared at me blankly, listening to the woman thank her for being such a humble and honest assistant to her husband and then ended the call. "What have I done, Rocko? What have *we* done? She should be mourning her husband, but she just praised me for being so loyal. I ain't shit." She hung her head feeling a rush of guilt. "They're gonna find out! I'm so scared!"

"Hey, be cool." I collared her up.

"Please don't hurt me," she gasped, then whispered with her eyes closed tightly.

"Ay, ma, cut it with the theatrics, yo." I felt myself losing patience with Lezlee because weakness wasn't something I handled very well. "How you talking about being with a nigga you can't even trust?"

I calmed down just enough to run game on her. After seeing her performance a few moments ago on the phone, I knew she wasn't the type of ride-or-die chick I could even keep around.

"I'm sorry, babe, but I was caught off guard." She tried cleaning up her emotions while wiping the tears from her face.

Too bad she can't wipe away my memories. I picked up my phone to hit Spade's cell while I allowed Lezlee to hug all over me, promising me to do better. I ran my fingers through her hair to soothe whatever feelings she needed me to nurse, but I had no intentions on playing the good guy much longer.

"Well, I'm gonna need you to get that shit together, Lezz—we're a team." I continued to gas her up. The trickery flowed easily out of my mouth 'cause I knew she was easily manipulated. "You already knew there was gonna be some questions, calls, concerns, and cover-ups you were gonna have to do behind ole boy's murder. Instead of you focusing on trying to get wifed—put all your eggs in the basket of trying to remain free."

"I understand, and I promise to do better next time. They won't break me." She rested her head on my chest.

Damn, nigga, what's really good? Pick up! Spade's phone continued to ring until it went to voicemail. I didn't know what he was off into, but I needed to holla at my manz quick, fast, and in a hurry.

"A'ight, ma, let me sit down and roll up so I can get my mind right. This shit ain't going right at all."

Jakia

"Hey, baby, I'm home," Spade called from downstairs.

I didn't bother to move or answer because I feared he might take my words and twist them the wrong way. After reading Juan's letter until the words were etched into my brain, I promised myself to stay strong enough and survive until his release. That was the only saving grace I could truly hold on to.

"You ain't hear me calling you?" He burst through the bedroom door. "A nigga trying to come in here and do right, and you trying to set me off." He dropped a gang of shopping bags onto the floor. "I got you all of this, plus a bunch of roses and shit downstairs."

I couldn't even front. As much as I wanted to give him the silent treatment and stay to myself because of the abuse I'd just gone through, seeing the Gucci bags I knew were for me brought sparkles to my dim eyes.

"Oh my God, baby, did you get the shoes?" I sprang from the bed and snatched the box from the bag. "You didddd," I sang, and then jumped in his arms. For a second, I forgot about the gifts and fell into his neck—lost in his Gucci Guilty cologne. He smelled so good and felt even better.

"Yeah, girl, ya manz did that. Plus, I got you the matching purse so you can stunt the next time we go out. Gon' and give me my props."

"I'll give you that, and much more." I hugged him again this time making sure to plant kisses all over his face. "I love my presents, Spade, even though I know you think I don't deserve them." I didn't want to bring up yesterday, but it just sorta slipped out.

"Naw, we ain't gonna ruin a good moment, Jakia. Even a knuckleheaded nigga like myself knows that." He pulled away from me, then leaned back against the dresser.

"I just wanted you to know—" my words were cut short.

"Let me talk, Jakia. I got some shit I gotta say, real talk, and I don't need you cutting me off."

I heard the seriousness in his voice, then instantly backed down. My only response was a nod as I took a seat on the bed while he gathered his thoughts and then continued.

"I know you don't think so, Kia, but a nigga got real love for you. Knowing that you'd give my pussy away like that had me spent, ya dig? I was feeling some type of way. That's what woke me up. Had me thinking and shit."

Spade wasn't as good with his words as he was with his fists, so I struggled to read through his jumble for a meaning.

"You ain't gotta worry about hitting the streets with me and Rocko no more. I'ma fuck around and catch a case behind trying to protect and make money behind you at the same time."

I couldn't tell if he was juicing me up or not. After all the punishment I've taken these last few hours, this could've been a sick joke.

"Please tell me you're for real, babe." My voice was soft, and so were my eyes. I wanted to be strong like the words in Juan's letter told me, but Spade promising me my dream made me feel weak.

"Naw, babe, I'm being real. It's time to tap you out. Do it look like I'm playing?" Spade pulled a small black bag from his pocket, then looked down like he was gathering his composure. "I don't really know how to do this shit, so, whatever—here it goes. Let's me try to do right by you. No more hitting, sending you out on the streets, or doing you how my pops did my moms. The white dude at the store said diamonds are forever, and this ring would get you to forgive anything I did wrong." He pulled a small red velvet box from the bag, then popped it open.

"Spade! I'm about to pass out!" I couldn't believe my eyes. Spencer Spade Johnson, the man whose heart was ice cold, was standing before me with a blinging-ass engagement ring.

"So, what's up? You with a real nigga or nah?" It didn't matter the moment; Spade kept his attitude straight gangster.

"Hell yeah, I'm down with you, Spade. You've been my whole life over this past year. With Juan gone and Phoebe cuddled up to that pipe, you're the only family I have. You're all I want to have." I was being real with him. I could handle a relationship with Spade as long as it didn't come with the pent-up aggression he liked to let rip on me.

"Make sure of that, Jakia. I meant what I said about you and another dude. If you ever doubt me, let last night be a reminder."

Spade put the ring on my finger, and I damn near melted. Maybe my prayers *were* being worked out. I held my hand up and admired how it glistened and symbolized him and me starting over to a new life. The longer I stared at the ring, the more I started to believe he was going to be a changed man. The bitter thoughts of yesterday became less clear as his promise to wife me up had me on cloud nine.

I put all of my reservations and our bad history to the side because I truly loved my man. I couldn't see myself giving up now—not when he was ready to do right by me and us. "You don't have to worry, Spade. I ain't never been cut out for helping you and Rocko do setups. I've always wanted to play house full time."

"Well, this ain't no play-play shit. I took you out of the streets, but that only means you have more time to cater to ya man. So nothing around here better be unkempt, and that coochie better stay just right. Matter of fact, get on over here and give me a taste of that. Let me get you barefoot and pregnant right quick."

I obliged and gave my man all that he wanted. Why wouldn't I? I was getting ready to be Mrs. Jakia Johnson. I couldn't wait to write to my brother about this.

9

Rocko

My cousin was out here MIA, blowing in the wind. I'd hit his cell up like a basic bitch from a one-night stand, but he wasn't answering. I ain't know what was up with him, but I knew things this way were heating up. The house catty-corner from me was ready to be hit off.

"Rocko! Rocko! Where are you?" I heard Lezlee screaming through my squat house.

Man, this chick ain't got no type of trait as a rider. She'll blow a nigga's whole steelo one hundred. I jumped up and flew into the house, making sure to bolt the locks immediately that I'd installed. "Hey, bury that damn voice. What up?" The more I dealt with Lezlee, the more I understood how Spade stayed snapping.

"The shit has hit the fan. I know you said you got this—but, um, Mrs. Taylor sending pictures to my phone of ole girl y'all used to seduce him. Plus two dudes with fitted caps—one looking a lot like you."

"What in the fuck? Give me that damn phone," I shouted, ready to bust a fuse. I twisted it out of her hand to read the messages for myself.

Mrs. Taylor: My husband's corpse is being checked for bodily fluids. I am on the next flight out and would like to meet up with you as soon as I arrive.

Mrs. Taylor: **Please call me ASAP.**

Mrs. Taylor: **The Detroit Police Department has just released the attached photo. Do you know this woman?**

The photograph was a woman in a black catsuit, large Chanel shades, and a long, blond, curly weave. To an unknowing eye on the street, this could've been a picture of any Detroit girl working the casinos. But I knew better and knew Lezlee was right . . . Shit was about to hit the fan.

This chick was without a doubt—Jakia. After forwarding the picture to my burnout, I sent it to Spade behind my last 911 message. If this didn't make him call back, I didn't know what would

Ring! Ring!

Lezlee's phone received another text message.

Mrs. Taylor: **Was my husband involved with her or these men?**

Even I lost a little bit of my composure as I stared at a picture of Spade and me coming out of ole boy's room with Jakia leading the way. Damn, it's about to get hella real. This dude better hit me back so we can do some serious damage control. I forwarded the picture to myself, then him as before, then headed toward my makeshift bedroom.

"Here you go." I tossed the phone onto the air mattress.

"Is this you and your boy?" She scrolled through her phone seeing the lady's last message.

"Don't ask me no dumb questions. Just hurry up and reply that you don't know the girl, and do they have a better picture of the men."

Ring! Ring!

"She's calling. Should I answer? What? What? This chick is relentless." Lezlee went into another panic mode.

Instead of telling her how to follow, I wanted to see how she would lead.

"I'm not about to answer or text her back." She sent the call to voicemail. "I'm about to take my money and dip. I'm not going back to Chicago, and I fa'damn sure ain't staying here." She made a move for her purse.

"You ain't doing nothing that I don't tell ya ass to do. Sit down and get comfortable until I figure this thing out."

"Naw, I'm straight. You can keep that phone and them blunts. I'm bouncing."

Whap!

"Sit your ass down. Please don't make me put my hands on you again tonight," I growled. I was pissed off to the highest level. This chick was taking me all out of character. I couldn't think straight with her yapping like a Chihuahua.

"Ain't nothing about ta pop off until I holla at my manz about all of this. So, like I told you earlier, fall back."

Spade

My pants were at my ankles as I shot nuts into Jakia like an Uzi. She was creaming, screaming, and throwing every bit of love she had for me back onto my dick. I didn't know how Rocko and I were gonna game niggas in the streets with li'l momma off our team, but somehow, someway, we'd make moves and make thangs pop. The way I was making moves on her right now, without a doubt she was gonna have a belly full of my seed.

Ring! Ring!

"Whoever that trick is, tell her your fiancée is about that life." Jakia looked back at me while grinning. "Our last names are about to be the same. You're all mine now."

"Gon' and turn that ass around and be about taking this meat." I smacked her on the behind until I juiced her all the way up. I could feel my dick going limp inside of her as my phone rang off the hook.

I assumed it was Tiff trying to meet up for our sex session, so I kept ignoring each call and text alert. For once, I had to devote 100 percent of my time to Jakia, my soon-to-be wife.

Mrs. Taylor

"She isn't answering the phone or replying to any of my text messages. I'm more than certain that Jezebel had something to do with his death," I shouted as I sipped on a chilled glass of white wine.

Over the phone, I could play my game well. But the truth was that I didn't give two shits about Robert being dead. His cheating behind had never been faithful. I'd just never had the guts to do anything about it.

I knew he stuck his penis into every woman walking in every city he did business in, but I was a well-kept wife with no worries. I let the money soothe my emotional pain—up until a month ago when my routine HIV test results rolled in. There are some things money couldn't fix.

"Well, ma'am, we're on the case, and a photograph has been sent out of the parties we believe are responsible for your husband's death. If his assistant was part of the ring, we will find out," he promised.

The officers continued to run down all of the information about where Robert's body would be sent, but the only information I needed to obtain was a death certificate.

Once the world knew Robert Taylor was deceased—I could collect the insurance money, wipe his name from our loaded accounts, and live swell for the rest of the days God allowed me to have on this earth.

As far as I was concerned—that's what he deserved for cheating. But this was my consequence for allowing it so long.

"Thank you for working so diligently on this case, Officer. I do understand Detroit is overwhelmed with gruesome cases almost hourly."

"Yes, indeed, Mrs. Taylor," he laughed lightly. "But no amount of crime could keep me from working around the clock on this one. Please call me once your flight arrives, and have a safe one."

"Thanks again, and I will." The call ended, and my celebration had just begun. I downed the glass of wine and stared at the woman in the photo one more time. "You're the *real* bitch in all of this. Cheers to you," I sang out, then danced throughout my loft packing.

I should've despised my husband's alleged killer, but I secretly praised her. I wished I could be her. If we ever crossed paths, I'd give her way more than the measly stash she got from setting him up. I'm sure she'll need a little comforting once her immune system starts shutting down.

Jakia

I was done taking Spade's dick and his nut. I walked with wobbly legs into the bathroom for a quick ho bath while Spade lay back on the bed tending to his phone. I still couldn't believe a karat-size rock was on my wedding finger, and I also couldn't believe Spade was trying to knock me up. With him turning over a new leaf, I didn't want to dwell on the past, but there was one lingering thought I couldn't block out no matter how hard I stared at my glistening ice.

Spade's come wasn't the only sperm swimming around in my insides. So was Robert's. Even though I wanted to nurse my soon-to-be husband's child, I couldn't take the chance of it being the dead man's baby. I had to get to the drugstore for the Plan-B pills. Some prevention needed to be done—and fast.

Spade wasn't in the bedroom, so I went downstairs to find him. A large smile spread across my face seeing my living room covered in rainbow roses. I rubbed my belly wishing the future he was suddenly trying to build didn't have to be tainted, but I knew there was no other choice.

Besides, with Phoebe being the only example I had, I wasn't sure I could amount to much in the mother department. I kept calling out to my new fiancé but wasn't getting an answer.

His car was still in the driveway, so he hadn't disappeared. Part of me wanted him to be dipped off with his ex-chick Tiff so I would have a sneak moment to hit up the local pharmacy. Getting rid of this problem before it became a bigger problem was a must.

"Jakia! I'm in the basement. Bring ya ass and hurry up," Spade yelled up to me.

I flew down into the basement without hesitation. The base and urgency in his voice could be heard even a flight away. "What's wrong? What's going on?"

Spade was stuffing wads of cash into a suitcase, along with clothes and shoes.

"Pack your bags. We're going on a trip for a few weeks until shit dies down in the D. I know you thought that was some random chick or Tiff blowing me up, but that was Rocko. They've got pictures of all three us." He showed me the screen on his phone.

I felt my lungs collapse and my heart stop as I stared at pictures of me leaning over Robert in the casino's eatery area. I saw straight through the disguise I'd thought was so foolproof, and I feared others would too. All it would take was for my picture to get plastered all over the television. I'm sure someone from my old hood would flip and reveal my identity if the reward were high enough, especially ole cracked-out Phoebe. I began shaking uncontrollably. The whole situation reminded me of the ordeal with Juan, and how helpless I was when his fate was sealed. I didn't want to go to jail, no matter how much I suffered with Spade.

"What's going to happen, Spade? Is this enough for us to get caught? Can they trace me with this? Will they be able to put his murder on me? I'm scared, Spade! I knew this lick was too dangerous for us." I was panicking and breaking down.

Spade's expression was cold and menacing. "So, what you saying? It's *my* fault the shit got hot?"

"No no no." I started fidgeting with my shirt. "I just don't want to go to jail, Spade." I was now crying.

"Then I suggest you get yo' weak and worried ass up out of here and pack yo' shit," he snapped and slid his phone into his pocket. "You already know I'm not taking no charges."

Five Long Weeks Later . . .

10

Jakia

I was curled up in the bed, and my body was drained physically while I was still in the dumps emotionally. Being down for the team and loyal to love wasn't working out in my favor. I was tired of being a prisoner in this room while Spade still got to run the streets free as a bird. Newlywed or not, this lifestyle wasn't my fantasy. The "new life as a wife dream" Spade sold me was officially a figment of my imagination. I felt like a fool for ever having faith in someone who has never given me a real reason to have hope.

Let me catch you up on what's gone down. After Spade showed back up at our house five weeks ago with a "mysterious" rental van I later found out was in Tiff's name, we rode out to the city of Toledo to elope, then checked into a slum-motel in the city of Monroe.

At first, I thought this was the rest stop until we vacationed for our honeymoon, but I've been stashed here ever since. The more I pondered on Spade's reason to marry me so quickly, the more I felt played. It didn't take many hours after scrubbing this once-filthy room clean to figure out he'd suckered my weak mind once again. Me taking his last name wasn't for my added safety. It was to ensure he continued to keep control.

After a few minutes of lying still, I sat up, grabbing the motel's notepad from off the nightstand and the Bible from inside the drawer. Propping myself up against the headboard, I took a deep breathe, then tried to meditate my stress away. Despite me not wanting to lay all my burdens and worries on Juan since he was locked away in the penitentiary, there was absolutely no one else in the world for me to confide in.

My tiny words were scribbled, and my hands were cramped from writing on such a tiny space. Still, I poured my heart out to my brother and made sure to express how much I missed him. I wondered if this letter would find him or if it was just a therapeutic way for me to survive another mind-fuck with Spade. Either way, I kept going until I felt relief.

Every ounce of emotion swimming around inside of me was lost within the letter. Every sour feeling I had toward Spade was bleeding through my pen. I was inking my bitter love story, and it felt good to release what I'd been bottling up for so long. The more I wrote, the more I thought.

Why not run and disappear? Why do you keep letting him control and manipulate you? Why don't you think you deserve more than what he's offering? Fuck this nigga; you can stand on your own. No matter what I thought, I never believed a weak link like myself could stand alone without Spade.

I've had plenty of times to run from him. It wasn't like he kept me handcuffed to the bed or cut phone cords when he left. Even though I was taking the risk of getting slapped up if he caught me out and about, I still disobeyed him whenever it was opportune and walked laps around the motel for fresh air. Disobeying Spade was how I confirmed my fate was tainted for good in the first place. That was my first and last trip to the store.

When I feared the white discharge, stomach queasiness, and food cravings were symptoms of me being knocked up, I ripped off a few dollars from Spade's pocket so I could walk to the nearest store for a pregnancy test. Before my pee could hit the stick, the two pink lines meaning I was pregnant were bold and bright pink. The results didn't shock me, though.

Since waking up the morning after getting ejaculated in by both Robert and Spade, I knew life wasn't good enough to spare me an "oops pregnancy." In spite of how I got pregnant, I wanted to keep this particular card that was dealt into my life. Good or bad, the baby growing inside of me was mine. It might've sounded slightly twisted, but at least if I really were to have a baby, he or she would love me unconditionally.

Closing my eyes feeling an anxiety attack coming on, it was hard fighting back my tears. No matter what I thought a few weeks ago, my heart was actually developing strings to the thought of being a mother. Regardless of Phoebe fuckin' up Juan and me as kids on the emotional tip, then Spade bringing it up on the back end, I still had a lot of love to give a child.

Rubbing my still-flat stomach, knowing there was a tiny human inside, I didn't know what to pray for. I wanted this baby to be the beginning of me, but the eerie feeling overwhelming my soul told me my fate was about to be the exact opposite.

Behind Prison Walls . . .

Juan Coleman

"It's count time, countttt tiiime," one of the officers of Jackson State Penitentiary announced over the loudspeaker.

Prison life wasn't for me. It was three o'clock in the morning, and even though I didn't want to be cuddled up in the stiff-board, twin-sized bed, I didn't want to be up waiting on some pickle-dick-prick to count me. For the whole year of me serving jail time, I've hated every single count time like the first. Whatever we were doing at whatever time the prison staff deemed it necessary, we'd have to stop and drop to be tallied up as the prisoners we were. It was dumb shit like this that's made me regret taking the bid for Spade. It was even more frustrating having to deal with the politics inside here knowing my sister was on the outside living hell.

A few hours ago, I'd read a brief letter saying she'd be in touch after their mini vacation and for me not to write until then. I've been itching to see my lawyer in addition to punching a few walls out ever since. Justice needed to be served swiftly, which started with the Coleman siblings reuniting. Spade's bid to ruin me was already in progress. I couldn't let history repeat itself with Jakia.

After count was over, I lay in the bed wide awake. My own rendition of Jakia getting punched like a grown man played out in my mind relentlessly. That nigga Spade owed me to take care of her since I was locked up as a favor to him. But instead, he was taking advantage of her having a bleak support system. Having a cracked-out corner mom and an incarcerated brother only made him prey on her more. The joke was gonna be on his shady ass, though, once I got up out of here. I'd already put plans into motion to see that nigga eye-to-eye. I just needed them to play out properly.

"Hey, Coleman, you good? Even your thoughts are keeping me awake," my Hispanic bunkie Gonzalo spoke in a low tone over the scurrying mice. He was from

Southwest Detroit and into his fourth year of a ten-year bid for a botched robbery too.

"Yeah, I'm one-hundred. Just over here thinking of a master plan to murk that nigga Spade when I get out." I didn't consider myself friends with anyone behind bars, yet I kicked it real with Gonzalo about the real deal concerning me.

"What are you about to do—dig up out of here with a rock hammer like in that movie *Shawshank Redemption?* Ain't no way in hell these racist white suckas are about to let you out a day before your sentence is served," he said as he tried breaking my spirits down.

"I've gotta get free. And when my lawyer feeds them the truth of what really went down that night, they'll have no other choice."

"Wow, Coleman, you've gotta be the only prisoner left up in here that thinks the system gives a fuck about the truth. You might as well get comfy in that cot and get to crossing days off your calendar. They ain't wasting another penny on a trial over a robbery that took place in the hood."

"Watch what I tell you, Gonz, I'm about to be sweet. You'll see," I reassured him while trying to reassure myself.

"Well, I've gotta catch some shut-eye before it's time to get up and give these cocksuckers more free labor. I'll holla at you in the a.m., bro. Make sure you keep hope alive," he sarcastically chuckled. "Oh, and if shit doesn't work out with that Great White Hope lawyer of yours, get at me." Gonzalo Ramos didn't have to drop any hints on what he could do. Even on the inside, my bunkie was powerful. The stories I'd heard about him and his Mexican crew that still did dirt on the outside were endless. Spade and Rocko were no competition to the heat those li'l fellas could bring.

The sun rose, but the prison walls I lived within kept life gray. After the morning count, I made my way to the shower, then to work. Since Spade only allowed Jakia to ration a few bucks to me now and then, I used the little pennies they "paid" us to keep on my books. It was barely enough to save up for much-needed toiletries and snacks from the commissary or random illegal contraband floating around, but I made do. Struggling and ending up with shit wasn't nothing new.

I rushed getting ready, which wasn't much to do. It was the same mundane routine day in and out. I would've killed for a pair of run-down Air Max shoes and handed down True Religion jeans right about now. Anything would've been better than this bright pumpkin-orange jumpsuit, prisoner badge, and worn down Chucks I'd paced the soles out of. I'd gone from being a dusty bum on the streets to a caged monkey up in here. Even if my little sister wasn't in danger, I had to change my circumstances.

I scrubbed toilets, mopped floors, and cleaned up left behind blood from brawls that went down. There were always inmates fighting, but I kept my head down and was doing my time the best I could. I was the type of prisoner that fell in line because I was scared of being hauled off and confined to solitary. Everything within the jailhouse was crooked. The guards, wardens, and even counselors should've been serving time with us for all the illegal shit they did daily. But no one cared about the common criminal. We were treated like trained dogs and humiliated as such whenever someone in charge had a bad day.

"Coleman, your lawyer is here," my supervisor shouted from his desk. I usually couldn't stand the crude bastard, but today, his words were like music to my ears.

The female guard who escorted me to the meeting room tried hitting on me a few times, but I shot her down with ease—knowing the game well. In lockdown, it wasn't unusual for male prisoners and female guards to get down on the low. Hell, even those peanut butter-loving cocksuckers got loved on up in here. We might've been locked up for not following rules; however, there weren't any to follow when it came to sexual relations. Folks liked to label us as deviants to society, but these hot-and-bothered supposed women and men of the badge kept juicy pussies or hard dicks and illegal contraband in exchange for our services.

I wasn't having no parts in getting written up on some bogus nonsense because I wouldn't cooperate in the game. I kept my eyes in my head and my dick in my pants. Fuck having my piece fall off from catching a slow-creeping disease. Even if this attorney couldn't pull a miracle out of his hat, I'd still be out in my late 30s ready to spray up some bitch with nut when I got out. From my first day in county, I've been doing my time the very same way—to myself.

"Mr. Coleman, how are you holding up in here? Are they treating you okay enough?" Popping open his black briefcase, he pulled a manila folder out with a stack of official-looking forms.

"It ain't shit like the 5-Star lavish life," I smartly commented. "Please tell me you've come with some good news that can get me up out of this hellhole, bossman."

My lawyer looked down, then began shuffling through his file of paperwork. I knew off rip he was about to come at me with some bullshit I wasn't trying to hear. If we were meeting in the privacy of his office, I would've fa'sho been across the table with my scrawny hands around his puny neck. My hands twitched as my eyes burned a hole through his head.

"Listen, Mr. Coleman, I can't get your story to check out. With the crime taking place over a year ago, and you refusing to give names back when it actually occurred, I'm not sure your chances of a retrial are good. Maybe you should focus on serving the remaining nine years of your term. With good behavior, I'm sure they'll let you out in maybe seven."

"What in the fuck? Are you crazy?" My outburst was loud and should've been expected.

"Watch your language, Coleman," the guard scolded me.

I nodded, then looked back at my attorney who had the nerve to be tight-faced. "So, it's like that, my man? You're gonna leave me hanging up in here when you know good and well I'm innocent? Spade and Rocko are the two most ruthless cousins in the D. If I'm out, I can help the cops get more dirt on them than I already have so you can lock them both up under here. I don't deserve to be here another day!" Hearing my words out loud, I was getting pissed at myself for begging to snitch even more. I'd already sung like a canary to him, and it hadn't meant shit thus far. In other words, my extra attempts were in vain and an embarrassment to me.

"Listen, boy, I've done everything I can for you, and I don't have a big enough heart for pro bono. Plus, I've got much more pressing city issues to handle. Check out the law library for some newbie lawyer out of school looking for practice. You and your kind like to live by the no-snitching rule—which has to be the dumbest thing my people have ever heard of. I wish you well and hope you follow my advice." He gathered his paperwork, but this coon-hating paste face was about to get set straight. Guard or no guard around, he had me fucked up.

"Fuck you, yo' wife, yo' incest-looking kids, and I even wish death on yo' moms—you fat, white bitch." Something in me snapped. Before I knew it, my attorney was dangling by his feet, and the guards had their weapons in my back. He was powerless to me as my hands tried choking the life from out of him.

"Release him, you piece of shit," the woman guard who'd just tried to fuck me demanded. When I didn't comply, she aggressively elbowed me in the side, then followed up her attempt at restraining me by hitting me in the back of my head with her metal flashlight.

It wasn't the blow I took that made me let the attorney go. Thoughts of Jakia out on her own came rushing back, and I realized I'd crossed the line. The male guard who finally showed up as backup put his foot in my back, then handcuffed me. Shaking my head, I knew my fate was sealed, and the system had fucked me. Gonz was gonna clown me hard once I got back from where I was heading.

"Tell ya friends that I'm the wrong one to fuck with— you got that Jew *boy?*" The last comment, I meant with every vicious feeling brewing within my soul. I wasn't anybody's boy—not even Phoebe's.

I was dragged down to solitary kicking and screaming. My voice was echoing throughout the prison. Fuck the Great White Hope. Time in the SHU only meant one thing—more time added to my sentence. Plus, I'd collared up a man of the law, technically, so ain't no telling how my black ass was about to burn.

Clank!

When the hollow metal door slammed, I stood against the wall continuously banging my head against the concrete. "Let me out of here! Let me the fuck out of here!" I knew my screams were pointless; nevertheless, I kept shouting until my throat went sore. Who knew when they'd come set me free from this small, sickening cell. Sliding down the wall, I could barely breathe as my chest began caving in. As disgusting and inhumane as it was inside of this cell, my heart and mind were heavier with a bigger burden. "Please, God, let me survive this so I can right my wrongs with my little sister."

11

Jakia

Spade massaged my back while we watched a movie on Netflix. We'd been having a good time enjoying each other's company, but I was fighting through each moment trying not to show that I was sick. My attitude was hot and cold, but to me, it didn't matter. I was entitled to it. The smell of the blunt he kept smoking, then putting out, was unsettling to my stomach even more. Plus, his usual Unforgivable cologne was making me want to gag. Bells were going off that I was pregnant—hopefully, Spade was deaf to them.

"Drink some of this. I wanna get you fucked up so we can have some drunk sex tonight." Spade pushed his cup of Hennessy with no chaser into my face.

"No, thank you. I'm good on that." I pushed the cup back toward him, making some spill out on his shirt.

"Damn, Jakia," he jerked back. "What's your problem? Why have you been acting funny all day?" Taking off his shirt with aggravation, I'm sure his attitude couldn't match mine.

"Nothing besides the fact that I'm tired of being cooped up in this stuffy-ass hotel room all day and night. You wouldn't know how I'm feeling since you get to rip and run the streets still," I whined like a kid throwing a mini extra tantrum. Spade knew what was up before he asked. This wasn't a new conversation; yet, I yearned for a different outcome.

"Don't start that shit, Jakia. You already know what's up and that you can't hit the D again until everything in the media about the 'Motor City Murder' dies down. Why do you keep having memory lapses and shit? I'm tired of hearing you bitch about something you can't change." He guzzled down the remaining liquor in his cup, then poured some more.

"Not as tired as me." I wouldn't drop the subject. I couldn't understand why Spade got to run back and forth to Detroit if I couldn't, especially if we left together. His rationale had holes in it, and it wouldn't shock me if he were lying. He was probably laid up with Tiff all day. "I'm starting to think you wanna keep me stashed out here in no-man's land so you can do your dirt in peace. There's no reason I can't at least hide out at home— especially since no one knows where we stay at besides Rocko." I folded my arms ready to have a full-blown debate. I didn't care about the open and unsolved case we were involved in. The circle to snitch on me was small since he kept me friendless and isolated. Besides him, Rocko, Lezlee, and I, no one knew of my involvement with Robert Taylor's setup/murder.

"*Whomp, whomp, whomp.*" He moved his hands like I was talking too much. "I'm tired of hearing your mouth about the next chick, so chill the fuck out," he said, sitting back on the bed.

I flicked him off, knowing I'd lost another battle to get more than ever weeks ago was a welco from out of down-river back to Detroit. The home I hated med joy right about now.

"So now that we've settled that, you wanna drink and fuck or what?" Spade looked at me with greedy eyes.

"Why not? It's not like there's much else for me to do." I rolled my eyes, then slid down toward his midsection. "I don't need liquor to fuck you right." Because I was pregnant, drinking was out for me. To make sure he didn't slip any in my system by force, I hurriedly pulled out his dick, then began giving him the best head job I could. Like any good woman, I knew my man—or at least I thought I did. Bobbing and slobbing on his dick and nut sac like it was my last meal, maybe if I swallowed a huge enough glob, he'd take more consideration into my pleas about going home.

"Yeah, that's right, wifey," Spade hummed. "Hold it right there and don't move." He firmly grabbed my head and held it still. All the sweat, funk, and stale come of another bitch's pussy was far up my nose, along with his scratchy pubic hair. The disgustingness of it all had me ready to gag. "Ah, yup; slurp it up and take every drop." A split second later, I felt Spade's hot come sliding down my throat.

Urargh! Urargh!

His come mixed with my slob and the McDonald's we'd just eaten rushed up and was now in puke form all over the bed and on his stomach.

"What the hell," Spade leaped up yelling. "I oughta make you lick all this shit back up."

"I'm sorry, babe. That Mickey D's must not have been any good." I tried playing it off while making my way into the bathroom. "Let me grab a rag to clean you up." My words were slurred. I was light-headed and dizzy. Whatever was going on with my body was taking over.

Before I could get the warm, soapy washcloth and spare towels to the bed to wipe him down, Spade was pushing me back into the bathroom and over the toilet. "You're about to take this dick the right way."

Bent over gripping the toilet seat, I was taking every inch of him deep in my gut, though I felt queasy like I was about to pass out. Since I knew Spade was relentless when it came to coming, I swallowed several times and fought back the urge to ruin his moment. Needing the moment to be fulfilling for him but quickly over for me, I twerked my ass with each thrust—a move I knew he couldn't resist. "Give it to me, daddy." I juiced his ego up with the intention of rushing him along.

Spade gripped my hips forcing me to arch my back. Slowly, he stroked me a few times while kissing me gently on the neck. Without warning, but much welcoming, he plunged into my wetness slowly. My pussy was making sounds to the dick-thrashing it was getting whipped with. No matter how much I loved to hate Spade—the long stroke Spade's been putting down on me the last five weeks has been leaving me with rubbery legs.

"Aaah, you—feel—so—fu-c—" before I could finish my sentence, the pleasurable feeling turned into pure pain. My body tensed up, so I tried repositioning myself, but he was digging in me too aggressively and hard. Spade wasn't coming up for air; yet, I was starting to lose all of mine. I tried scooting away from him but was snatched back and held down hungrily.

"Take tha dick, wifey; quit running." He and I got down rough, so in his mind, he was just sexing me right. "This pussy feels extra wet and sloppy tonight."

I bit down on my lip and fought back the woozy feeling that was starting to become too overwhelming. This secret pregnancy and my raging hormones, of course, had me sick off the dick. Why couldn't it just be a change of foods like for most women? It's like everything surrounding my life was cursed to be the absolute worst.

"The more 'pleasing" Spade thought he was doing for me, the more I was continuously swallowing and taking plenty of small breaths. Whoever said "mind over matter" is smart as hell. The beatings I'd taken for not "behaving" were on my mind, so none of the spazing out my body was doing mattered. Holding my shit together was essential if I didn't want Spade to nut up in a bad way. When his speed and stroke increased, I prayed to God he was nearing the finale. And he was. A second later, I felt his creamy nut shoot up inside of me.

"Aaah, aaah, damn, you feel good," he murmured.

Releasing an exasperated breath when he pulled out, I hurried to lift the toilet seat lid, then vomited everything I'd been holding in. "I swear I'm never eating a Big Mac again." I rested my head on the side of the toilet.

"Ugh, that's gross as hell." Spade sounded disgusted. "I'm about to take a shower and bounce. I ain't got time to be catching whatever cooties yo' ass got."

"Please don't leave me. You know how I get when I'm sick," I begged, using reverse psychology.

"I'll slide back through with some chicken noodle soup or some shit like that, but nothing more. It's money out in the streets, so me and Rocko are about to be out."

Spade stayed spinning me. For the first few weeks of us being married, you couldn't pry him away from my good loving and attention. All of my desires were catered to, even though we were cramped up in this small space. He had me living on cloud nine because the Spencer Johnson I'd given my heart to from back in the day was showing face. Unbelievable as it may seem, he'd given me a million reasons to forget what was going on outside of these motel walls. When the newness of being married died off, so did my occupancy in a dream world.

When Spade first began making up excuses to roll
out with Rocko, I chalked it up to him going stir-crazy.
But when the outings turned into overnight stays, I
knew he was back slipping to the D and into that trick
Tiff. A woman's intuition was a bad thang—especially
when it was accompanied by a seeking hand. I stayed
going through his phone and pockets finding receipts
from Detroit businesses. When I found a used Magnum
condom with no come stuffed inside of his denim jeans
pocket, it was all the proof I needed to know he was
officially back to his old ways. It was cool, though. I'd
been mentally preparing myself for the downfall anyhow.
Spade could be my guest to run up out of here. The more
time he strayed, the more time I prayed. Wife or not, it
was essential to find my road to peace.

After hurling all of my insides out, then brushing my
teeth, I made my way to the bed, then prepared for a
nightcap session. Lighting a blunt to soothe the oncoming
nauseating feeling that was creeping back up, I didn't feel
bad for drugging my unborn child since I wasn't keeping
it anyway. I was a sinner living in the imagined life of a
saint.

"A'ight, Jakia, don't wait up. And don't forget to keep
your antsy ass still along with the rest of my rules," he
cautioned, then slammed the door.

He and Rocko couldn't have been out of the parking
lot before I was reading scriptures about forgiveness. My
soul needed healing in the worst way.

Spade

I stepped foot out of the stale-smelling room we'd
been taking refuge in for five weeks knowing exactly
how Jakia felt. We were staying in one of the grittiest

motels between Toledo and Detroit. Located in Monroe, a downriver city, all they required was cold hard cash in order to check in. It might've been a 1-star dump, but the "don't ask—don't tell" policy accommodated us better than any 5-star hotel could have.

Some occupants were truck drivers, some were homeless heads or prostitutes passing through, but we were paying heavy for silence and solidarity. As soon as things died down with the pending case of Robert Taylor, though, we'd be up and out here—back in the D for good.

12

Rocko

"Hey, man, watch your left and right. I got you covered from the back," Spade spoke over my shoulder.

Boom! Boom! Pop-Pop!

Kicking in the door, then landing my first two bullets into the first house soldier that greeted me, I stepped over his jerking body as blood poured from his chest. "I'm passing out bullets to any buster that wanna try me."

It was too simple to go that smoothly. But either way, Spade and I had taken over the house I'd been watching for weeks. Just as they ran their establishment on the outside—sloppy and out in the open—is exactly how the inside operated. What was bad for them was gravy for us. The few naked girls that were packaging baggies scattered in fear, while the dudes sat pissed and grim faced.

"You pussy-ass, faggot-ass, no-hustle-having-ass niggas! I can't stand thieves. If you wanna put in work chomping this crack and making this cash like a real boss, get at me the right way. Unmask yo'self, you clowns," the biggest talking moneyman made himself known.

"All that talking ain't got you nothing but a front-row seat to yo' funeral."

Pop-Pop!

Two quick ones to the center of his head, ole boy fell to the ground. Then, like dominoes, the boys that held his back down threw their hands up surrendering to my gangster. An eerie silence fell over the house as their leader took his last breath on account of his last words.

"I don't think I'ma have to make the speech on shutting the fuck up and doing as you're told. Right?" I walked over his body while waving my pistol around the room. As the last three boys and two girls in the room agreed to conform, I moved through the rest of the house checking for hidden workers. Putting a chair up to the basement door so I wouldn't have to waste time running up and down the steps, within seconds, I was back in the main room snatching gold chains and jewels clean from off their necks.

"Yeah, we want all that product, partna! Dump everything you chopping up back in that ziplock bag, then, hand it over." Spade held his gun to the dome of a random hustler's head. The worker was shaking and shivering while trying to follow Spade's demands.

"And move fast, muthafuckas. As you've seen, we ain't against leaving no bodies behind." Pacing through the house like a madman with two pistols drawn, I wasn't worried about none of these flashy-ass Negroes whipping out with any heat.

"Light that blunt up, li'l nigga," Spade taunted one of the workers by flicking the freshly wrapped cigarillo from behind his ear.

The boy lit it up quickly, then passed it to Spade. When the boy smirked after Spade took a long hit, I knew some shit was in the game.

"Aye, li'l homie, what's off in this 'rello?" Spade held his pistol toward the boy's chest. "Why in the fuck are my lips tingling?"

My assumption was right. Cuzzo should've known not to trust a cat from the other side. He was slipping on another tip, so I had to keep it cool and keep my eyes on the crowd.

"Me and the dude yo' boy blazed dead do 151s. It's called Christmas cookies," the young boy proudly responded. "Ain't nobody around here blowing on normal blunts," the kid smirked, proud of being slightly strung out. "That's why our spot jumps triple over every spot around this hood!"

Whap!

A third young and black body was left jerking on the floor. Spade might've cracked his cranium with the handle of his pistol for the boy slipping him, but he was also still puffing on the cigarillo like he hadn't heard it was laced with crack. *The fuck, man! What is this nigga really up to? I see he has graduated from just popping a few pills.* Not wanting to put him on blast and seem divided as a team, I shook off what I was seeing, then went into my own zone. There was still a major robbery to pull off, and as always, the only person I could count on to hold shit down successfully was me.

"The rest of y'all—strip. I want them Jays, those Rock Revival jeans, and that Gucci belt," I pointed out the clothes I wanted that the street solders were dressed in.

Ninety seconds later, I had every pocket of each hustler in here turned inside out with their gear inside of a laundry bag. Spade and I carried two bags each out of the house—full of product, guns, money, and the clothes off their backs. The only things left inside were dead men and fellas with wounded egos. Once I hit the final step off the porch, I trucked it over to the rental van and tossed the bags into the back. Whether or not they were armed, the house stayed cranking, so we had to go.

"Yeah, man! This right here is the only way to live life." Spade jumped in the van singing his words loudly. "You popped them niggas like it wasn't nothing," he imitated how I was shooting, then fell back into the seat as I floored the gas pedal. A blind man could see that Spade was floating. He must've been on more than those few hits of that 151. Taking a quick look at his face, I saw the white residue underneath his nose. No doubt, my cousin snuck a sniff, fa'sho.

"Calm yo' hyper ass down, man. I can't think straight."

Shaking in his seat, he damn near sat on his hands to keep from moving around so much. "Swing by Tiff's crib so we can stash this come-up, dude." He wiped the small sweat beads from his face. "Damn, it's hotter than a muthafucka! Turn on the air. We got that fire up in here!"

Spade was spazing out jumping from one subject to the next, and there wasn't shit I could do but roll out with his plan. Since new blood was on my hands, I needed a little downtime to chill out, smoke, and get my mind right before going back to Monroe. Just today, I'd dropped two bodies more, and ole boy's corpse from the hotel probably wasn't even in the soil yet. I tried to shake the uneasy feeling since we'd cleared the crime scene without getting popped. However, a man of the streets can always sense when death's lurking around the corner.

Officer Brickman

"There have been multiple shots fired and several calls coming in from neighbors for what's suspected to be a drug house in the 48223 District. Is there a squad car available to respond?"

My heart raced to the beat of fighting crime. Flipping on my siren, I prepared to answer back to the dispatcher but was sidetracked by my ringing phone.

"Hey, Cap, let me call you back so I can answer this call-in about a shoot-out in Brightmoor," I picked up, prepared to hang right back up.

"Scratch that call, Brickman, and let another officer get it. I need you back at the precinct now," he demanded.

"But, sir—" I tried speaking but was cut off. I wasn't ready to come out of the field. Locking up deserving criminals was a thirst I loved to quench.

"But, sir, my ass," he mocked me. "What I told you was an order, so hurry up, Brickman! Your job is on the line," my boss hollered into the phone, then hung up.

The captain was getting on my last damn nerve putting the weight of this case on my shoulders. I'd been working on it tirelessly but coming up with zero leads. Robert Taylor wasn't the only one who couldn't be touched in the flesh; his assistant was up in smoke too. This made me feel like she was the number one suspect in this murder—not that pretty prop them two thugs put in place. I've been doing police work for over twenty years and wasn't ready to slack for this case. But with funds trapped in a funnel for this mayoral campaign, amongst other twisted problems within the city of Detroit, I'm sure I was about to get fucked out of another case.

"You made perfect time, Brickman. Come in and shut the damn door. What progress have you made on the Taylor case?" My captain was a jerk that didn't value or honor real police work.

"No change from the last report, sir. The picture float-ing around in the media hasn't gotten any hot hits, and the few prints in the room were from previous guests and housekeepers. The fingerprints and bodily fluid sam-ples found on Mr. Taylor have come back with zero hits from the system. Whoever our perp is—is a first-time offender."

"Well, that's nice." The captain was definitely uncon-cerned. "Make a thorough report of everything you and your team have found. The mayor called while you were out and put his foot even further down on my neck. He's sending over his right-hand man this afternoon to get briefed on the details to take over—so you know what that means."

"Bullshit, Cap! I'm tired of that crooked-ass political party. If it ain't one roundabout act to keep the city ill-in-formed, it's another." The city of Detroit was much worse than the murder capital of the world; it's a melting pot for organizational conspiracy. They weren't reporting real crimes. Unfortunately for the tax-paying citizens—and even those that struggled in the slums—the real news was cleaned up and reported how the Republic saw fit. The D was undergoing a takeover and for a major crime to go unsolved on such a hot main attraction was a cold sore on the city's surface. "I became a cop to fight crime and find the bad guys and not a damn thing else. I'm tired of being their fuckin' political puppet!"

"That's enough, Officer. You're way out of line. Now, you've got your orders—write that damn report, and if you want your job tomorrow, tame that spitfire attitude you've got going on. Don't nobody around here, espe-cially the mayor of Detroit, owe you shit, Brickman. You better perform like a dancing dog if they call down the order." Staring at Brickman with anger in his eyes, he continued trying to break him down. "And the last time I checked, *you* don't assign my cases. *I* do. If you want a real tip on how to do police work and keep a redneck like me off your neck, solve your case in less than five weeks. Now, leave my office quick—just as you came—and get to work!" He waved his hand, dismissing me, then looked back at his computer screen, probably at some sadistic porn.

The more mayoral terms I got to witness from working inside of DPD precincts, the more corruption I became a part of. "Whatever you say, boss," I sarcastically spat. "I'll be at my desk if you need to bark out any additional bullshit orders."

13

Spade

Rocko swerved up in Tiff's driveway, and before we made it to her side door, she'd swung it open, holding it wide for us to enter. I kissed her on the lips as I walked through with the bags headed toward the basement. Tiff remained at my beck and call and always on time, even when she hated me. She'd been blowing up my text with every vile message her ghetto-girl mind could muster up over the last few weeks. Nonetheless, here she was, ready to hold me down.

"A'ight, dude, I'm about to blaze up and watch TV until you get done with ole girl. Do me a favor and waste that 'rock energy' on her pussy so I don't have to deal with all that on the road." He let me know, not so slyly, he'd peeped my secret indulgence.

I gave him a play of acceptance and agreement, then snorted a pinkie-nail full of coke from the secret stash in my pocket before joining Tiff in her room. Truth was, I liked the rush it gave me. One hit of the Christmas Cookie blunt at the house had me hooked. So much so that I'd sniffed a bit, plus snuck a bit for me to sprinkle my blunts with later. This was a new addiction, a far better thrill than pills.

On the center of the bed, Tiff was sprawled out in one of my tee shirts going wild with a dildo. My eyes popped open, my dick got hard, and the coke settling in my bloodstream gave me an instant euphoric feeling. The lethal combination had me ready to fuck. I devoured Tiff like I hadn't just busted a massive nut with Jakia.

I plowed into my ex feeling like a true pimp with each thrust. Her pussy felt hella good, and she was taking my meat like a pro. I went for so long that I dried her up. Flipping Tiff over 'cause I was still urging to go, I tapped her lips with my mushroom thick tip, then felt her swallow my dick whole. Licking, slurping, then gagging, I held her jaws still and let my load off into her throat while my high came down simultaneously.

"Where yo' slick ass been at anyway?" Coming up from the face-to-dick position, Tiff couldn't wait to swallow my nut so she could start a round of questioning. "I ain't heard from you since I rented that van. I started to report it stolen." She rolled her eyes.

"Don't play with me about the police, Tiff. That shit ain't never gonna be funny." I made my point clear. "You know me, Rock, and Kia had to lie low until shit died down with ole boy from the casino," I replied, agitated.

"Uh-huh, nigga, whatever. I'm not stupid. You've been somewhere exotic and cake baking with that bitch," she backhanded me in the chest. "*I'm* the one who helped y'all pull that heist off, for real. If it weren't for me putting that room in my name in the first place, y'all would've been fucked. Plus, you didn't catch me with a dick twisted off up inside of me." In addition to throwing what she'd helped me out with back up in my face, Tiff was going hard on Jakia like any bitter ex with her hand still off in the cookie jar would.

"Damn, since when did you start getting so territorial over a nigga? Jealousy ain't a good look on you, babe," I chuckled at her.

"And being a dog is looking real bad on you right about now," she huffed.

It was then I knew any chance of getting a runner-up head job was out of the question. Stuffing my now flaccid penis into my boxers, I moved on to get control over the situation. "Aw, chill out and settle down, girl. Why you wanna go and fuck up the good thing we got going on?" I wasn't trying to beef out with Tiff, but she knew the rules to the game we were playing. I wasn't about to change my position. Jakia was my main lady, and all other chicks fell in line afterward—Tiffany being first.

"'Cause I'm tired of getting the short end of the stick, Spade. It ain't been a solid month of you fuckin' with that young girl that you haven't been over here all up in my face. It's not gonna be too many more times of you shading me for her—trust and believe!"

"Should I take that as a threat, Tiff? You know I don't do well with threats." Up until this point, I was letting Tiffany have her choice of words with me. Out of all the women I dealt with, she's always had more room to talk recklessly. But first love or not, the yapping was getting played out. Even my wife wasn't allowed to sass me.

"Take it how you wanna take it, chief," she smartly backed up. "But just know that I'm serious about you shading me and mine." Pulling up her shirt, she exposed a pudgy belly with the words "Hi Daddy" written with blue lipstick across it.

"Aye, Tiff, what the fuck type shit are you on?"

"Read it and weep, nigga. The fuck is ya girl gonna say now?"

"I swear to G—if this is a so-called pregnancy prank you call yo'self pulling, I'ma put one in you."

"Say *what,* now? Since when do I play games? And you putting one in me is the reason I'm gonna be set for life, nigga. Can you say 'child support'?" Tiff's ghetto attitude started pouring out in every word that she spoke. "Oh, and don't sit over there acting like it ain't yours, by the way." She had her argument prepared from every angle.

"How in the fuck do I even know you're pregnant? We both know how you like to hit niggas over the head and shit. Please don't have me put my hands on you." Tiff knew how I got down. She was the preliminary reason for me being a villain. With her, I was only a monster.

"Would you question that sneak bitch, Jakia?" When I didn't respond fast enough, Tiff took it to another level. "Fuck all this conversation, Spade. I can show you better than I can tell you. Come on, let's make a run."

I whipped Tiff's car around the few corners necessary to reach the Family Dollar Store. Jumping out of the passenger seat with the crisp twenty I'd handed her, she disappeared through the doors, then reappeared a few minutes later. With a bottle of water in one hand and a plastic bag containing the detection test, she sat back and guzzled her H2O with a smirk painted on her face.

Tiffany was all too eager to piss on the stick in front of me. She pulled off her drawers, plopping down on the toilet, all while staring me dead in the face. I watched her rip the package open, pull the purple plastic cap off, and urinate on the absorbent strip. When she was done damn near drenching it, she replaced the top, then tossed it toward me. "It don't matter how many sticks I pee on, nigga; they all will read 'pregnant.' I've been missing days on the pole 'cause this seed has got me sick as hell. It's a shocker I'm not throwing up right now."

"Man, Tiff, real talk. You've got me royally fucked up. You already know I'm not trying to have no kids. So what cha' talkin' about doing?" I wasn't the type of dude to hint toward an abortion—I gave it to all my girls straight, with no chaser.

"Wow, okay—So after you send me off to the chopper, will you come back to tamper with my abused coochie? What am I? A garbage disposal?" Tiff was getting emotional, when all along, even before Jakia, I never campaigned to be her baby's dad.

"Regardless of how you wanna play the game, your ass better be scheduling an appointment at the scrap house on that," I pointed my finger toward her stomach, then dusted my hands of the mess. Balling my fists up, I walked toward Tiffany so we could bump noses. She was feistier than Jakia but was still no competition to my weight. "Unless you want me to kick that muthafucka up outta ya!"

Rocko

"I swear that nigga has found his match in that one," I spoke out loud while wiping sweat beads from my forehead. He and Tiff have been going head up for the last forty-five minutes straight; and from the sound of it, she wasn't about to back down anytime soon. Whatever popped off between them, though, wasn't my business, so I kept low in her basement getting stone-cold high. I didn't have time to focus on the drama that Spade loved to dwell in. The deeper we got off into robbing cats, the more bodies I claimed under my belt. Shit was getting crazy. And even though I didn't mind popping a cat, I detested not having control.

After I smoked the first blunt down to the nub and rolled another, I broke out one of the laundry bags of product, then dumped the contents onto the floor. Every piece of jewelry, crack, dollar bill, and pistol we robbed from them punks was well worth the blood on my hands; but Spade wilding out had me on another level. The plan was for us to empty the spot and flip the weight into more for us. We'd done just that, but Spade smoking 151s meant his turnup was about to be our downfall.

Instead of stuffing it all back in the bag and into the stash spot, I took a few stacks for myself, then snuck it out into the van. It was obvious that Spade couldn't be trusted, so I wasn't about to let him snort my come-up away. His new addiction wasn't about to be my downfall. I knew my blood cousin better than his mother even did. We grew up like brothers, but him as a snorter was a stranger in my eyes. As bad as I wanted to be loyal, it was time for me to start separating into my own individuality.

"Aaah! Rocko! Come get this nigga up off me," I heard Tiff yelling from two stories up.

I was hesitant to get into their drama, but she continuously kept yelling, and objects kept smashing into the wall. Because I didn't want the cops to get called by a nosy neighbor, I sprang up and rushed toward the sound of their voices.

"I'ma have somebody do yo' ass in, nigga. Get up out of my house."

"Call who you wanna call. I ain't leaving till you leaking. I know you snuck me, ho," Spade shouted.

When I got to the top of the stairs, I froze, then fell out laughing. "Aye, y'all two are clowning." As a grown-ass man, I didn't follow reality shows, but the legendary Joseline and Stevie pregnancy scandal was the funniest gimmick on earth. And here right before my eyes was Tiff waving a piss test. If he knew like I knew, a wrath was coming if she didn't get her way with that seed she claimed was brewing in her exposed belly.

"Don't just stand there laughing," she tried cutting into me. "Get your damn cousin to chill out or get him up out of my crib."

With a front-row seat, I fell back for a moment watching them beef. Tiff might've been a rider, but the head-ache she continuously brought to Spade's table wasn't worth it, in my opinion. And from the looks of it, he'd slipped up and fucked himself for at least eighteen years to life. It wasn't my place to judge, but Tiff was the last type of woman you wanted to breed kids with. He should've been back at the room putting some babies up in his wife.

I tuned back into their argument with Tiff threating to get even with Spade. That was my cue to get both him and me up out of there. "A'ight, cuz, let's shoot that move up back up the highway. I ain't with all the threats ya girl spitting." I kept it real. I've never been a fan of Tiffany's—Spade was well aware of that—so for her to be talking wild had me ready to react.

"Yeah, gon' to wifey so you can tell her she's got a stepson or -daughter on the way," Tiff giggled, then darted into her bedroom—slamming and locking the door. "Take yo' ass on, Spade. I'll be here when you get back," she screeched from the other side.

Before Spade could even get a head start running to kick down the door, I grabbed his shirt, shoving him into the wall. "Cuz, quit tripping on ole girl. She ain't going nowhere by the looks of it, and we need to bounce. Right about now, this right here is a no-fly zone. I ain't with that bitch making threats that can get me caught up in y'all's crossfire."

I could see the cold glare in his eye in disbelief that I'd yoked him up so quickly, effortlessly, and aggressively—but the act was done.

"That's cool. I feel you. I'll take care of Tiff on my own. But, um, try falling back when it comes to putting yo' hands on me—real talk," he grimed me, then straightened his roughed up collar.

Spade

Every word coming out of Rocko's mouth might've been legit, yet and still, my eyes couldn't stop icing him. This nigga must've been getting high off the same supply I was while he was alone in the basement to be putting his hands on me—let alone collaring me up against the wall. Between him and Tiff, I was about ready to pop off.

"Do me a solid and make sure the product is stashed properly. I'll be out right after I take a leak," I lied, truly wanting to sneak a hit. After all that's gone down, I felt I needed a pick-me-up.

"A'ight, but don't take a long time. I'm itching to get on the road and ain't got time for the soap opera that's titled 'you and your sidepiece,'" were Rocko's last words before he flew down the stairs.

Who in the hell told this fool he was boss? He better be lucky he's blood, or I would've put one up top with his name on it for his ass. My thoughts raced and became more irrational as I laced a blunt for the road. Too much occurred today making me need the Christmas cookie, so the hood called 'em, to mellow me out.

"Hurry yo' sneaky ass up out of that room and lock this door, Tiff," I yelled upstairs, then walked out.

By the time I got in the passenger seat, she was standing in the front door with a ripped mug set into her face. Rubbing her belly with a look of bitterness, I knew Tiff meant business about having that baby. My messiness was about to catch up in the form of Karma.

Tiff: I've been throwing up all day—every day, nigga! Since you've been gone, it's been nothing but eating, sleeping, and vomiting.

We hadn't been on the road for ten minutes, and already Tiff was texting me. At first, I swiped past her messages, refusing to read the madness, and then I began putting two and two together, comparing her and Jakia. The same way I'd left Jakia earlier in the room—sick as a dog—was the same way Tiff claimed she'd been for the last few weeks of me being on a hiatus. That had a player like me shook. Buzzing or not, I felt some type of way. Since I had the remaining pregnancy tests in my back pocket, my questions weren't about to remain unanswered for long.

"Hey, Rocko, you can't drive no faster? I know this a grandma van and all, but, damn." I was over the pleasantries. I'd peeped how he'd cut into me earlier, so it was clear we needed new formed lines and boundaries. Plus, I was burning to get back to the room.

"You better smoke you some; be cool. I ain't in the mood to spaz out with you again 'cause you beefing with yo' bitch," Rocko put me on blast.

"Nigga, whatever. You gonna quit coming at me sideways. Save some of that big talking authority for that trick Lezlee. *She's* the one that needs to be checked."

"You have no idea how the tables are about to turn," Rocko spoke underneath his breath. "You better believe me when I say—the game is about to change."

"Whatever, dude. You ain't said nothing but a word," I blew off whatever he called himself trying to say. My own drama was overwhelming enough. I didn't have time to figure out Rocko's riddles.

Jakia

"Hey, Jakia, get yo' ass up and pee on this stick!" So caught up in writing Juan, I hadn't heard Spade come in. I tried sliding the notepad underneath the blanket, but he was too slick for my game. I looked up at him waving a single pregnancy test in my face. First and foremost, where was the rest of the pack? "Hurry up and get yo' slick ass up and into the bathroom. I ain't got all night."

What else does he have to do—that his dirty ass ain't already done? Reeking like marijuana, Spade was either tricking cash at the strip club or on his stripper ex-chick Tiff. Either way, I couldn't figure out how either one of those things had to do with him cutting into me like he was. Did he put two and two together from earlier? Not having a choice but to leave my letter to Juan unattended, I slid out of bed and moved like a turtle toward the bathroom. I was trying to delay him finding out, though I knew that was no longer possible. I pulled my pajama pants and panties down, sat on the toilet, then let a few droplets fall onto the stick purposely holding the rest back. If only this test could come back a false-negative, I'd have more time to figure shit out.

"Don't fuckin' play me slick; piss more!" Spade wasn't playing the stupid role like I needed him to.

Two minutes later, Spade was looking over my shoulder as I read the word "positive" on the EPT Digital First Response pregnancy test. My knees were weak, and my eyes began watering instantly. I might've been attached to the strong thought of being pregnant, but I was no fool—Spade was about to crush that want.

"You will pay for trying to keep a secret from me." He squeezed my shoulder blades tightly. The intensity shot up and down my spine, then settled in the upper discs of my back.

"I wasn't trying to keep a secret from you. How could I when I just found out myself?" Yeah, I was lying and playing it dumb—every woman knows her body, plus I'd snuck a test already. And right down to the milky white discharge, I knew a baby was forming inside of me—or a helluva STD.

"When is the last time yo' fat ass been on the pad? Come to think of it, I haven't brought none to this damn room! Don't think you about to trap me with a baby, Jakia." Spade was fuming as I moved quickly through the room from any hits he wanted to serve me up with. He was hot on my trail with such little space to maneuver through.

"*Trap* you? I thought the vows 'till death do us part' meant you were dedicated to being trapped," I sarcastically spat, not caring about the consequences.

Whap!

He slapped me across the face. Like a soldier, I took it without dropping a tear, then fell back onto the bed. If he wanted to beat my ass, he could. But from here on out, I'd have a voice. Shocked and appalled by my reaction, from the look on his face you'd think he could read my thoughts.

"Flip through these yellow pages and find a clinic for me to take yo' black ass to in the morning. When I'm ready to give you a baby, *I'll* let you know." Kissing my stinging cheek gently, I fought back spitting on him. If he only knew. . . .

I flipped each page with as much attitude as I could muster up. Looking him boldly in the face, Spade no longer looked like the scary monster I'd been terrified of for the past year. I mocked Vanessa Bell Calloway on *Coming to America,* knowing it would piss him all the way off. She was the subservient bride-to-be that Akeem never married. Bowing my head in agreement, underneath all this humor was burning pain. *"Of course, Spencer . . . You can have whatever you like."*

"Let's see how many jokes you have when they're snatching that bastard up out of ya. Stay put—I'll be right back." Spade walked out of the room with a blunt in his hand.

That's when the storm of tears I'd been holding back rushed from my eyes. I hated Spencer Spade Johnson with a burning passion. I went from wanting my baby to wanting Spade dead. No further thought on the subject was needed.

14

Rocko

"I'm so tired of spending night after night in this dump, babe." She leaned up trying to kiss my lips. "Why can't we take both shares of our money and dip? It can just be you and me." Lezlee's pleas were in vain.

Spade and I had just gotten back from hitting up Detroit, plus getting into it. It was time for me to start cutting the strings I had to people. "You can quit talking that nonsense," I flipped her off. "Be patient. We'll be up and out of here in a few more days, at most." I was tired of pacifying Lezlee. It was time to murk her and get it over with already. I was tired of having her lurking around as a liability.

"I swear time ain't ticking fast enough," she huffed, then flopped down onto the bed. "If you don't make good on your word to get me up out of here within the next few days, I'm leaving on my own," she threatened.

Whap!

Before I knew it, I'd lost my cool and openhandedly smacked her in the back of the head, making her fly like a ragdoll across the room. She looked up shocked, but I wasn't done. "I've been trying to take it easy with your smart-talking ass, but you're taking me to the point of no return quickly. Don't make me do you in like I did your boss." My hot breath was harsh in her face as I spit each word out unforgivingly. My evilness needed to be etched into her memory. I wasn't the man of her dreams if it consisted of me being a punk.

"Okay-okay," she cried out, curled up in a fetal position on the bed. Whimpering lightly for a few minutes, she looked up at me for pity. "Can you go grab some shower gel from the front desk so I can take a bubble bath? Maybe that'll help me relax."

"Yeah, why not? I'll at least give you a chance to get your mind right. Blow on this blunt too." I passed her the swisher I'd been getting lifted on.

After grabbing the cash to pay the attendant for the next few days of our stay, I left Lezlee peeling herself off the floor looking pitiful.

Mrs. Taylor

All of the things in the condo Robert and I shared were either sold off or packed up. For the rest of my days, I'd be spending it underneath the sun in California. The Windy City hasn't given me anything but misery and lonely days. Once Detroit finished pussy-footing around with the investigation and autopsy, the insurance company could close the case on their end and forward me the remaining balance of Robert's policy. I was eager to get the check and add it to the money that wasn't gambled up.

Ring! Ring! Ring!

"Hello, this is Carolyn Taylor," I answered my sounding cell to the private calling number.

"Hi, Mrs. Taylor, this is Lezlee, your husband's assistant. I'm in a lot of trouble and need your help." Her words were fast, run together, and at a whisper.

I pulled the phone from my ear and stared at it in disbelief. This young girl has been refusing to answer my texts and calls, plus is a prime suspect in Robert's infidelity and murder, yet she was contacting *me* for help. She must've been high on some cheap street drug to be reaching out for my help.

"Mrs. Taylor, are you still there? If you help me, I can help you. I know who killed your husband."

I let out a long, exasperated sigh, then rolled my eyes out of frustration. I was going to bury Robert more than six feet under, just to make sure he didn't rise miraculously and start back haunting me with dysfunction. I've been dealing with side chicks and his revolving door of sleazy assistants he hired and fired. "Come on now, honey, it's obvious you're part of the crew who robbed and killed my husband. You've already helped yourself to his dick, money, and life—what's left that I can help you with?" I purposely left out that she'd helped herself to the HIV Robert never told women he was infected with. Homewrecking hoes deserved ill turns of fate to hit them upside the head unexpectedly.

"It's not what you think, Mrs. Taylor," Lezlee tried, begging me to listen.

"Sell your game to the cops whenever they catch up to you. I could care less if your parents have to bury you first, to be honest." I hung up in her ear, then called Officer Brickman again. When he sent me to voicemail, I left a detailed message that I'd contact him once I landed, then powered my phone off knowing there was no one else for me to talk to.

Honk-Honk! Honk!

The taxi was here. It was time to dismiss everything from my past and live whatever future I had left. I was tired of living the life of a bitch. Climbing into the backseat, I smiled—ready for a new adventure. "O'Hare International Airport, please." I folded my hands in my lap, all proper like.

"Yes, ma'am," the driver replied, then pulled away from the curb. It goes without saying; I never glanced back over my shoulder. Carolyn Taylor was officially signing off.

Rocko

Lezlee was so busy begging the dead man's wife for help that she didn't hear me crack the door open or tiptoe inside. It was hard not to choke the soul out of Lezlee's body as I listened to her beg for help and attempt to turn me in. My fate could have been sealed had Mr. Taylor's wife been willing to be her savior, but she shut Lezlee down and hung up on her. It was time to get her out of the way—for good.

"Hey, baby," she purred when I finally walked back into the room. "What took you so long?"

Already naked, I would've pounced on her ass like a hungry dog if my plan wasn't mapped out to murk her. Instead of thinking with my dick, I thought with my mind and chose to play mind games with her for fun. "I fell back for a minute to think about what you wanted, and you might be right. Both shares of cash might be enough for us to start off in another city." I was enjoying every second of looking into her eyes and lying through my teeth. This bitch had no meaning to me and no space in my heart. A stone-cold killer was stroking her.

She screamed to the top of her lungs out of happiness, then jumped in my arms celebrating what she thought was a sentimental moment. "Yes-yes-yes, Rocko, you just made my night. Those are the only words I wanted to hear."

"Here, go take your bubble bath. I'll be in to rub you down in a minute." I gave her the final kiss she'd ever feel or receive from a man.

When she got into the bath, I went into the mind-set of a killer—no longer the lover she adored or wanted to be on the run with like Bey and Jay. Since she couldn't help but break the rule and use the phone, it only seemed right for her to die by the same weakness. I unplugged the phone cord from the receiver and the handset, then stuffed it inside of my pocket.

"Come on in here, baby. The water's getting cold," she called out for me, not knowing what she was asking for. I was heartless when I entered the bathroom. Her smile flipped an even colder switch in my soul, which made me know it was time to take hers. "What did you call Chicago for? Tell me what your plan was, Lezlee," I spoke in a condescending tone.

She recognized the trouble she was in. Lezlee tried jumping out of the tub. "I'm sorry. I'm so sorry," she sniffled and yowled violently. "I promise I didn't tell her anything, Rocko. Baby, please don't kill me," she begged for her life.

"Shut the fuck up with all your lies!" I shoved her with all of my power. She tripped over the edge of the tub, hit her head on the wall, and then fell. I felt a tinge of satisfaction. "Your words mean nothing to me, Lezlee.

Save whatever explaining you gotta do for your ex-boss when you meet him in the afterlife."

All I saw in front of me was a snitch bitch as I pulled the phone cord from my pocket and wrapped it around her neck. Lezlee's body jerked as she fought, scratched, and kicked in an attempt to loosen my grip. My wrath couldn't be contained, though. The harder she tried fighting for her life, the more I pushed to take it. My mission was to make the thick plastic slice her skin open, but I let Lezlee's limp body fall to the floor after I felt her lungs collapse from her last breath. Regret was written all over her face when I dropped her lifeless body into the tub of water and began cleaning up the murder scene.

Officer Brickman

I was sitting at my desk looking at the detailed report of the Taylor case when the captain shouted through the precinct for me. I almost spilled my fresh cup of coffee all over myself and the report. He'd been tap-dancing on my nerves all morning. Turning around annoyed and ready to spit out more slurs, I was forced to have a change of mind. The mayor's do-boy lackey lawyer stood side-by-side with my boss wearing a devilish grin. All lawyers were crooked, but this jaw-jacking Jew was getting rich by helping Detroit fall deeper into corruption. Each time his falsified paper-carrying-ass waltzes in and out of here with that black briefcase, the city I worked so hard to clean up regresses.

"Hello, Brickman. Good seeing you again but under such horrible circumstances," the lawyer routinely greeted me. The guy was always transparently fake and a jerk.

I tried swallowing my pride by speaking and shaking his hand, but the dislike between us was mutual. As always, the tension between us could be cut with a knife. On my cop stance, I looked him up and down and noticed red marks around his neck. I wanted to question what the hell had happened, but being a crooked political official in Detroit—any repercussion was possible. Letting the thought go, I followed him into my captain's office.

"Take a seat, Brickman. You know the rules," Captain barked at me.

"I'm not interested in digesting any more bullshit, plus I'm solid on the routine. I think I'll sit this one out." Before he could respond, I dropped my report onto the lawyer's black briefcase, then my resignation letter onto the captain's desk. "To be real firm with both of you fine officers of the law, I'm tapping out on all of this. If you have any questions about my report, I'll be clearing out my desk for the next ten minutes or so."

"Slow your fucking roll, Brickman. Close that damn door and glue your fat ass to that seat. *I* will let you know when the force is done with you. Until then, it's time to start covering up some crime."

Detroit was doomed. When the mayor's crooked attorney shut his black briefcase and shook my hand, my last official deal with the devil was done. I'd signed off on trumped up police work that would lead to the Taylor case closing under illegitimate pretenses. Three prop people will accept the charges and sentencing for Robert Taylor's death under aliases, but won't serve a day. My falsified reports in addition to the attorney's affidavits were enough to keep red flags down, plus a trial wasn't needed. The mayor closed all of his high-profile crime cases the same while managing to keep the media at bay.

And the true criminals, of course, would never stand up. It was a win-win situation for everyone—but me.

"I'm so sorry to see you go, Brickman. The mayor and I thought you worked wonderfully as a part of this team. The city won't be the same with you gone," the attorney spoke sarcastically, then rose to leave. "And, Captain, I'm sure my boss will be in touch. We're aiming to close this one out immediately so the ratings won't be a bad look, of course. The city has taken enough hits over the years with black folks running it down. It deserves an honest chance at getting cleaned up."

"That it does. Indeed, the city does," I sarcastically agreed.

"Good day, gentlemen," the attorney snickered, catching on to my wittiness.

Only two steps of the lawyer being out of the door, my ex-captain began reading me up and down. "Your ass is fried in this town, Brickman. You better hope you can survive on whatever pennies you've got saved up because any of your hopes of a recommendation from this desk or this city are certainly out of the window. What possessed you to come in here busting your balls like that?"

"Like I said earlier, I'm tired of this flimsy-ass police force. I mean, damn, aren't you tired of having the mayor's hand up your ass like a puppet?"

"Money makes the world go 'round; and you're old enough to know that, Brickman. Drop your badge and weapon on my desk; you're free to get the fuck on."

"And you're free to go fuck yourself, sir." Walking out of his stale-smelling office for the last time, his words or the career I'd been making for myself didn't mean anything in the twelfth hour. I swiped everything off of my desk into a box, then followed his last order efficiently—I got the fuck on.

Today, of all days, the sun beat down on my pale, white skin when I stepped foot outside of 1300 Beaubien's door. A weight was lifted from off my shoulders for sure, but I felt like a letdown to the city I swore to uphold and protect. The mayor was so wrapped up in keeping his political tenure pristine that whatever blemish showed up on his crime stats couldn't linger without being solved. My chest wasn't covered with a badge of honor, and my waist wasn't suited with a protection piece. For twenty years, I'd been a man of the law. But now, my life had changed.

Buzz, buzz, buzz!

Without a holster on my waist, it was easy to retrieve my vibrating phone. The out-of-state Chicago number flashed on the screen again, but Mrs. Taylor's business was no longer mines. Slamming the company phone onto the concrete, I stomped on it to ensure every bit of metal broke up. Before climbing in my car, I hawked a big glob of saliva onto the cap's car, then pulled my dick out and pissed all on the side of the door. I didn't care who saw because, in this city, you'd have a hard time getting a soul to snitch. It was fuck the captain, the mayor, that crooked-ass Jew lawyer, and any crime that went down in Detroit. I was out.

15

Jakia

"Get the fuck out of my way before you get run down. Y'all ain't got bumpers," Spade yelled out of the rolled down window to the right-to-life picketers. Once clearing the path into the clinic's parking lot, he turned in my direction and began running down the rules. "Hear me good, Jakia. We are here to get rid of this li'l fucker and not a thing else. Go up in here like the trooper I trained you to be and handle yo' business. Don't drop a tear or a hint that you want it. Do we have an understanding?"

"Yeah, whatever, Spade," I whispered, reaching for the door handle. He didn't have to continuously prepare me for going to kill our kid—or what might've been ours. I knew what he wanted and didn't see a way to get what I desired. So, like tradition, he had it his way.

"Don't think for one second I won't snatch yo' wig back in front of these white folks, girl." His last warning could've gone without him saying.

My feet were barely on the ground before the same mob of protestors started running up to the car and making a huddle around me. Everywhere I looked was a lady yelling in my face about being pro-choice and giving my baby a chance at life—or a dead fetus, or photographs of God and religious stuff. I was overwhelmed and saddened by all of it, especially since I wasn't torn about having an abortion but being forced to. I knew I couldn't reach out or accept the pamphlets. I knew Spade would snatch me back into the car and beat the baby out of me if I tried reneging on this abortion. My heart ached as I pushed past them.

"The Lord won't forgive you, my dear child. Take this pamphlet and think about your choices. Don't kill your baby. You will be a murderer, and God will not forgive a murderer," a gentle-looking lady tried persuading me.

"Aye, Grandma, get back with yo' shit before I crack your head." Spade knocked the pamphlets from her hands. She stumbled backward while looking at me for sympathy, but I couldn't give her any.

"All you honkies better back up off me and my lady." Spade threw a towel from the motel over my head and damn near suffocated me while dragging me inside. "Stop harassing us and leave my wife alone before I start dealing out ass whoopings!" By any means necessary, he was going to get our kid out of my womb.

Once inside, the receptionist immediately began apologizing for the protestors, then handed over a stack of medical history forms for me to complete. Spade stayed close to my side but at no point was he comforting. He wanted to make sure I didn't write any help letters or answer any questions that would make the staff think I was being forced to abort or a victim of domestic violence. I initially skipped them but was nudged in the side. I knew better, so I answered "no."

"Jakia Johnson," the nurse called. That was the first time I'd heard my married name since the minister announced it at the courthouse.

Spade and I met with the doctor who was signing off on my abortion. He and Spade seemed to bond as he slid the $475 across the table, then pocketed the receipt. At no point did the doctor look at me or ask if this was something I wanted to do. Every day of my life, if nothing else, I learned cash ruled this evil world. And, yup, since I was with Spade, it must've ruled mine too.

"Right this way, Mrs. Johnson. And, sir, you can have a seat in the waiting room. Once the procedure is over, your wife will meet you back out there," the nurse kindly spoke.

"Oh, hell naw, lady. I ain't going nowhere till I see to it this abortion pill I paid good money for is popped," Spade snapped, then grabbed my hand.

"You have to sit out here, sir. It's against HIPPA policy. Your wife may be okay with you being a part of her procedure. However, this clinic cannot, under any circumstances, allow you to violate the privacy of other patients." She opened and held the door for Spade to walk out, but he refused to move.

"You better bring those pills up in this muthafuckin' room right here, then, 'cause I ain't about to separate from my wife, yo." He was determined to have his way.

The nurse looked at me, then spoke in a condescending tone. "Ma'am, is this something you want—or he wants? At this point, you can still get a refund because nothing but paperwork has been done."

I thought about telling her the truth. Hell, I *needed* to tell her the truth. Killing my baby was the last thing on earth I wanted to do. If I went through with this medication abortion, I'd be killing part of myself. On the other hand, if I kept it, I'd be starting trouble with Spade, plus possibly breeding a dead man's child. I answered knowing I couldn't truly have this child, though I wanted to. "Of course, this is what I want. If I didn't wanna get this li'l fucker up out of me—I wouldn't be here."

She rolled her eyes like she could sense I was lying but shut the door anyway. "Okay, this is the only compromise I can make. Ma'am, you come with me to finish your labs and ultrasound; and, sir, you wait here for us to return with the medication. Take that deal, or I'll get the doctor in here to take care of your refund. I don't have time for the back-and-forth."

"Naw, I'm good with that. I'll be right here waiting. Toss me that remote." Spade sat down crossing his legs. He always got what he wanted. I was sickened to my stomach, and not because I was pregnant.

The nurse was rough and short with me as I went through a physical, more laboratory tests, and an ultrasound to determine the exact location of the baby. With the monitor turned to her, she took a few pictures and didn't speak a word to me—even for casual conversation.

"How far along am I?" I couldn't help but question her.

"Why do you care? You just want the li'l fucker up out of you, right?" she hissed, using my exact words against me.

I fell back on the table and kept silent. I was in a catch-22. But woman to woman, she should've treated me with a little more grace. From that point on, I only spoke when spoken to. I focused my heart, mind, and soul on detaching from the child I wished I could keep. And when I popped the first pill with Spade by my side, I knew then I'd never be the same. Handing me a bag of after-care instructions, including when I would administer the misoprostol to myself, along with antibiotics, the nurse released me back into the mob. The world was cold and lonely for me, even with so much going on around me.

"Baby killer! May the Lord have mercy on your soul!" they shouted, taunting me.

Throwing the towel back over my head, Spade rushed and shoved me into the car. I'm sure he ran a few folks over burning rubber out of the parking lot.

Spade

With one kid on the chopping block, I felt a little stress relieved from off my shoulders. As soon as I got her settled back at the room, I'd be making my way back to Detroit to do the same routine with Tiffany. I don't know what the fuck I was thinking nutting in either of them, because I'm not trying to have no seeds out here sprouting and needing a nigga to hold their hand.

Jakia sat in the passenger seat with tears and snot smeared all over her face. I loved her, yeah, but I wasn't weak to her emotions. Baby girl could'a gone and chopped this seed up as a loss. "You know you did this to yourself, right?"

She turned and gave me an ice-cold glare, then rolled her eyes to blow me off. "What the fuck? Do you want me to humor you? Inevitably, I don't see how I've had any control over my destiny, Spencer. But you already know that. I'd rather not talk about any of this."

My anger was boiling over at the way she was addressing me, but I was trying hard to contain it. I was itching to pull over and shove her wannabe badass out of the passenger seat.

Ring! Ring! Ring!

Instead of shooting Tiff to the voicemail, I wanted to piss Jakia off even more. I was sick of her slick comments and trying to act tough. "What up, T? You good?"

Jakia's head whipped in my direction with a menacing glare. With pursed lips, I could tell she was biting the shit out of her tongue, trying to swallow a few cutthroat words. She'd been around me long enough to have picked up on my aggression.

"Hell yeah, I'm good! I'm trying to find out if you and Rock are straight," Tiff was yelling with a panicked voice into the phone.

"What you mean? A nigga like me stays one-hundred." I spoke like a boss trying to get under Jakia's skin.

"Well, it's all over the news. They've arrested the perps responsible for the Motor City Murder, so the bitch I love to hate must've finally went down." Tiff's words threw me into a shock. I was seldom shook, but all of sudden, my head was throbbing, and everything around me turned into a blur.

"What in the hell did you just say?" Trying my best not to repeat Tiff's exact words, I didn't want to set off any alarms with Jakia until I had all the details. In a flash, I turned the volume down as low as it could go, hoping to drown out her response.

I listened to Tiff run down the breaking news story that, according to her, was on every news-reporting Detroit channel. She claimed the Detroit Police Department apprehended the suspects regarding the murder and closed the case officially. Which seemed crazy to me 'cause at least two of the four—plus Tiff—were still living free. Or at least I thought.

Flooring the pedal, I coasted toward the Knights Inn hoping not to pull up on State Troopers surrounding the scene. If Lezlee and Rocko were in police custody, without a doubt, the cops would still be waiting around for us too.

"I can't believe you answered the phone with that dirty ho," Jakia twisted her lips up after I hung up on Tiff. "If you don't respect me as your wife, why should I respect you as my husband?"

Whap!

Slapping her quiet was the only way I could think straight. I was confused and nervous from the phone call and pissed I didn't have a Christmas cookie. Jakia needed to find and get into her place. "For every other reason that you exist—'cause I said so. Now, sit back and relax—there's bigger shit on the table to handle. Supposedly, they've got the ones responsible for ole boy's death in custody."

Jakia

This must've been the morning that Satan was sent to earth. First, I pop pills to start the killing process of my baby; then, I find out I might be going to jail. Utterly confused by Spade's words, I grabbed my chest and tried taking deep breaths. In just two seconds flat, an anxiety attack had set in.

"What do you mean, Spade? How could that be? Do they have Rocko and Lezlee? Did they drop the ball on us? Is your trick side bitch lying?"

"How in the fuck would I know? You were sitting right here when I got the call. And this nigga ain't answering," he snapped, then honked the horn at jamming traffic. "Get the hell up out of my way!"

I held on to the seat belt for dear life but not knowing why I wanted to live. I knew Rocko was loyal to at least

Spade, which meant me too. But as far as Lezlee went—
that stranger danger ho wouldn't dare take a bid for me.
She might've rubbed my back and played nice to me last
night, but a friend I knew she was not.

The closer we got to the Knights Inn, the deeper my
heart sank into my stomach. Between my anxiety and
the subtle cramps that were sneaking in and out like
contractions, I secretly longed for my body to give up and
pass out.

Unexpectedly but thankfully so, the scene was just as
mundane as when we left. Thinking there'd be cop cars
surrounding the entrance and both rooms rented to Spade
and Rocko, only the fiends and early rising prostitutes
were posted up. Instead of surveying the land and at least
circling the block, Spade pulled in with no fear.

"I don't know what's going on. But keep your ass in
this car until I say otherwise." He grabbed the keys from
the ignition, got out, and slammed the door.

Spade

"What up, Rock, you good?" I tapped on the door a
few times but didn't get a response. "Aye, cuz, I hear the
TV and shit, open up."

"Damn, nigga, I'm good up in here. Quit sweating
me." He swung the door open. "Ain't nothing going on
but me handling some lingering business. Did you take
care of your situation with what would've been my li'l
cuz?"

"Dude, I'm gonna give you a pass since you obviously
don't know what's going on. Where's Lezlee?" I pushed
past him into the room. Instantly, Clorox and Kush bud
fumes shot up my nostrils, damn near choking me out.

"She ain't here," he nonchalantly replied, then slammed the door.

I got to going quickly about Tiff's phone call. "Aye, come on, we gotta split, Rock. Tiff just called saying they arrested the people responsible for the Motor City Murder. So if that bitch Lezlee is in the wind, it won't be long before the cops are on our heads." Rushing to the window and pulling the curtain open, I waved for Jakia to come inside. I didn't want her out there by herself if a State Boy did roll up.

"Calm down and say what? Have you been smoking that shit again?"

He moved throughout the room looking for the remote. That's when I noticed the entire room's linen was stripped and everything, including the drawers, lamp shades, and living space chairs, were pulled out or flipped over.

"Naw, I haven't. But don't worry about my side sniffing when you've been up to some ole action adventure MacGyver shit. What's going on up on here?" Pointing at the random clutter of the room while he found a local channel to report the Detroit news, I ran him through an investigation.

He threw his hand up with a smirk on his face, then passed me the blunt. I hit it with no problem, then opened the door for Jakia to come in. Just like me, she covered her nose coughing from the fumes, then looked around not knowing what was up.

We watched the news report featuring the captain of the Detroit Police Department along with the attorney working for the mayor. Just as Tiff ran back on the phone with me, they were claiming to have those responsible for the crime me and my team committed awaiting sentencing in their custody. Before I could speak up about my suspicions of what was occurring, Jakia broke the room's silence.

"Where's that snake you fucking, Rocko? I know that bitch is down there singing like a canary to the cops." She jumped up, pacing the room.

We both looked at her shocked that she'd gone nuts and taken that tone with a man linked to my blood. She knew better, but given the circumstances, I was trying to give her a slight pass.

"I can't take this. Oh my God, I'm about to be sick." She darted for the bathroom. "Aaah! Aaah! Spadeee!" Her piercing screams sent shivers through even my spine. Out of instinct and concern, I ran to be by her side. I didn't know what the problem was, but being human, I understood this whole ordeal must've been traumatic for her.

"Have you lost your fuckin' mind, Rock?" Slouched in the water was Lezlee's lifeless body. When I got a closer look, I saw the phone cord wrapped around her neck and her eyes bucked wide.

"The weakest link attached to our hip is dead. I ain't crazy. I'm precautious. We've taken too many risks already." Rocko was answering to what he'd done but was drowned out by Jakia's wailing.

Cupping her mouth to enclose the screaming, I led her out of the bathroom all the while side-eyeing Rocko. He'd been flipping the switch all day but never did I expect for him to ice Lezlee. From one extreme to the next, the life I lived was mad crazy, fa'sho.

Jakia

Hyperventilating and trying not to pass out, the image of Robert Taylor's dead body had been replaced with

Lezlee's ghastly looking face. I was flushed with regret for wishing her dead because from the looks of if, she suffered horribly. Spade passed me the blunt he was smoking as Rocko sat across lighting another one.

"She had to die. When we got back last night, I heard her talking to that dead man's wife. I couldn't trust her ass to be around me for not a second more." He brushed off killing her like it was nothing. All this time, I thought Rocko was the good guy. But lately, he was turning out to be more scandalous and heinous than Spade.

"Is that why they're saying they've caught the Motor City Murderers? Did she tell his wife we did it? I don't understand any of this."

"Ain't no telling what was said during their conversation—and we sure can't find out now." Spade cut Rocko off from any answers he was willing to give. "What's real is that we've gotta get rid of her body and get out of here. So quit all that whining and get your game face on. You've been around a dead body before." Spade downplayed the situation.

"Plus, if the cops knew your identity and our whereabouts, they would've been here by now. Our best bet is to get up out of here," Rocko cosigned.

He and Spade kicked it between themselves as if I weren't in the room about the next moves we'd make. In the middle of me trying to meditate and wrap my head around Lezlee's sudden murder and my involvement in her mutilation, I overheard Spade making plans to uproot—falling off the grid from Detroit for good. Rocko agreed, so nothing more needed to be discussed. As usual, I didn't have a choice in the matter, but truthfully speaking, I didn't feel comfortable going back to the city anyway. In my opinion, the DPD was on some shady shit that could blow up in my face later.

Young and dumb, I've been a ride-and-die girl in a lot of Spade and Rocko's reckless missions; however, disposing of another woman's body took the cake. Despite the cramps, pounding headache, and overwhelming nerves that were fighting to take over my being, I used whatever potent concoction Rocko mixed up to clean the walls again. Using gloves, I made sure not to leave a fingerprint of mine. Since I knew the police didn't have the guilty party in custody, my fretfulness wouldn't settle.

When Spade barked out orders for me to help move Lezlee, I followed his orders but couldn't help throwing up at seeing her dead again. She was wrapped in sheets, but her limbs stuck out from the sides as if they were taunting me. I trembled at the sight of death, then thought about what Spade would do to me if *I* became a threat. If only I could endure, Juan would be home to save me. Only able to help carry her to the door, having her dead body under my touch freaked me out, making me let go. No matter what Spade thought, I couldn't help them toss her in the dumpster.

Spade

In addition to me peeping Jakia couldn't handle the task at hand, I needed to get some space from her so I could blow a blunt. After everything that's gone down today, especially her abortion, I knew she wanted to smoke with me, and I didn't want to get her hooked on Christmas cookies. Come to think of it, though, if she kept acting up, an addiction might be in her future.

"Clean the bathroom from top to bottom while we go dump her around back. We'll be hitting the road shortly after we get back," I ordered Jakia to work while Rocko and I prepared to ride out with a dead body.

"I'm feeling kinda dizzy, Spade. I'll clean it after I get a few moments to rest," she softly spoke, curling up on the floor.

"Naw, ain't no time for that. You can rest in the car. Think about how you feeling the next time you quit popping them birth control pills with yo' sneaky ass."

Yanking her up, I stood and monitored Jakia cleaning the room for a few minutes until I felt comfortable leaving her alone. This wasn't the time for her to get weak with another murder hovering over us. I wasn't tripping on Rocko, though. Lezlee was a liability and had to go.

Rocko and I carried her around back of the Knights Inn motel as discreetly as we could. In the alley, there were a few battered-looking working women giving slob jobs to tricks, but no one paid the slightest attention to us. With only a little strength exerted, we tossed Lezlee's body into the trash container, then threw a few bags from other receptacles on top of her. Since her body was wrapped in white sheets, maybe—just maybe—she'd go unnoticed until making it to the county's final disposal site. We returned to the room and found Jakia finishing up in the bathroom.

"Go ahead and attack our room the same way. We'll be loading the van up." I sent her on her way so Rocko and I could talk in private.

The door hadn't slammed behind her good before I commenced to dropping my hand with Rocko wanting to know what was up. I wasn't built to go against the grain in front of Jakia, but I wanted to know the words of the last conversation he had with Lezlee just as badly as she did.

"Let's kick it right quick before we make this last haul up I-75. Real talk, it would be nice to know what ole girl said before you iced her." I kept it real.

"She didn't tell much because the dead man's wife wasn't trying to hear nothing. From what I did hear, she was willing to tell it all."

"I told you that broad was trouble." I couldn't help but throw that fact in his face. "But bros before hoes, so it's no skin off my back."

We gave each other plays, then chilled for a second making sure we were A1 swell. Everything within the last twenty-four hours had been insane, and both of us sensed the slight tension. In place of having a bitch session and calling out flaws, we acknowledged things needed to get better by handshake, then agreed to move on. As family, I couldn't be petty to him. Flat the fuck out, he was the only person 100 percent in my corner.

"Let's be out and get back to the city. If she did throw them some leads to us being here, I don't want to be around if the boys come snooping. You can stay at my crib until we make our next move."

"A'ight, cool. Maybe we can hit a few more licks to add with what's stacked at Tiff's. We'll need it once we get to a new city and start back on our grind." Rocko was truly feeling the idea of leaving his hometown for good.

"I'm with it, fa'sho," I agreed with no hesitation. "If I can't take care of my problem with Tiff, I'm gonna have to leave town for good anyway," I joked in all serious-ness. With all the craziness going on, I still remembered the daunting alleged "pregnancy" I was responsible for.

Giving the room a thorough once-over to make sure nothing was left behind, we walked out with one more stop to make before leaving the Knights Inn for good.

Rocko

"Yo, Hakem, let me pay you up front for me and Rock's tab for next week." I walked into the front office flashing a bankroll to the hotel's attendant.

"Okay—okay, not a problem, bro." He popped open his safe as I laid the bills across the counter.

Instead of paying with big bills like every other time, I left Hakem to count stacks of fives, tens, and a few twenties so I'd have time to survey the premises longer. There were a few cameras that I assumed weren't working, but I didn't want to take any additional chances. I was trying to think and move differently since the casino hit went wrong. Finally making count to the last bill, Hakem looked up to the barrel of my gun.

"We had an agreement. What are you doing?" he stuttered, trying to push me to rationalize my actions.

"I know, and I appreciate your hospitality. Unfortunately, I can't leave you dangling, knowing how I look, Hakem. You understand, don't you?"

"No, no, I wouldn't talk to the cops. Look around. Everything around here is an illegal operation. Please don't kill me. I have no reason to give you up," he pleaded.

Pop! Pop! Pop!

"Ay, dude, you ain't got all day to be negotiating with his scab ass." Spade lowered his pistol from firing three swift shots into Hakem's upper body. "Grab our cash off that counter and whatever's in that safe and let's go!"

Pushing Hakem's body off our money, I swooped it up and put it back in the bag I carried along with the contents from his safe. Before running out for good, I snatched the tape from the recorder and the camera from the wall, just in case.

"Come on, y'all—let's truck it back to the D." I jumped in the van and slid the door closed. "Our presence in downriver, I'm sure, is no longer well received."

16

Juan

"Coleman, let's go," the prison guard's voice bellowed into the eighty-foot room when he opened the door.

"I'd rather skip my hour of exercise today." Not bothering to turn over, I couldn't face another sixty minutes of torture being teased with time outside of this cage. That's the only time I was allowed once a day to step outside of this room while the remaining twenty-three were reserved for me to go mentally crazy.

"Get up, Coleman, you're leaving SHU."

I hesitated.

"Coleman, if you don't get your good-for-nothing black ass up, you'll be locked down for the rest of the day at least."

I flew off of the cot and was at his feet before my heart could pump another beat. My ears hadn't heard wrong. I was officially being released back into the general prison system. However, I was carrying ten more years on my back.

"Damn, homie, I ain't never think you were gonna rise from solitary. I was worried you weren't gonna make it. That shit is meant to break you down mentally." Gonz welcomed me back into our prison bunk. "Young bucks like you ain't made to serve hard time."

"Real talk, homie. That shit faded me. I think I cried by the twelfth hour," I couldn't help but admit. "By the end of the first week, I'd completely gone numb. My sister is on the outside getting whopped up on, and that punk-ass attorney of mine got me ten more years pending on my sentence that the warden personally delivered himself."

"I told you about believing in the Great White Hope, homie," he chuckled. "Me and my people don't fuck with no man that takes a code to abide by any law of this America. All they asses want is for minorities like us to be locked behind bars. And can't no man truly do for his family behind bars." Gonz fed me knowledge. "My offer still stands."

He offering twice was too much. If I would've hollered at him instead of snitching, this mandatory extra ten wouldn't be a dark cloud lingering over my head. Plus, to make things worse, the warden promised me a transfer upstate. From the horror stories other inmates told, that's the worst type of time to serve. "Hey, Ramos, real talk, I'ma need you to hold me down on this one." Those were the same words Spade used when asking me to serve his time.

"Say no more." He nodded, then stared me in the eyes. "For my help, you owe me one. In here, that's all we got."

"If you can guarantee my sister's safety, then all is fair." I stood, shaking his hand and should've felt a sense of relief. However, something deep down inside made me fear I'd made a deal with the devil.

"Write who needs to be taken care of, their facial and physical descriptions along with anything else that my men will be able to use to locate him. Please don't hand me that sheet until you're absolutely certain you want them handled. Regardless, though, you're still in debt to me a favor." Gonz called heavy shots, but my need to protect Jakia was too great.

"Hey, yo, Coleman, welcome back." One of my fellow prisoners acknowledged my return from solitary.

I nodded, then turned back to the small television screen. Since the situation with Jakia was semitaken care of, for once, I could sit in peace and watch what was going on in the world. At some point during my isolated confinement, I'd come to terms with turning into an old man in here.

"Breaking News . . . The Motor City Murder has been solved. Detroit can now sleep with a little more peace knowing the perpetrators responsible for such a heinous crime are behind bars," the news reporter broke through a commercial. *"Live, reporting from 1300 Beaubien at Detroit's Police Headquarters . . .*

"It's been a long five weeks, but after tirelessly scouring the city, all parties involved in the Motor City Murder have been apprehended and are awaiting official sentencing. The mayor along with his staff would like to apologize and thank the city for standing beside the administration and officers who have worked the case."

The city of Detroit was just how I left it—under complete distress and bullshit. They never cared about the citizens unless it meant collecting revenue from us for tickets and citations. Not having a long list of choices to keep me occupied in this hellhole, though, the breaking news story conference had become the highlight of my day. That's until the devil himself appeared on the screen.

So that's why his chunky paste face ass couldn't help me with my case. Oh, Mr. Big Shot aka the False Great

White Hope was too high profile for a slum like me. Anger ripped through my body as I fought hard to contain myself. When he leaned on the podium and promised his dedication, commitment, and trustworthiness to the city of Detroit—I was revving up from zero. When I spotted his tricky black briefcase, I lost my cool straight to one hundred.

"Detain the prisoner! Coleman, have you lost your mind?"

I'd tossed the steel chair I was sitting in straight into the television, shattering the screen into a million pieces. I knew I was getting led back to the SHU.

Jakia

Being home was much better than being cooped up in that ratchet motel room, but the whole feeling was bittersweet. I couldn't get settled and situated when I didn't know when for sure we'd be pulling out. Juan wanted me to pack. However, the first thing I needed to do when I got enough strength was to write to him. We had a lot of pen pal catching up to do. Not to mention, I had to break the news to him that I'd killed his first niece or nephew.

Trying hard to play the mind over matter game, I rolled around on Spade's and my king-sized bed trying to get comfortable enough to bear down until the cramping subsided. I tried visualizing butterflies and flowers, counting backward from 1,000, and even talking to God out loud. My efforts were in vain because no form of hope brought me a moment of relief. Moving my hand around in the bed for my phone, I called Spade but knew he couldn't be my last and final resort.

"You think I give a fuck about you cramping? That's on you for trying to sneak a nigga with a baby. I bet you'll think long and hard next time you wanna go around forgetting to take your pills while cheating with the next nigga. I don't know what in the fuck you thought this was." Spade was going in on me and hadn't paused to re-up on his words.

I guess my punishment for fucking around on him was never going to end. He might not have brought it much yesterday, but I was paying for that neglect today.

"I thought you were ready to work on a family," I responded, almost too low for even me to hear.

"What?" he shouted into the phone. "Have you been sniffing out of my dope packages on the sly? You sound like a fool if you think I'm trying to have kids. I ain't ready for no kids, especially by your ditzy ass. Besides, for all I know, that could've been that dead man's baby. And I fa'damn sure wasn't about to have a hand in raising that."

Spade was going in on me like I wasn't his wife. The rude remarks and disses didn't stop with Rocko's encouraging laughter in the background. I wanted to go in on him, but I didn't have the strength. My body simply couldn't handle the extra stress or consequences that would come from trying to be tough.

My head was banging, I could barely open my eyes, and my stomach was pushing clots out the size of my fist. I'd soaked through ten superabsorbent maxi pads in two hours. Something was drastically wrong. Instead of Spade being an insensitive thug for his no-good-ass cousin, he should've been at home nursing and catering to me—the woman he vowed to cherish and love. But the joke was on me. If I wasn't careful, I'd end up like Lezlee.

"Hello! Earth to Jakia," he yelled, noticing I was off into another world. "You better say something, girl."

Naw, not this time. Fuck what I got coming 'cause it can't get any worse. He's already sent me to the baby chopper and got me pushing the fetus out in our bed. I'd taken this struggle to the head alone so far, so I guess I had to continue doing so.

Spade kept screaming my name into the phone, but I refused to respond. I wasn't getting ready to waste what little energy I had left in my body defending my character, loyalty, or love to him. When he left me here alone to finish the medical abortion and insert the remaining RU-486 pills alone, I lost all hope our marriage would stand the test of time.

"Hey, dude, you might have to swing me to my crib. This bitch might've tapped out for real."

Whatever else he said wasn't heard. I left the phone in the bed as I crawled and slithered across the floor to the bathroom. The cramps were making it impossible for me to stand up straight, plus I felt extremely light-headed and nauseated. I didn't need a doctor to tell me something wasn't right. I needed a doctor to save my life. Within seconds of me sliding my pajama pants and shirt off, I was hugging the toilet and vomiting, which turned into dry heaving my stomach insides and blood out. Shit was bad—really bad.

The cold, ceramic tile in the bathroom felt good against my hot skin. The touch of my skin was scalding hot. Not having enough strength to venture downstairs for the thermometer, after a few more minutes of resting in the same spot, I crawled over to the tub and turned the shower water on. Not only did showers and baths usually soothe and make me feel better, but also it was imperative

I wash away the reeking smell of dead baby blood. The odor was horrific and making my healing process more unbearable.

Once clean, I'd figure out my next game plan. If Spade wasn't here by the time I was out and dressed, Checker taxi services would be the only resort I had to the hospital. He would kill me once he found out I'd gone without his permission, but if I waited here too long, I'd be dead anyway. If it weren't for him trying to keep me under his microscopic eye under lock and key, I could've had the surgical abortion and been in and out. This whole RU-486 option was turning out to be the worst experience of my life—next to getting twisted up with Spade in the first place.

Spade

The timer on the phone was still counting so I knew Jakia hadn't hung up in a rage. Something might've really been wrong, and even though I didn't give a fuck, I didn't need her tapping out. Deep down inside, my gut feeling told me that baby wasn't mine in the first place. Had it been, Jakia would've jumped at the opportunity to tell me the news like Tiff did. All the hiding Jakia did only made her story less believable, and I was back on the tip thinking about the night she cheated on me. After returning the rental to Tiff and retrieving Rocko's and my stash, I was in the wind on her ass too, at least until I got my mind right out of town. These hoes ain't loyal is more than just a hook to a song. However, on a new grid, I could re-up on a whole new flock.

"Hey, swing me past Walgreens Pharmacy right quick so I can pick this broad up some pads and shit. I'm mad as fuck about her trying to trap me, yo!"

"You silly as fuck, man." Rocko bent the corner on two wheels. "How do you come up with the crazy stuff you say? Jakia's your wife—wives can't trap husbands and shit!"

"You a lie. And I'm gonna sign off on the death papers for every single baby Jakia thinks she's about to bring into the house. Do I look like a car seat carrying type nigga to you? Hell to the naw!" I'd gotten hype and was now biting Rocko's head off.

"Keep going; don't stop! I swear you fooling tonight." Rocko was drunk, just as I was.

He was ripping through traffic doing damn near 100 mph as I leaned back sipping from my fifth of Patrón and puffing on a Christmas cookie. We'd been partying on the profits we'd robbed from the doughboys a few days ago, and only to Rocko's knowledge—I'd been having a love affair with white powder. One of our last celebrations in the D was in full effect—until Jakia called with her "woe is me" speech.

"But on the real, nigga—why'd you marry homegirl if you weren't about to at least treat her right? I know you're still hung up about ole boy we murked, but that cold case ain't our worries anymore. Let it go 'cause the cops sure did!"

"Why not wife a bitch that don't make you do no better? What other chick am I gonna find that's as loyal as Jakia? Real talk, if she stays around long enough, I'm gonna renew our vows to do right by her."

Rocko damn near crashed into a parked car pulling into the Walgreens parking lot. "Case and point proved—

yo' ass is a dog and is straight vicious." He shook his head.

"Says the man who killed Lezlee in cold blood and bubbles," I sarcastically reminded him.

He cut his eyes at me, then took a swig from his bottle. "Case and point proved again. Hurry yo' ass up so you can take care of yo' problems."

I climbed out of his cashed-out Chevy Impala and ran into the drugstore headed straight for the pharmacist. A nigga like me wasn't getting ready to search through no aisle of feminine products. "Hey, yo, I need some help real quick." I rudely cut past the few people standing in line. It wasn't no thang 'cause if they wanted a problem I could bring one. I lived for setting shit off.

"It'll be just a few minutes, sir. There are a few customers I need to help that were waiting in line before you." The attendant looked up with an annoyed expression on her face. "So if you could please step to the end of the line, I'll help you once it's your turn." She popped her white pharmacy jacket like she was some type of boss.

"Nah, I don't think so." I leaned over the counter blatantly staring at her chest. I wanted her to feel more than uncomfortable as I put her on blast. "Crystal, right?" I thumped her name tag with the upmost disrespect. "What I'm gonna need from you right now is to hear me loud and clear. Shut that register down or call for some immediate backup. A nigga like me is not waiting. You got that?"

By the time it was all over, I had walked out of Walgreens with bottles of Motrin, bags of maxi pads, cans of chicken noodle soup, and plenty of bottles of Gatorade to keep Jakia hydrated. Crystal, the same snotty-ass pharmacist, even had to fill the script the abortion clinic prescribed. I should've dropped it off, but my street world was much more important. The minimum wage-working clerk stocked me up with a care package that should have Jakia feeling better in no time.

"Damn, nigga, did you buy the store out?" Rocko laughed, handing me the blunt he was blowing on.

Jakia

The shower was giving me back a little life, but I was still passing large blood clots. As I sat in the tub letting the shower water run directly over me, I didn't care about my hair napping or my makeup running. Looking pretty and covering my battle wounds was the least of my concern. As I spread my legs and pushed out more clots, I was trying to speed up the process and hopefully pull myself from out of my misery. The nurse from the clinic said the pain should subside soon, but six hours didn't equate to "soon" in my book. The shower water had gone from scorching hot to lukewarm and was on its way to icy cold. I didn't care 'cause I didn't want to get out and face the world. A blunt would do me so good right now.

"Jakia, where is yo' ass at?" I heard Spade yelling through the house and commanding Rocko to search for me too.

Now I'm about to be really embarrassed. Why can't he tell his psycho cousin to find another squat house until it's time to leave Detroit? I leaned my head against the wall and held on tightly to the towel rack, bracing myself. Every part of me hated Spade to his core, but I was happy he'd come home to rescue me. I needed his help badly.

"Hey, I found her," he called out to Rocko as he rushed into the bathroom. "What are you doing in there? Damn,

Jakia, you sure know how to ruin a nigga's night." He
turned the water off, then pulled me out of the tub.

Usually, Spade and Rocko stay on the sticks playing
video games, but Spade got me dressed instead. He
wasn't comforting or gentle as he roughly slid my socks,
pajama pants, and shirt on.

As he scooped me up in his arms, I cried like a baby.
The feeling was bittersweet to have him coddling me, but
I knew him comforting me would be short-lived. Spade
wasn't the type of man who wore his feelings on his
sleeve. "It hurts so bad, babe," I whimpered. "I wish you
wouldn't have made me kill our baby."

"Okay, shh. Just breathe and chill out."

"Please take me to the hospital."

"Hell-to-the-no! You don't need no damn hospital.
The woman at Walgreens said this stuff should be enough
to comfort you until the cramping is gone." After handing
me the prescribed meds from the abortion clinic, he
dumped a bag of maxi pads, pain meds, and a few cans
of Campbell's soup onto the bed. "I'll grab you some
water to pop those pills and the remote so you can get
comfortable."

"No, please don't blow this off, Spade. I promise you
I need medical attention. I'm pushing out clots the
size of your fist! If you leave me here with this bogus
bag of feel-good, I'll bleed to death. Ain't none of this
shit gonna stop blood from gushing out of my uterus!"
By this time, I was screaming and crying loudly. I didn't
care about being humiliated in front of Rocko 'cause my
struggle with Spade wasn't a secret anyhow.

"Shut up all that loud shit," he yelled back at me. I
could tell from the rise in his voice and the way his left

eye twitched that he meant business, but I was too far gone into my tantrum.

"But I can't. This shit hurts so bad! I can't believe you made me kill our baby. It's because of you I'm going through all of this in the first place. I swear to God I hate your black ass!"

Whap!

Spade sent his open hand right across my face. "I told your ass to shut the fuck up. And, bitch, who the fuck knew or not if it was mine? I don't want to hear another word about that flushed out bastard!"

It's like he smacked my cries back into my soul. What was coming out as loud wails were now swallowed deep in the pit of my stomach, along with the terrible cramps. Spade hated me.

The feelings were mutual.

Knock! Knock! Knock!

"Hey, man, I ain't trying to be in y'all business and shit, but let me holla at you for a second."

"This ain't the time, Rocko. Matter of fact, I'll hook up with you after I take care of my wife. You can hit chill downstairs until I'm done." Spade stood over me fuming. I could tell the postabortion problem was about to be second on my list of issues. He was about to whoop off into my ass.

"Naw, nigga, come on out or I'm coming in. Let me holla at you!" Rocko was persistent, and I was thankful. It was about damn time, and hopefully, this wasn't the calm before the storm of him murking me like he'd done Lezlee.

"Your ass better not move," Spade said as he grabbed and mushed my face before shoving me onto the bed. He watched me with an evil eye as he walked across the room. I dared not move a millimeter. "What up?" He cracked the door open to see what was up with Rocko.

"Shit, man, you on a nut. We been drinking, blazing, and popping off all day, so I know you amped up. Let me save you from doing something you'll regret tomorrow, and let's drop her off at the emergency room. Don't let ya wife die up in there." Rocko tried talking some sense into my husband.

"Did I give you slack about killing that Lezlee chick?" Spade shot back. "I've got this, dude. So like I said before, I'm good, and I'll get at you once I'm done taking care of my business."

He tried shutting the door, but Rocko pushed it back open. I still sat quiet as a church mouse waiting on the drama to unfold. The cramps were kicking my ass, but I knew disobeying Spade wasn't an option.

"No. But I know you're off on that shit, and I can't let you go out like that." He spilled Spade's business out onto the floor.

I was thrown for a loop hearing Rocko's words, but there wasn't a free moment to question him or respond. Spade looked beat at his own game, then turned to face me.

"Get your stanking ass dressed. If you ain't at the front door in three minutes, you're gonna bleed out on that damn bed and die. Either way, me and Rock are about to be out."

17

Rocko

Breaking every speed limited and traffic law, I flew through the streets of Detroit trying to reach Sinai Grace Hospital. Jakia was in the backseat curled up in the fetal positon crying while Spade barked orders into her ear. I never liked to play the middle man when it came to getting involved in their shit, but Jakia was more than just his girlfriend at this point. Spade had officially made her my cousin, so to some degree—I had to protect her like family.

"Yo, nigga, climb yo' ass back in the front seat at the next red light so we can finish getting blazed. Give her a break already," I intervened, then raised the Patrón bottle.

After the next half mile was up, Spade joined me in the front seat but didn't let up on screaming the rules Jakia had to follow over his shoulder. The few times I looked in the rearview mirror, she was nodding and wiping her face, recognizing his wrath. *If only Lezlee could've been just as compliant. . . .*

"Aye, Rocko, this is close enough. She can walk the rest of the way." Spade threw his hands up for me to stop the car.

I slammed on the brakes as ordered, even though I knew what was going down was wrong. We could've at least dropped her at the front door, but I wasn't about to go against my homeboy's wishes. I pitied Jakia, but it was up to baby girl to stand up to fend for herself. Unlike Lezlee, she'd been loyal to no limits, but every deed was in vain. Pulling my baseball cap brim down lower, I pulled off once Jakia crawled from the backseat and away from the curb. I made sure she made it to the vicinity of the hospital, but the rest was on her.

Jakia

Once Rocko and Spade sped off leaving me at the curb, I limped as far as I could up the walkway before falling into the flower bed. Thankfully, I was only at the edge of the parking lot when they dropped me off.

"Ma'am, are you okay? Someone call security," I heard a spectator say. "Ma'am, is anyone here with you? Do you know what today is? What is your name?"

Before I had a chance to blink or breathe, the same voice who'd called for help was now standing over me trying to see if I was coherent. "Yeah, I'm okay. I just lost my balance." I ignored all of his questions trying to stand up. I didn't know who he was, but I knew Spade's word was law—and that was not to get friendly with muthafuckas.

"No, no, no. Don't try standing up. Chances are, you'll fall right back down there. I'll come down there with you." The stranger was being far too nice.

"Please don't do that." I slid away from him. "I said I'm good." I frantically looked around for Spade. Knowing him, he was probably posted somewhere inconspicuous, watching my every move alongside Rocko. I didn't want to get caught talking to a stranger that wasn't on his roster to get set up, even though he was only trying to help me.

"Okay, not a problem. But please, just stay down there until security gets here with a wheelchair."

Through the cramping and discomfort, I looked up at the man noticing his soft features. It had been awhile since I'd encountered someone being genuinely nice to me. Even though I couldn't welcome it, the temporary feeling felt extremely comforting.

"Thanks, but you don't have to wait. I appreciate it, though." Still staring around in a frenzy, I was more panicked now than I was in pain.

"I could get in trouble for letting a pretty woman like yourself stay in distress alone. Until whoever you're waiting on gets here or at least the security team arrives to rescue you, I'll wait." I smiled at his compliment and generosity.

It wasn't long before a security guard came with a wheelchair and, as promised, the mystery man disappeared into the hospital. As they wheeled me to the trauma unit's nursing station, I regretted not thanking the stranger for being so kind and helpful. Who knew how long I would've been stretched out in agony in front of the hospital if it weren't for him calling out for help. I appreciated him for being my lifesaver, although I wasn't showing it.

"Okay, ma'am, you seem to be in pretty bad shape, but I have to ask so we can have complete paperwork, and I can get you the help you need. On a scale from one to ten, with ten being the worst, what's your pain level at?"

"A ten," I responded with no delay. "Please get me some drugs to knock me all the way out. I can't take this pain anymore!" I looked up at the nurse like a wounded dog hoping she'd pity me even more. I knew they saw cases like this all the time, but, of course, to me, mine was the most severe. My loads of mental, physical, and emotional abuse were killing me.

"We're going to take good care of you, ma'am. Don't you worry about that." She helped me out of the wheelchair onto a stretcher. "The doctor will be in momentarily, but I'll need to get some pertinent information from you as well as check your vitals. Let's start with your name." The hospital's intake staff was quick and efficient.

"Jakia Johnson." I leaned back onto the stretcher, thankful I was about to get the medical attention I was in desperate need of.

"And what brings you in today?"

I had to be careful about how I responded. Spade was specific in telling me to keep my mouth shut on anything outside of the botched abortion, so I couldn't throw any red flags out about me being a victim of domestic abuse and certainly not the deaths I've witnessed. "Um, I went to the clinic yesterday to start a medical abortion. Everything was fine until I inserted the final three pills this morning. They said I was supposed to cramp and bleed heavy, but I've been like this since early this morning. I couldn't take it anymore."

"Okay, relax. It's a good thing you came in. Let me get your blood pressure and an IV line started. The doctor will more than likely send for some pain medication for you," the nurse reassured me.

"Can the doctor be a woman? I've kinda got a thing about men doctors being all around me *down there,*" I lied, knowing it would be believable.

"That's understandable." She appeared to be relatable. "I'll inform the head nurse. They should be able to accommodate the request. Let's get started so we can get you more comfortable." She started the light exam but continued questioning me about the clinic, their procedure, how I inserted the pills, and what follow-up care I might've administered to myself.

I was truthful about everything pertaining to the abortion. Nerves will make you do that. I was scared out of mind that my body was fed up and ready to take itself out of the game. With Spade misusing me, forcing me to exploit myself for his gain, and me not knowing how to defend myself—maybe this was my body's way of saying, "Hey, bitch, this is it."

"Okay, Mrs. Johnson, the doctor should be in shortly. Please get fully undressed and put this gown on. Here's a bag for all your belongings."

I checked my cell seeing Spade hadn't called, then tucked it back into my purse. I didn't have any friends or family to call since he made sure to keep me isolated. So it was a time-out for having someone to help me kill time. Through the pain, I managed to get undressed and prepare for whatever procedures they had to do.

Knock-Knock!

"Yes, come in," I answered the taps coming from the other side of the door.

"Hi, Mrs. Johnson. I'm the emergency room physician, Dr. Wang. What brings you in today?"

Dr. Wang listened intently while I explained my experience and everything I'd told the nurse. After questioning me explicitly about their procedures, my internal feelings, and what follow-up care I received, she prescribed a drip of morphine, then put me on the list for the next available examination room. "Please get some rest, Mrs. Johnson. Something tells me you need it." She winked, then closed the door.

Once the morphine was inserted into my IV line, euphoria took over. I was doped all the way up. My eyes were heavy, the crucial pain in my abdomen was starting to subside, and for the first time in years—I felt at ease. This was the safest place for me to be right about now 'cause I knew Spade wasn't coming nowhere near it.

Juan

Sweating like the caged animal I was, I lifted my muscular body up and down doing a countless number of push-ups to let off steam. Time wasn't the real factor in this prison, but Jakia's well-being was.

"I see your counselor forced yo' hot-headed ass to find another way to let off steam." Gonz approached me on the yard.

"Hell yeah," I responded, leaping up to face him dead-on. "Anything is better than solitary confinement. I made every promise I could think of to change my act when I thought they were taking me back down to SHU."

"I feel that, man. In here, every move made is for survival." Gonzalo's words were always weighted. "It's best you're learning that now so you can use another prisoner to your advantage if and when the time comes. Never forget that behind here, we all operate by the barter system."

Gonz noticed me thinking over his statement, and then when I didn't respond, he continued.

"Well, here's a little news that might make your days here a little easier." Gonz put his hand on my back. "Your sister is back in Detroit along with those two men you wish dead."

He'd piqued an emotion and my response. "How long have they been back? Is she okay? Has your team seen that nigga Spade touch her?" Now, pacing the yard like a wild man, it was a good thing there was nothing but air to attack. If Jakia was back from her mini vacation not writing or emailing me, something must've been wrong.

"Wow, slow down, Coleman. My men only reported that they saw the people you described touch back down at that address. I've got them on the watch but not for your sister's personal bodyguard team. Their only purpose is to shoot and kill."

"Well, tell 'em to make it fast and make sure they spare my sister." I ended the conversation, then started back exercising.

Gonzalo wasn't accustomed to me being the one to brush him off. Usually, he manipulated or controlled the conversation. But I'd earned a shitload of stripes being locked down in solitary—he owed me respect—or at least space I needed to work through my built-up frustration.

"I'll see you later, bunkie." He turned and walked away.

Spade

"That's my bad for tripping out earlier. These broads got me on another tip." I took a cop apologizing to Rock.

"Real rap, it might be them laced blunts you keep blowing on. You know I'm gonna hold it one hundred with you no matter what—and yo' hand been showing. That Christmas cookie bullshit been having you do some real wild and sporadic shit lately. You've always been crazy, but I haven't been able to calculate your moves lately. Some shit don't seem right, bro."

The words coming out of Rocko's mouth might've been hard to swallow, but they needed digestion anyway. "Maybe I'll quit this shit cold turkey and leave it in the D when we pull out." Wishful thinking or not, I wanted to believe my own words. Crack was no one's friend and a hard monkey to get up off your back.

"Yeah, you can sell another nigga a boat and Jakia a bag of dreams. Me and you go back to diapers, and you've got that addiction shit from yo' moms, honest— no diss on auntie, you feel me?" Rocko was throwing jabs; nonetheless, it was an intervention I needed to hear.

"You're right. Say no more." I issued my flag of defeat to my cousin. I wasn't giving my Christmas cookie fix up anytime soon, but I made the promise to control it. Whatever that meant. . . .

We rode around the city chopping it up about old times while planning for our dip out of the city. Detroit had been our playground for doing dirt so long that it was gonna be sad saying goodbye. People who lived in the crime jungle either hated it or loved it, but surviving as delinquents made our value for the dirty D much more. I'd starved like a homeless man, then ate like a king—all within the same week hustling in these streets. Maybe after a few years passed, I'd be back to call it home.

The turnup at Rouge Park was unreal. With Belle Isle turned into a state park swarming with state police, every young black male and female stayed clear of even Jefferson Avenue. Downtown Detroit had become a mecca for businessmen, white folks, and new money. None of us underprivileged nonvoters wanted to be caught up doing dirt or made an example out of. A new day was rising in the supposed bankrupt city—one where the white man felt safe to show his face and return. I might've been deep in the streets looking for ways to fuck up, but even the shadiest criminal knew what was up.

Rocko cruised through the strip with the sounds on bang, the sun roof open, and the windows halfway cracked. Blowing out Kush fumes to pollute the earth, we blended in well 'cause everyone was getting doped up. By nature, I took in the scene and scoped people from head to toe. Everyone was out dressed in their best top-of-the-line gear, flossing in waxed up cars, and peeling off big bills from knotted stacks for freak dances. Even the ice-cream truck man stepped out in a pair of Red Bottoms. The Gator Capitol was truly the stunt haven, leaving Rocko and me like squirrels trying to catch fat nuts. The show-off didn't mean shit to us—the come-up did.

"Let's park, get lit, and watch them hot-and-ready THOTs." I pointed to a group of loose-looking girls on the prowl for attention.

"Fuck it, why not? I could go for some 'goodbye Detroit coochie,'" Rocko joked, turning the ignition off.

Within no time, I'd called a few chicks over and cashed them out in advance to get it popping. I loved a girl with a little ego willing to do strange thangs for chump change. The four of us got bent for hours. Dusk was setting over the park; however, the party was nowhere near over. Neither Jakia nor Tiff were on my mind as I got lost in the impromptu going away festivities surrounding us.

Blunt after blunt, plus two bottles of Patrón later, one of the girls was popping her hips on my dick while the other gave Rock some head. It was becoming hard to say good-bye to my hometown.

Rocko

I ain't had head like this since Lezlee. Baby girl was now just a mere memory while the new girl was serving me up. The guarded feeling of someone watching us was coming and going the more lit I got. And the sloppier the freak got with her head job, the more I was willing to let go. Gripping the steering wheel, I enjoyed the view of her bobbing for my nuts. When a strange feeling rushed over me, I looked up in just enough time before getting blasted. Before the li'l nigga in my peripheral even got a chance to let loose, I'd already jerked the gearshift into drive.

Pop! Pop!

The girls started screaming, and even Spade ducked when bullets flew, and I took off. Whoever ole dude was let off two shots aimed at one of our heads, but I'd already floored the pedal. I was a criminal by nature and a killer at heart. I always sensed when someone was close on the watch.

"Drive this muthafucka, Rock." Spade rose up from the floor with his pistol in hand. "I'm about to smoke these clowns." In the same minute, he was sending bullets out of the back passenger window.

Taking his lead, I flipped the glove compartment over and pulled my piece from inside. Aiming it out the window behind me, I let off my own round of shots until the clip was empty. Our efforts didn't stop them from ripping holes through my car, though. I felt the impact of each bullet tearing through the metal every time. It was easy to see Spade and I were coming up short in an area we were usually aces in.

The crowds of people who were once just living the vicarious life were now running for their cars, trucks, or some form of cover. With bullets flying in both directions, anyone could've been struck as an innocent bystander.

Pop! Pop!

Two simultaneous bullets shattered what was left of the rear windshield.

"Oh, shit." Spade ducked right before both girls rang the car deaf with their horrifying screams.

If I would've had bullets left, I would've blasted their trick asses and collected my money back. Nothing irked my soul more than a chick with no street intuition or mentality. As gutter as they got for a few dollars, they should've been more accustomed to hood tactics. And a shoot-out surely qualified.

I'd temporarily lost control of the car, almost swerving into a tree. It only took a split second to get right and gain our distance back on them. The police were nowhere to be found as I felt the car floating in the air from us going so fast. In all our years of doing crime, I was feeling strange on the opposing end this time.

"Cuz? You good? Don't tell me you caught a hot one," I shouted out into the car once my bearings were together.

"I'm straight, chief, but get us out of here quick. I'm out of shells!"

Without hesitation, I leaped the curb, hoping not to burst the tires, and then burned the grass up speeding toward the nearest main street. If these cats wanted me dead, they were gonna have to drag me up out of this car and send me to glory. I wasn't getting buried from a bullet to the head, neck, or back.

Spade

One minute I was getting the nut rode out of me—the next minute I was ducking and dodging bullets. Detroit was sending me off with a blast—if not in a body bag. My clip was empty, and the bullets I usually kept in my pocket had been replaced by my sniffing stash. On any other day, I would've brought the heat to the mark busters chasing us, but today, I'd fallen short.

Slouched down in the backseat, I held the door handle as Rocko manhandled the car in what had become a high-speed chase. Whoever was coming after us seemed to be the mob, 'cause they were coming extra hard.

"Hold on," Rocko warned, then turned on to Plymouth on two wheels.

When the car rested back on all four, he took off with the best effort he could make to get up out of Dodge. We were halfway to the freeway when we noticed the shooting stopped. All four of us rapidly looked around checking to see if the coast was clear. Like ghosts, what seemed to be an entire carload of shooters had vanished. Even the area seemed cool, calm, and peaceful.

"Did you ID them niggas, Rock? I wanna get back at 'em, dog." I sat up with a chip on my shoulder. There was no way I should've been caught without at least another round.

"He was a little Mexican cat," the random rat I was banging spoke up. "And they were driving a raggedy pickup truck that looked to be spray painted."

"Bitch, what? You saw him creeping and didn't say shit?" Before I could catch myself, I'd slapped her across the face.

"Damn, nigga, I was only riding you facing the back right before it all popped off." She grabbed her face with an unrelieved look in her eyes. "I didn't get a chance to say anything because it happened too fast."

"Well, what else did you see? And you better get to talking quick, fast, and in a hurry," I warned.

"Like I said, a short Mexican cat in a spray-painted pickup truck," she shot back. "It ain't nothing more I can say because it was nothing more that I saw. Matter of fact, you can pull over and let my girl and me out. I ain't with all this extra drama, especially since I've made enough money for the night."

"Not a problem." Rocko slowed down the Impala. "Hop y'all thirsty THOT asses out."

I took my place in the passenger seat; then Rocko skidded off into the wind. "Hey, nigga, what Mexican cats have we hit up? I know I been blazing that shit lately, but I didn't think it was iggin' with my memory that bad."

"We haven't; that's why I'm racking my brain. Don't get me wrong, I know we cut it thick with a lot of brothers east and west, but never into Southwest territory. This hit don't seem right to me if ole girl saw correctly. The way them cats was chasing us, it was most definitely on some retaliation type shit. But for what—I don't know." The wrinkles in Rocko's face were all the explanation I needed to show he was really at a loss for what just went down.

"I think it's time we make our way up out of the D sooner than later. The streets have died out on showing love and being fools." I wasn't trying to punk out, but getting popped definitely wasn't a feasible option.

"I swear I want blood shed over what just happened."
Rocko slammed his hand against the steering wheel. "If
I catch them fuckos before Jakia gets out of the hospital,
it's not gonna be a body spared."

"She won't be there long—" I was cut off.

"Trust, they'll be back." Rocko sounded sure of
himself and his words—all the while checking over his
left shoulder.

I dropped the subject because all things that should
be, will be. In other words, I was gonna let things play
out and be prepared if my gangster was tested again. On
the way back to my crib, we tried coming up with a plan
and a city we could touch down in. Atlanta and Baltimore
were the cities to choose from since they had room for
our reckless behavior. Cutting up was a must wherever
Rocko and I went 'cause that's the only life we knew how
to live.

18

Jakia

I could hear the monitors distinctly beeping in the background as my body began waking up. Since I stayed, I was hyping up my pain level, even though the aches were starting to subside, and requesting stronger narcotics so I could stay all the way doped up. Anything was better than being coherent in this cruel world. I'd gone through a boatload of tests and bloodwork and was awaiting the unfavorable results. Dr. Wang had already told me she was on the concerned side because my white blood cell count was high, which meant there was an infection in my body, and coupled with some of the symptoms I reported like constant sore throats and sore joints, the infection could be serious. I always thought I was in pain because Spade was beating my ass, and that I always had sore throats because he stayed choking me out. I couldn't help but hope those were the reasons for me being sick.

From head to toe, I felt slightly better, but my mind and spirit still felt flushed. What I was experiencing wasn't anything an emergency room doctor could fix. But that didn't mean I wasn't about to hit her up for a few scripts of anxiety and depression medication. The fresh abortion was a perfect excuse to cop enough pills for when we hit the road.

"I'm glad to see you're up, Mrs. Johnson," the same male voice I heard earlier returned. "How do you feel?"

"Much better," I said through squinted eyes. I was caught off guard yet happy seeing the same man in my room from earlier. He deserved a proper thanks for his pity toward me hours ago. Not having the distraction of Spade, I looked him dead in his face, then couldn't help but automatically feel self-conscious. I would've never felt less than gorgeous around a man so attractive if I was dressed to impress. However, I was laid up with a napped ponytail and no gloss . . . probably a basic bitch in his eyes.

"And about earlier—I'm sorry I came off like that. I truly appreciated your help." My discomfort in my beauty didn't prevent me from being nice. Blood gushed out of me as I repositioned myself trying to get comfortable. The nasty feeling made it seem like I was soaking through the sheets, so I jerked still for the remaining conversation.

"That's good to hear. You were in pretty bad shape, so they must be taking exceptional care of you." His statement was more like a question, but I nodded because either way, it was true. "Is there anything you need or is anyone coming to visit you that may need the schedule?"

His sudden burst of questions reminded me of how he introduced himself earlier, which wasn't by name or affiliation. I might've been in bad shape, but a fool I wasn't. "Okay, this is a bit much. Why are you being so nice? Who are you? What's your name?" Instead of focusing on his sexiness, it was my time to overwhelm him with questions.

"I'm Mr. Peterson, one of the social workers on staff here at the hospital." He walked over placing a card on

my temporary nightstand, then extended his hand for me to shake.

"Oh, wow, you're the sneaky type." I barely touched hands with him, and then rolled over to secure myself within the thin blanket. I needed a barricade for the bullshit of "good" advice he was getting ready to give me. Social workers were the worst type of people. It's like they felt their degree gave them the right to judge you. I felt stupid for initially being engrossed by him.

"Sneaky? What do you mean by that?" He appeared to be caught off guard as he smiled widely, seeming innocent.

"Nothing." Spade's strict orders were not to fraternize with any hospital employee more than necessary, only be treated by a female physician, and by no means do anything he wouldn't approve of that would find me in trouble. Talking to Mr. Peterson meant I wanted to feel Spade's wrath—and please, believe me, that was *never* the case.

"Aw, come on now. You can't leave a brother hanging after calling me out like that." He tried being down to earth. Fooling me wasn't an option. I knew being relatable was part of the job.

"And you should've started the conversation off earlier with you being a social worker."

He laughed, knowing I was right but continued to play me for more conversation anyhow. "What's wrong with social workers?"

I was played and opened up. "They're pushy as hell." I might've been talking, but each word I gave him was either harsh or straight to the point. I didn't want him to feel like I was welcoming of this conversation for real.

"That's because we do care, Mrs. Johnson. We wouldn't be in this line of work making pennies and dealing with horrible attitudes if we didn't have big, genuine hearts." The thick speech he was pouring on wasn't working.

I've had my share of shit bag state social workers when my mom was scamming the system for stamps and cash. They didn't care that catching her up in her fraudulent schemes meant I would go hungry. The same type of happy-face social worker came into our home for a routine evaluation, cited my mother unfit, and had Phoebe placed on probation until she cleaned up her act. Everyone knows a head can't drop their habits cold turkey, so she dropped the state aid, making Juan pick up the slack on his own.

"I'm not trying to be rude but can you let me get some rest, please? I'm feeling my body start to cramp again."

"People that start their sentences off with—'I'm not trying to be rude' usually are," he laughed, taking a seat in the guest chair across from me. "Either way, I have to do my job, Mrs. Johnson. I will be out of your hair as soon as you complete this questionnaire."

"Are you serious? I'm not about to do a questionnaire or be bothered with any of this." I copped an attitude again.

"I apologize but the doctor requested a social worker be assigned to your case, and you won't be discharged without being cooperative with me."

"Won't be discharged? You can't keep me here if I don't want to be kept." I bit my lip, hoping what I was saying was true.

When he saw the look on my face, he abruptly went across the room to shut the door. "I will be honest with

you right now, so you don't blame me later for being sneaky. They are concerned about your mental health and safety. How you answer these questions will determine your eligibility for counseling through the psychiatric ward of the hospital, in addition to many helpful services. Now, you don't strike me as a woman who has a mental health issue. However, you *do* strike me as a woman that needs a little support. No woman, especially one as beautiful as you are, should be sitting in the hospital alone. But that's just *my* opinion."

I blushed at his compliment but swallowed hard at the rest of information he'd just laid on me thick. "What's your first name, Mr. Peterson? If I'm going to tell you my deepest and darkest secrets, we must be on a first-name basis." I started to work him like Spade taught me to—a mark buster in the game.

"Xavier."

"Nice meeting you, Xavier." His name rolled off my tongue. "Let's start." I didn't have a choice, plus I felt slightly wooed.

"Not a problem. The first concern the doctor noted was that you didn't mention the handprint welted across your face."

Oh, shit, I'd forgotten all about that. Damn. Panicked, a lie couldn't come out of my mouth quick enough. Mr. Xavier Peterson's sneaky social working ass kept calling me beautiful even though I was sporting another one of Spade's bruises. If I didn't feel insecure, scammed, and uncomfortable, I surely did now. All of my emotions became overwhelming at once, signaling a rush of tears from my eyes. No matter how hard I tried, I cried my eyes out—draining a year's worth of hurt.

"It's okay, Mrs. Johnson. Crying is the first step you must take to heal. I promise you a safe zone in here if you open up—just take your time. I'm here to help." He spoke with sincerity in his eyes.

For once, I needed a man to be telling me the truth wholeheartedly. There was something about his words that made me truly feel safe, relaxed, and ready to open up. I hadn't felt this at ease since before Juan went to jail. Before I knew it, I had diarrhea of the mouth and was telling him everything about my brother and almost everything about my marriage with Spade, making sure not to incriminate myself. I sugarcoated the story when it came to me helping Spade set suckers up.

I led Mr. Peterson to think I was nothing more than my husband's bottom trick—not the slithering snake I'd grown to be from getting in bed with him. By the time I finished running down my life story, he was gripping my hand, apologizing for Spade's behavior. The expression on his face wasn't one of judgment, but one of pure shock and surprise. He was soft with me—something I wasn't accustomed to feeling.

"Wow, Mrs. Johnson, you've been pretty strong to have endured all that you have."

I looked up at him, staring into his deep brown eyes, and wished he could read further into my soul. "Are you sure? In my opinion, I'm actually weak as shit."

"Trust me, Jakia, a weak woman would've crumbled by now. Unfortunately, you've been built to fight. The hard part will be getting you to understand that you don't have to."

Juan

Since coming in from the yard, I'd been looking for clues in Jakia's inked stories. She always wrote to me three to five pages at a time but never once did she paint such grave tales until the last few. I couldn't wait until I got to see my family again. I tried emailing Jakia today at the last known address I had for her, but it returned as no Web address with that name was available. If they're back in Detroit residing at the same house, I couldn't understand why she hasn't reached out. Even in jail, Jakia and I were close, so I couldn't fathom a rational reason about why she'd break ties with me.

"My men went head-hunting today." Gonzalo walked up into our bunk disturbing me with good news—or so I thought. "They came close to taking care of your problem for good. Let's just say it won't be long before your problems are handled on the outside, my friend."

"Wow, they move quickly." I shouldn't have been surprised. "But what do you mean by 'came close'? What happened out on the streets, Ramos?"

"The charges are in the details. Let's say this—my men moved too quickly and sloppily and didn't execute. From where I come from, failed missions aren't accept-able. Rest assured, there won't be another fuckup from this way."

Jakia

"You haven't been talking to them cocksuckers, have you? It's crazy out here in the streets, babe." Spade sounded paranoid. "Me and Rock are tripping out here like who to trust."

Reclining the hospital bed back with a smile on my face, I was at peace with not having to deal with their drama. Both Rocko and Spade had Karma coming that was gonna be dealt honest, whenever it came. I was glad they'd dropped me off.

"Not more than I have to. They had a lot of questions, though, since the abortion was botched, and my face was red."

"What the fuck you mean botched?"

"Don't worry; they've taken care of it. I had an emergency dilation and curettage, which removed all of the dead baby from my uterus. Problem solved." I kept it gritty 'cause he always gave it to me raw.

"Hell yeah, that's a problem solved. So what time do you want me to pick you up?"

"Um, I haven't gotten my release papers yet because my bloodwork showed some abnormalities. Besides that, I'm still in a lot of pain and can't hold down food. I need this rest, Spade." I tried pleading with him.

"Fuck all that, Kia! I ain't got time for my wife to be laid up in the hospital with the streets retaliating. Did you not hear me when I said I got shot at last night? Me and Rocko are trying to get up out of here faster than planned. Tell that doc to fall back, and yo' ass better quit being a crybaby. You cramp every month, so this shit right here should be a cakewalk."

I fell quiet because I knew my wants and needs were of no real concern to him. When I heard taps on the door and it cracking open, signaling someone was entering the room, my voice came back as I tried to rush Spade off the phone. "I've gotta go; here comes the nurse."

"Naw, don't hang up. Keep the phone in your lap while they go over whatever bullshit scam you're running on them. You ain't slick, Kia. I know you trying to get a break from a nigga, low key. But let me be clear, there's no way in hell you're gonna walk away from a nigga living. Tell whoever that is you wanna be dis-charged right fucking now," he yelled loud enough for the whole hospital to hear.

I was so thrown off and in shock seeing Xavier Peterson standing by my bedside instead of the shift nurse, that I dropped my phone into my lap, when I should have hung up.

"How's the beautiful Mrs. Johnson doing?" Xavier asked sweetly.

My eyes bucked, and I was shaking. I was nervous as hell Spade had heard him. I didn't want him popping up here.

"Is that him?" he whispered extremely low.

I nodded with my eyes bucked out wide. My words were stuck in my throat as I listened to Spade yell my name over the receiver. I was so afraid that my heart was damn near pounding out of my chest. Spade was going to have my ass in a full-body cast—or worse.

"Hello! Jakia!"

Mr. Peterson grabbed the notepad from off my eating tray, then scribbled a message down for me, which read: *Calm down. I'm here, and I won't let him hurt you here. This is a safe zone.* It was clear he didn't know Spade.

I hesitantly picked the phone up and listened to Spade going ham before speaking. "Hey, babe," I tried playing it off. "I'm back."

"Hey, yo, Jakia, who in the fuck was that? You ain't hear me calling for you? I thought I told your ass no male doctors or nurses. I know you're not up in that hospital getting cocky and forgetting who the fuck I am." Spade was making me nervous through the phone.

"I told them, babe. That was my roommate's father." I shrugged my shoulders at Mr. Peterson as he laughed.

"Yeah, okay—I see you think a nigga is dumb. I better not find out you're lying, baby girl, or the repercussions are gonna be more than severe. Don't forget—you are skating free as a bird right about now, and I'm not the only one with my hands dirty," he spitefully reminded me of my involvement in crimes, which I didn't need—then the line went dead.

Even though I hadn't been the one to send someone for him, I knew what Spade's words meant, and that I better find a new way of living soon.

"Jakia, what did he say to you? Did he threaten you? Are you okay?"

Turning to Xavier with tears in my eyes, for a split second I regretted telling him anything about me, Spade, and even Juan—but then I found comfort in the fact that he knew. For once, I had someone to talk to that was totally on my side. "Please, can you find me somewhere safe to go that he can't find me?"

Spade

"Hey, cuz, you should take it easy on Jakia. Real talk, I don't think Jakia is the mastermind behind the hit on us today. If I would've known you were on that tip, I wouldn't have let you call her." Rocko was spitting some shit I wasn't trying to hear.

"The fuck is up with you always playing 'Captain-Save-A-Ho' for Jakia? In all of this shit, you should've learned your lesson. You advocated for her to go to the hospital, and then as soon as she's from underneath my thumb, gunshots fly. She has the right amount of bitterness for the right amount of reasons. Don't tell me shit about that gun play and chase we were lucky enough to live through being a coincidence."

"I'll give you that, it does seem odd." He nodded, then continued. "But doesn't it seem odd that right after Tiff threatened to have someone do you, someone actually *tries* it? In my opinion, you oughta be using some of that energy to check out her ghetto ass." Rocko had a point. His wise words had me thinking.

Without hesitation, I called Tiff to see how she'd play her attitude and position, but I was directed straight to voicemail. Her phone didn't even ring. Sitting back in the passenger seat, I was mentally fucked up not knowing which bitch had set me up.

Back at my house, Rocko and I swapped cars because the plan was for him to hit Southwest Detroit to find out information about that particular rusted, spray-painted pickup truck. We weren't worried about splitting up because if we weren't meant to meet our Makers, having company with one another didn't matter. Besides all that, I had to try touching base with Jakia and most definitely Tiff again. Rocko had my mind going. These li'l Mexican cats had me fucked up. And the girls I'd been controlling for the last year like puppets were starting to play back. Naw, I wasn't feeling the changing of the guards at all.

19

Jakia

Xavier was gone for the night, but all I could think about was how good it felt to have his calming presence and aura around. After dealing with Spade's alter ego for so long, this breathe of fresh air felt like heaven touching down. Mr. Peterson spent damn near his whole eight-hour shift within the small confines of my temporary hospital room listening to the horrific story about Spade's and my dynamics. I'd left out incriminating parts about myself—but had no shame when it came to dragging Spencer's name through the mud. I was fed up and fucked up behind the traumatic year of our relationship; and for once, it wasn't feeling like something I couldn't overcome.

Feeling the urge to pee, I slid my numb legs around and dangled them on the side of the bed in an attempt to wake them up. I'd been in this bed for so many hours, my whole body was restless, and my joints were starting to cramp up. Okay, get it together. You've had your body feeling much worse. After the two-second pep talk, I carefully stood up and dragged the IV pole into the bathroom with me. I damn near pissed on myself when I saw whose cold and menacing eyes were staring back.

"My sweet wife," Spade's voice was raspy and menacing. "It's time to check out of here."

"Sp-sp-, what are you doing here?" My words were caught deep in my throat as I stuttered. So much so, I couldn't finish the syllables in his name.

"Come on now, baby girl—you know me better than that. Let's be real. You knew I was coming when I heard that nigga in the background. Where's your roommate, by the way?"

Giving me the side eye, I bowed my head defeated to the lie. The single room I was set up in wasn't equipped to handle more than one person.

"See, that's why I need to keep my eyes on you. It's a wrap on this whole hospital bullshit." He stood up ready to make his word bond.

"But the doctor said I'm severely dehydrated, and she's unsure of some test results. Until I clear these IV bags and speak to her tomorrow, she said it's best for me to stay in that bed and rest." Trying to manipulate the situation, I didn't want to leave the hospital with this man I'd grown to hate. Not only was it against the doctor's orders, but it was also against what I really wanted. Love no longer lived in my icebox heart—at least not for Spade.

"This is not a game. Get this shit up out of you and let's go." He flipped the light switch on, then ripped the bandage off my arm. I yelped in pain, but he cupped my mouth closed, grabbed a towel with one hand, and pulled the IV needle completely out. "Hold this down on your arm. You know how that shit goes."

I felt like we were starring in a twisted remake of *What's Love Got to Do with It.* I was Anna Mae Bullock before she became Tina Turner, while Spade was Ike busting me straight from the hospital. Unlike the leading actress, however, I wasn't smiling looking forward to marriage. Dressed with my hospital gown underneath my clothes, I walked out of Sinai Grace Hospital only foreseeing hell.

"I ain't stupid, Jakia. I know you went to that hospital running yo' mouth like a wounded puppy." Spade chased me through the house yelling. "Who did you send after me and Rock?"

"I don't know what you're talking about." I continued to leap over furniture, dodging whatever household item he flung my way. "You're crazy as hell, Spade. I'm sick of you," I shouted to the high heavens.

The more I stayed from within his reach, the more infuriated he became. I was truly clueless about what he was talking about because there was no way he could've known about me and the social worker's conversation. Whoever went after Spade and Rocko came for retaliation owed from the dirt they did in the streets, not from me running my mouth.

Spade eventually tackled me from behind and served two quick punches to the back of my head. The impact from his fists made me see stars as I fell to the ground, then felt his weight suffocating me.

"Who in the fuck did you send for me, bitch?"

"I said I don't know." My lungs felt heavy from him sitting on top of me. "But whoever it was, I wish they'd come back to finish the job."

Grabbing the back of my neck, he lifted my head, then smashed it against the carpet with no remorse. "Well, since you putting death threats on people, how 'bout

I finish yo' brazen ass right here and right now? Fuck airing yo' ass out to the cops."

"Then I'll haunt you in your sleep," my words were muffled, but I refused to be silent.

"If you've never learned a lesson from fucking with me, Jakia—you'll learn tonight." He leaned up but kept his knee jammed in my spine.

Moments later, I heard him flick the lighter on, then smelled Kush buds burning. I closed my eyes and tried inhaling the little smoke he was puffing out, but the pressure from his knee had my chest caving in. Every time I moved, his knee dug deeper, and the pain became more excruciating. However, I still tried fighting to get up.

I should've sensed that was the calm before the storm. As soon as I blinked, I felt an indescribable pain, then felt Spade cover my mouth as I screamed. Right beside my ear, Spade put the fire of his blunt out. First, he kept tapping it against my skin, torturing me; then he laid it flat, smashing it down. I jerked and fought him off as hard as I could, but my weight was no match. Until he was done using my face as an ashtray, I was at his complete mercy.

Once Spade got up, making the sorry assumption that he'd won the war, I rose up swinging—with the same lighter he'd used to light the blunt. When my hand got close enough to his body, I flicked it on trying to set him on fire.

"Ah, you crazy bitch!" He jumped backward, finally moved by me taking a stance.

"You ain't seen crazy." I kept talking with no fear. With a hollow stomach to match my hollow heart, it finally felt good standing up to him. I swung at him two or three times the same way but came up short each time. He moved quicker than I did . . . Yet, the fact that I had him on the move meant I was scoring.

That night, I gave Spade the fight of his life. I didn't win by far and even caught a few smooth punches to the face, but at no point did I back down. Each time I fought back, cursed back, or stepped out of the passive position he'd created for me—he came harder with aggression to knock me down. All of the pent-up anger, pain, and hurt I'd been bottling up since watching the judge send Juan away was boiling over to a point where it couldn't be contained. For once in my weak life, I borrowed a lion's heart and stood up for myself. When the fight finally stopped, we were both icing cuts and wounds.

Spade

"While you're sitting over here looking like you want your ass kicked again, iron my outfit real quickly." I disrespectfully tossed my clothes at Jakia. "And make sure the pants have a crisp pleat."

"Naw, I'm straight on that. If you want a crisp pleat, the spray starch is underneath the kitchen counter." Jakia threw her hand up.

"See, all that talking back and newfound confidence you brought home from the hospital reassures me you were up in there singing like a canary." I took a step toward her as she took one back.

"Whatever the fuck ever," she raised her voice. "Do you know how stupid you sound? You make it known time and time again that I don't have anyone but you. Yet, somehow, I've rallied up a crew in just a few hours to take you and Rocko down."

I went to respond, then cut my own self off. Phoebe was somewhere cracked out on the corner while Juan was serving charges on my behalf. The only person she could count on was me, and I'd made it be that way. Yeah, she might've had a point.

"Exactly, Spade." Jakia began her grand finale like she could read my mind. "You sound dumb as fuck."

The more I let her words sink in, the more I realized she wasn't trying to pull a slick move. But being cut from an "I don't give a fuck" cloth, I still continued to go hard on her until I felt justified.

Ring-Ring!

"What up, Rock? Talk to me," I answered the phone, then tossed my clothes back in Jakia's face whispering she better get to ironing.

"Have you talked to Tiff yet? I did a ride through around Southwest and peeped that pickup truck. Let a few heads lingering tell it, that's the Ramos gang. It's a family of little Mexicans who run the Southwest territory hard. I don't know how we've got beef with them cats, but they're trying to settle the score permanently."

"Naw, I haven't talked to her but pull up on me so we can shoot a move over there. It's weird she ain't trying to holla back at me." I knew she was probably trying to avoid me so I wouldn't force an abortion on her.

"A'ight, I'm about to pull up and blow. Come out, so I don't have to be in between some more of you and Jakia's drama," he requested; then we hung up.

I was amped up and ready to go. Now that we had a name to go with the men who had a hit on our heads, I felt slightly more at ease—but more revved up to pay them back. Rocko and I might've been leaving the D initially because of the shifty way the cops "solved" "The Motor City Murder," but at this point, I felt like we were getting run up out of our hometown. No matter how I flipped it, running like a coward wasn't sitting well with me.

I snatched my clothes back from Jakia, then rushed to get dressed. "Aye, ma, when I get back here—you better not still be acting like a bitch," he growled. "Me and Rocko are about to get in the streets to see who gunned for us. If any roads lead us back to you—it's gonna be a muthafuckin' problem." I didn't care how much I've already tortured Jakia in the past; she was gonna catch death like Lezlee if she'd crossed me.

"Just like you sounded dumb as fuck then—you sound dumb as fuck now," she flipped me off, then went into the other room.

Rocko

"So, what's the word? How's Jakia, or did you even ask?" Rocko questioned me as soon as I got into the car.

"Ain't nothing new up with her. She's still playing sick like there's something wrong with her. I ain't buying that bullshit, though. This hospital saga is only a stunt for Jakia to get some attention and pity. Ain't nothing wrong with her that my Christmas cookies can't fix." He spoke like he was plotting.

"Damn, cuzzo, don't do her like that." I tried taking up for his wife once again. It was starting to become a trend. "Anyway, let me not overstep my boundaries. Let's make our way to Tiff's so we can get our stash and see if she knows who these Ramos cats are."

Jakia

The moment I heard Spade and Rocko burn rubber out of the driveway, I jumped up from the bed and ran through the house searching for my purse and the minute phone. My heart and mind were heavy, and the only person I knew who could help sooth it was Xavier. I knew he'd come into the hospital room expecting to see me but ending up being surprised that I'd vanished. I had to let him know I was still among the living and all right.

I peeked out of the blinds checking to make sure Rocko and Spade were still gone as the phone rang in my ear. I hoped I'd memorized the right number, and if so that he answered. I needed his help badly, and I was hoping he was still willing to offer it.

"Hello, Mr. Peterson," he finally picked up. His strong voice soothed me through the phone. I closed my eyes and pictured his intriguing eyes.

"Hi, Xavier, this is Jakia from the hospital. I was just calling to check in and let you know I was living." I tried to sound sweet and sexy, but I was tense and on edge. I'd never been on the phone with another man in the house Spade and I shared before, but apparently, there was a first time for everything.

"Oh my God! I'm so glad you called. I was more than worried about you when I got to your room and saw you'd unexpectedly disappeared. The nurse's station didn't have any record of you checking out. How's everything? Why did you leave like that? Are you okay?" I could tell he genuinely was concerned.

"I didn't have a choice but to leave like that. Spade showed up, ripped the IV from my vein, then escorted me back into the free world." I left out the part about why I didn't fight back or get someone at the hospital to help. Spade was absolutely right when he said my hands were just as dirty as his. There was no record of him holding a gun to my head to being a setup queen. To anyone looking at it, it seemed like I was a willing participant. I didn't know how I was going to do it, but I wanted to clean my hands of all the bad I'd done alongside Spade and Rocko.

"Well, what now? Are you safe? Do you need my help? Even if he's being gentle now, Jakia, he will turn on you the second he feels you're weak or fooled again." Xavier tried coaching me on a play I was already ready to execute. "You know that man is a monster, and that you deserve better." Xavier had no idea that he didn't have to coach me out of the relationship anymore.

"I'm ready to make a move, Xavier. No, I'm not safe. Yes, I need your help. And I already know things will never get better between us." I answered all of his questions. "Of course, since Spade popped up unexpectedly, I didn't get to research any of those shelters you told me about. Can I just pop up, and can you give me a few addresses?" I wanted him to offer me more, but I'd take living homeless if it meant not getting burned with blunts and beat senseless again. Every day with Spade was less livable than the day before, and at this point, I didn't want to die with Spade. He was so heartless that he probably wouldn't even give me a funeral but just ditch my body in somebody's trash rubble. I couldn't wait to get away from the monster that I'd been calling my man.

"Are you really ready to leave, Jakia? I mean, honestly, in your heart, can you leave your husband and not go back? That means you can't give in and go back even if he comes running after you with empty promises. If so, I will help you leave and get a fresh start in life. I've told you from the moment I saw your beautiful face that I would be there to help you, and I meant it." I remembered back to being stretched out on the concrete in front of the hospital, and the moment before when Spade told Rocko to pull over so I could roll out of the backseat. The memory of it was bittersweet but also strengthening.

"Yeah, I am. I can't take it anymore. This nigga's love is gonna send me to the grave, more so than it already has."

"Okay, then without a doubt—my offer is still on the table. I will help you in any way possible. What do you need me to do right now?"

I breathed a sigh of relief and started moving through the house so I could hurry up and get out. Xavier's willingness to help was vital to me leaving. "Oh my God, thank you! Please keep your phone on and your volume up. I'll be calling you as soon as I'm able to get out of this house." I whispered like I wasn't in the house alone.

"Okay, I will. And be safe. If you need me to help you get out of there, I'm here."

"Okay, thanks. I'll be in touch shortly." I hung up and ran upstairs.

It was time to make a break for it. I grabbed my oversized Gucci purse and proceeded to stuff it with a few pairs of panties, Spade's cash stash for emergencies, and some toiletries to start me off with. Then I threw a few outfits and shoes into the matching backpack and slipped it on. This wasn't nearly a sixteenth of my belongings, but without a car, I had to travel light. I wasn't sure I even wanted any of the things I'd accumulated with Spade because they would be memories of our relationship—or the crimes we committed.

I don't know why, but when I went to walk out of our bedroom, I felt strings tugging at my heart. Then my mind started playing tricks on me, and I started hearing Spade's and my voice arguing, him yelling, and my screams begging him to have mercy on me. I couldn't leave without doing something rebellious. I dropped my bags, darted toward the closet with hate in my heart, and started ripping everything off the hangers that were Spade's. I got his favorite shirts, pants, jogging outfits, and sneakers, then tossed them all into our bathroom and poured Clorox bleach all over the top of them. I emptied the entire bottle, then grabbed some other random bathroom cleaning solution and dumped all of it in as well. The smell was so strong and overpowering that I felt light-headed and had run out of the bathroom before I passed out. I wanted everything of his ruined. If I could've gone out like *Left Eye* and set flame to his shit, I would have, but it would've been pointless without him here in it to burn to death.

As soon as I was done running through the house and breaking random shit, including all of Spade's video game systems, I peeked through the blinds so I could see which neighbor might tell Spade I'd left. Although I'm sure they've heard my pleas for help, they've never sent the cops, so I figured they'd tell Spade I ran away too. I knew his nutty ass would be on some door-to-door shit trying to find me. I wanted a clean break.

It might've not been the best decision, but it was my only decision, and I didn't have time to plot out another. There were only two doors I could go out of: the back door and the front door. The front door had my neighbors outside of it chatting, and my back door was dead bolted with a gate up to it because Spade wanted to make sure no one ran in on us. The only move I could make was out of the window. And since the alley was in the back of the house, I was able to run down it and get away from my block unnoticed.

The wind felt good hitting my body as I ran from the house I'd been a prisoner in. I'd learned to live with Spade for so long, that I didn't think I'd ever have the courage to break free, but I was, and I didn't have any intentions on being weak enough to run back. I sucked and swallowed on the brisk air as it hit me in the face like it was giving me some energy. The farther I got away from the house, the freer I felt. But each time a car zoomed past or revved the engine in my ear's hearing, I feared it was him and ducked down, petrified of getting caught. My heart sank when I saw a bus pulling up to its stop. I didn't know its final destination, but I knew it was going away from the house. Reading the route listed on the front screen, I pulled my cell out and called Xavier to let him know how to trace me. Had I had more than this bootleg Obama minute phone, I could've used my GPS or Maps application to lead me to his house.

"Oh my God, thank you," Xavier answered after the first ring. "Jakia, I've been worried since we hung up. Are you okay?"

"Yes, yes," I gleefully replied. "I'm at a bus stop waiting to get on. Stay on the phone with me until I load so I can ask the driver where it ends or at least where you can pick me up." I ran down the route information on the front of the bus hoping it was enough for him to start searching for its route.

"I'm already on Google looking up the information. I'll meet the bus in transit, if necessary. I'm proud of you, Jakia. You're doing the right thing because you deserve better. This Spade cat is nothing good for you or your future."

His encouragement was giving me the extra juice I needed to keep pushing. Up until meeting Xavier, I hadn't had the ego even to think I could survive on my own. "I know; trust me, I do. But it feels good to hear you say it."

The passengers in front of me were taking too long to load the bus, but I knew I had to be patient and wait my turn. Nervousness was bubbling inside of me, and I wanted to scream out that I was on the run from my abusive husband and could they speed up, but I kept quiet as one of the women ahead of me wrestled with her toddler children to get them on the bus.

"What's going on, Jakia? Everything good?"

"Yes, I'm just waiting to load still. I'm so scared." I pulled my shirt up over my nose and ducked my head down so my face wouldn't be so out in the open. I felt too vulnerable.

"Okay, be calm. Try to breathe and watch out for your surroundings. I don't want to scare you, but you're going to have to stay alert." Xavier was trying to coach me through the process. I was glad he was on the phone.

"I'm trying." I tried breathing, but my chest was heavy with anxiety. "Do you need help, miss?" I tried asking the lady, but her kids were yelling too loud.

Right before I got the chance to put my shirt back up to my nose, I looked up . . . to see Spade staring me directly in the eyes. "Oh my God! Oh my God! No! Please don't let this be happening right now," I cried out.

"What's wrong? Jakia! Talk to me!" I heard Xavier screaming to me through the phone, but my mouth felt paralyzed.

All I could do was hang up so I could run. I clutched my purse and took off. People were honking their horns as I ran across traffic carelessly and recklessly, looking for a way to get away from Spade.

"Hey, bitch, I'ma kill yo' ass," Spade yelled his threat across traffic.

Pop! Pop!

Yes, indeed, this nigga wanted my blood on his hands because he didn't care who saw what he was doing. Spade was sending gunshots in my direction, and if he caught up with me, I knew he wouldn't spare my life. I'd come too far to give up without going all the way out.

"Jakiaaaaa," his voice echoed.

Pop! Pop!

Please don't let him kill me. Please don't let me die. I've come this far. God, if you ever wanted to show up, make it now!

I'd run out of my shoes trying to get away from the man I used to want to spend my life with. Glancing over my shoulder, I saw he'd bust a U-turn already and was trying to maneuver through traffic—all while sending bullets flying into the air. I cut down a side street, then ran into an abandoned house. It was full of trash and smelled like death, but I was out of options and needed to hide from Spade. Xavier had been calling me back-to-back since I'd hung up, but I was too scared to slow down so I could answer the phone. I couldn't wait to get him back on the phone.

"Hello, Xavier, sorry," I whispered in a panic as soon as he answered. The phone didn't ring all the way through once. "Spade saw me and was shooting at me as I ran. I'm scared. If he finds me, he'll kill me, I know."

"Shooting at you? Man, this punk-ass nigga needs to see a *real* man," he shouted. For the first time in any of our interactions, I heard his gangster match Spade's. I didn't know what to think of that, but this wasn't the time to ponder it or have an opinion. "Do you know where you're at? I'm already in the car and will come straight to you."

I gave him the address, then begged him to be fast. "But be careful. You don't know my husband—he's crazy as hell," I warned him.

"Jakia, whatever you need, please tell me, and I'll help." His voice sounded just as passionate on the phone as it did at the hospital.

"Trust—your husband doesn't *want* to know me. Keep your phone on and answer it when I call. I said I'm coming to help, so I'll be there. If you weren't on a minute phone, I'd let you breathe into my ear until I arrived." He made me giggle.

We hung up, and I kept still and quiet until he pulled up. I don't know why God was blessing me all of a sudden, but I hoped he kept doing so.

20

Spade

I tapped my gun against the dashboard while blowing on a Christmas cookie blunt. I know I told Rocko I'd cut back, but I'd save that feat for the moment we'd pull out of Detroit. I needed to calm down because it was about to be off with everyone's head in this neighborhood because no one had any answers for me. A woman on foot running—someone should've seen. But everyone shrugged me off claiming not to have seen a thing.

I went from being pissed than a bitch that Tiff wasn't home to being relieved. Had she been, I would've never come back home or caught Jakia red-handed running away from me. But now back to reality, that meant there were *two* bitches loose in the world for me to catch up with.

"Where you at, cuz? I just got done riding up and down about twenty blocks, plus going inside a few stores, but I'm coming up dry." Rocko delivered me bad news.

When we got back to the house and realized she'd dipped out, I jumped back into the shot-up Impala, and Rocko got in his truck to help me search for her. Jakia being missing was a bad thing for both of us. Just like Lezlee snitching to the dead man's wife would've been a negative domino effect on us too.

"About to be on my way to the crib. I've been creeping around too but ain't come up with shit. At this point, she better stay tucked away 'cause I'll probably pop her disloyal ass."

"Chill out, cuz. Something tells me she won't be gone for long. These streets will eat her up. I'm about to fall through." Rocko ended the call. I hoped his words were true.

I didn't like the sense of control I was losing. Cuzzo was trying to play things down, but raw reality was staring me boldly back in the face. There was no doubt I felt Jakia was responsible for them random Mexican cats trying to gun Rocko and me down. At this point in the game, you couldn't tell me shit differently. Now she held the fate of Rock and me in her hands since Lezlee was already a goner.

In one quick motion, I wiped my nasal passages clear, then snorted the fine white powdery substance off my steering wheel. The instant high felt just as good as coming. So much so that my eyes rolled to the back of my head as my body craved to enjoy each moment. "Jakia, my sweet baby, Jakia," I moaned out into the car still in disbelief she'd gone against the grain. Expected or not, I was fucked up.

The more the high settled in, the more I wanted to sniff. Jakia might've been missing, but this coke-a-licious goodness was taking her place. My reflection through the visor mirror was hard. My eyes were bloodshot red, and the white residue from the continued snorting I'd been doing was caked underneath my nose. Wiping it way, I put a few droplets of Visine into each eye, then pulled away from the corner I'd been posted on.

Back at the house with enough time to check for Jakia's damage, I saw that she tried pulling a *Waiting to Exhale* scene by a bleaching a few of my clothes. I didn't let it fuel my anger though 'cause she'd pay for it later, for sure. Other than that, she hadn't taken much of anything, so I knew she'd be back. There's no way she could survive out there without any money, necessities, or my strong hand to keep her in check.

The few dollars of my pocket change she'd swiped wasn't going to get her more than a few extra value meals and a couple of nights at the Days Inn—at best. I knew Jakia. And as many nights she's spent around here nursing bruises, she wasn't about to take the struggle of the streets. Phoebe had given her enough of being poor growing up. If I cared to think about it in the morning, though, I'd ride through her old hood to see if she was that desperate.

I stripped down to my drawers, then grabbed a bottle of Moët from the fridge. Guzzling from the rim, I walked through the house with my piece in one hand and the bottle in the other. If Jakia was low-key hiding, she wouldn't be for long. I knew better than that, though. I'd seen her get ghost with my own two eyes. Hell, baby girl damn near committed suicide in traffic trying to get away from me. The high had me twisted, but I wanted more.

I dumped another line of coke onto the windowsill and snorted it off hard. Since I didn't have Jakia to work my anger off on, my secret, pricey drug would have to do. The higher and drunker I got, the more enraged I became. I couldn't believe she had the audacity to leave a nigga out here bold.

Instead of taking another sip, I tossed the champagne bottle into our glass living room table. The sound was

piercing as the glass shattered and flew across the room.
A few pieces cut me in the process, but I was floating
off coke and aggression—nothing mattered. Having this
emotional reaction was something new to me. I couldn't
help but to spaz out. "If you want out, bitch, be out," I
shouted into the empty house, stepping over broken
glass.

I took two steps at a time up the stairs, burst through
the bedroom door, and began giving Jakia exactly what
she wanted. Pulling all of her clothes from the closet and
dresser drawers, I was going mad crazy tearing up the
expensive things I'd allowed her to floss. Had it not been
for my setup skills, she would've still been living bold
with old-head Phoebe's ass.

"You ain't flossing nothing for another nigga that I
made possible. Fuck you and him with a sick dick," I
shouted, throwing a tantrum induced by both emotions
and drugs. Shoe boxes and old shopping bags fell from
the shelves, and that's when I stumbled upon the one
thing I'm sure Jakia didn't mean to leave behind. My
eyes lit up like a kid in the candy store as I raced to read
Juan's letter to Jakia from prison.

> *Jakia, baby sis . . .*
> *Thanks for the cash on my books. But I'm so
> sorry for sending u to that bitch nigga. It was hard
> reading the type of shit u out here doing.*
> *My word, when I'm out, he gonna have 2 explain
> his beef with u. I swear to Allah I'm gonna take
> care of shit, sis, better than b4. I been learning shit
> in here no man can take away, and fuck that nigga
> for putting his hands on u.*
> *I wish him death b4 I get out cuz payback gonna
> be a bitch. Have u seen Momma in them streets? I*

*gotta get my whole fam right. Be strong, sis. I talk
to my lawyer in a few days to give up Spade and his
ho-ass cousin.*

*4u, I'ma let the grain hold itself down and come
out like a snitch. I love u, sis. It's cool. Ain't no man
worth my time. Be strong 'cause u got that Coleman
blood.—1*

Juan

"I oughta kill her ass." I threw the letter down, not
believing what I'd read. I looked at the date seeing it was
a little over five weeks ago—before we'd even dipped off
to Monroe or gotten married. That means Juan has seen
his lawyer, divulged whatever information he was going
to use as leverage, and could even be out by now. *No
wonder Jakia seemed so comfortable coming at me like
the little gangster I've trained her to be. She thinks Juan's
dumb ass is coming home. . . .*

Jakia obviously told Juan everything she could regarding our relationship, and he was sitting up with nothing
but time on his hands taking it personally. If that nigga
thought he was about to send me to the pokey on an old
charge, he'd end up shanked in the showers first. I was
sure there was somebody from the hood locked down
who wanted their books kept filled for handling his rat
ass.

Rocko was on his way, but I couldn't wait for him to
arrive to enlighten him about Jakia and Juan. We had
to figure out a game plan to take care of Juan sooner than
later. Just as I got ready to hit "call" on my cell, my text
notification went off.

Tiff: What up, nigga? You been trying to get at
me?

Before I could send a response to check or question her about her whereabouts since I was suspicious about her being with those Ramos cats, she texted me again. And this time, it was along with an attached picture.

Tiff: I was at the doctor about our baby; doesn't he/she look cute?

I opened the photo mail, saw the sonogram, then felt foolish for believing she'd set me up. The more I studied the blurry gray, black, and white photo of what looked like nothing to me, I knew it meant the world to Tiffany. In other words, this baby meant she'd eat for eighteen years with no worries. Tiff wasn't stupid enough to have me murked, knowing I wasn't a man with a life insurance policy. To her, I was better alive than dead.

Instead of taking another hit of straight coke, I lit a flame to a Christmas cookie blunt and tried to get my mind right. Tiff was indeed gonna keep the baby, Jakia was in the air, and these Ramos cats were on my head. I should've been trying to piece the puzzle together of why they were trying to kill us and for whom. Instead, the harder I thought, the harder my dick got. I needed to release a nut, so maybe the tension within my body could lighten up. I texted Tiff back.

Me: Make your way to my crib. It's 100.

She must've had the phone in her hand because she texted back before I could set the phone down.

Tiff: Don't play, nigga. Pregnant pussy is the best pussy, and my hormones are raging. I want it with you. Don't gas me up.

Me: No games. Nothing but porno-type fuckin'.

Tiff: OMW.

The thirst of some females didn't amaze me. Tiff knew how I rolled and didn't give a fuck. It was Jakia who needed a reminder of who was boss. When the doorbell rang ten minutes later, I jumped up and pulled my dick out—fired up and ready to get my dick glazed.

Jakia

I was quiet the whole way over to Xavier's house because I didn't know what to say, how to act, or even how to breathe. I was so used to Spade controlling every part of me, that I didn't necessarily know how to be Jakia without him. Xavier kept asking me if I was okay, and I kept nodding that I was, but I knew the social worker in him sensed the truth.

Xavier's condo was definitely a bachelor's pad, but it was nice, nonetheless. It was furnished with oversized brown leather furniture in the living room, with a flat-screen television that had to have been seventy inches. It took up half the wall it was mounted to. I wasn't judging, though. It felt good to be free from Spade and around a man that was gentle.

"Wow, you watch a lot of movies." I tried making small talk about the large DVD collection that was lined up on a shelf underneath the television.

"Yup, I do. And I can't wait to watch a few, or two, or all of them, with you." He smiled and rubbed the center of my back. "I know you're tense, Jakia, but I just want you to relax and make yourself comfortable. Are you hungry? My food is way better than that hospital garbage we were forcing you to eat."

My stomach grumbled right on time. "Some food would be wonderful, as you heard," I laughed. "And thank you again for welcoming me into your house. It's very nice."

"Don't thank me, Jakia. You're more than welcome, and I'm sure I'm going to enjoy having you around."

"Okay, but, um, do you think I could take a shower or bath? Being stuck in that abandoned house made me feel icky and dirty." I'd been feeling like my skin had been crawling since I first went into the uninhabited house.

"Of course; you can take a bath or shower. You can take both if it'll make you feel better. Please don't be shy about asking me for anything. Right this way—let's get you settled in."

I followed behind him and took in the few pictures he had hanging on his wall. None of them looked like ex-girlfriends, but family members, because he wasn't cuddled up with any of them women. I figured they were probably his mom, grandmom, aunt, and favorite cousins. Some of them were even group photos.

Okay, Jakia, stop reading into this man's personal life when you've barely got a life. I thought about my diagnosis and fought back the tears. I wished I would've met Xavier a very long time ago—when I had time to be treated right.

"Okay, here's the bathroom. The towels and extra toothbrushes are in the linen closet in there, plus feel free to use my deodorant, soap, or anything else you need. I'll be in the kitchen fixing us something to eat. Then, maybe we can crash in front of the TV and watch a movie?"

All the time I'd wasted fighting back my emotions had been for nothing. I couldn't hold back the overwhelming feeling of relief anymore. I leaned in and hugged Xavier as tightly as I could. I could tell he was caught off guard, but he still put his arms around me and hugged back just as tightly. My body melded into his because it felt secure and trustworthy, a feeling I realized I'd never felt with

Spade, even when we'd first started fuckin' around, and I thought I loved him.

"Are you okay?" he asked.

"Yeah," I kept my face pressed to his chest. "And I know you don't want me to keep telling you, but thank you so much for everything that you're doing for me. I don't care how many classes you took to earn your degree. You have no idea how it feels to be abused or rescued. I won't even say I can pay you back because I'm sure that I'll never be able to at this magnitude." My stomach fluttered as I opened up to him.

"Wow, you're going to have me crying." He pulled me in tighter. "I can't imagine what you went through, but I know I'll do my best to protect you from ever going through it again. And I promise I don't need you to thank me again. People who truly do nice things from their heart don't require residual cheers from a person. Everything is going to be fine, Jakia." He gently kissed my forehead and wiped away my tears. "I know you're worried and relieved at the same time, but trust me when I say that it'll get easier by the day."

"The last man I trusted tried killing me."

"And the next man you trust will save your life." He lifted my chin and made me look him in the eyes.

"Meet me in the kitchen when you're ready, but please take your time. You can feel completely at ease to move at your own speed around here. My guest room is down the hall on the left. I'll leave the door open." He left me alone but feeling extremely secure.

I stripped down naked and was forced to remember I hadn't finished bleeding. I didn't know if Xavier smelled it or not, but the amount of old, dried up baby blood was kind of funky to me. The doctor said my body should be back to normal within a couple of weeks, which was too damn long for this nastiness, but it was normal for a woman's body to take this much time to heal completely. I took the sanitary napkin off, wrapped it up in a bunch of toilet tissue, and then put it in my clothes to help mask the smell. I was going to ask Xavier for one of his tee shirts and some jogging pants so I could get rid of the clothes anyway. They'd be too big, but that would be better than wearing some dirty clothes that smelled of trash.

I remembered reading about stress creating more blood and clots, so I climbed in the shower and spent a full forty-five minutes scouring my head and body. In my mind, I was trying to wash away the sins I'd committed with Spade. Xavier was promising to help me start a new life and save me, and I wanted that dream to come true more than ever. His words made me feel stable, while his touch made me feel secure. He was giving me a reason to smile, and when I thought about it, I hadn't ever had a reason before to smile. I was way too vulnerable.

Once I was done with my shower, I cleaned the bathroom back up the way I found it. I then tiptoed down the hallway to the bedroom Xavier said I'd be staying in and found total tranquility inside. A few candles were burning that smelled like they were vanilla scented, light jazz playing through the television, and a note on the pillow saying his house was my house. I had a grin plastered on my face that was a mile long. *So this is what it feels like to have a man cater to me. . . .*

Knock-Knock!

"Are you okay in there, Jakia? There's no rush—I'm just checking on you," Xavier continued to be a gentleman.

"I'm more than okay. You set it up in here so nice." I was careful not to say thank you again. "I'll be out in a few more minutes," I responded, then put a little pep in my step. I smiled, knowing he was truly concerned about me. Xavier was something new, and I liked it—a lot.

"Okay, think about what type of movie you want to watch. I have everything from comedies, to dramas, to documentaries, to horror flicks." I could tell he was eager to spend time with me too.

I had some Bath & Body Works lotion in my purse that I rubbed over as much of my body as I could; then I finished the rest with a bottle I'd found in Xavier's cabinet. I was happy he didn't have a funky men's lotion, but some Cetaphil. Xavier already knew I'd need something to put on, so he'd laid out a few pair of jogging pants and shirts on the bed, along with socks. I swear this man was more thoughtful than I think I'd be if I were in his shoes. After I swooped my hair back in a ponytail, I put on some concealer to help mask the dark circles underneath my eyes and some lip gloss on my crusty lips. *Damn, I've gotta get to someone's spa.* I hadn't felt like a bad bitch since going to see Robert Taylor. Once I was done throwing my woe-is-me party, I finally made my way to the front room where Xavier was returning to the kitchen.

Seeing him with his back slightly turned, I admired his side profile and became attracted to the idea of having him as my man. Everything about him was appealing to me. As he prepared a meal for us, I stood in the shadows and watched him move in the kitchen with precision. Never in my relationship with Spade had he cooked for me. It was always me slaving over the hot stove, then getting slapped up over juice. Xavier was surpassing every desire of a man I'd ever imagined. Spencer only kept me locked up in a nightmare.

"Whatever you're cooking up smells delicious." I finally walked into the kitchen to join him.

"And you're looking radiant," he said, looking up, making me blush.

I didn't feel sexy, pretty, or the least bit attractive; but the way his eyes danced across my body made me feel beautiful. The only experience I had with men was when it came to me setting them up. Without my makeup, game plan, or my mentality set to rob him in mind, I'd morphed back into the innocent girl who once lived under Phoebe's roof. "The room was set up very nice, Xavier. Thank you so much." I tried breaking the ice.

"No worries, you're more than welcome. I insist that you make yourself at home."

"Why are you being so nice to me? I mean, as a social worker, I'm sure you run into women who need help all the time. Do you help them all?" I noticed that at first, I sounded ungrateful, which was the furthest thing from the truth. And even though I called myself cleaning it up, I still stumbled upon a good question.

He laughed, then walked around the kitchen counter to stand beside me. My breathing intensified the closer he got. "I help everyone that crosses my path, Jakia. It's my job, yes—and one I love. However, I don't invite just anyone into my house. I figured you'd be a beautiful touch." He leaned over, kissing me on the forehead. Shivers went up and down my spine. "You've been trained to doubt your worth for too long."

The rest of the night, we watched movies, told jokes, and even played one of his video games, *Call of Duty*. It was true what he said about how killing the bad guys would make me feel better. I didn't want the night to end, but his eyes were getting heavy, and so were mine.

Spade

"Welcome home, daddy. I know you feel how juicy this grapefruit is for you," Tiff panted.

She was right. This pregnant pussy of hers had me busting nuts back-to-back. "If you got room to talk, I ain't fucking you right."

"Then I guess you better get to fucking me better."

Tiffany had no idea how damaged my ego actually was. For a split second, my mind went blank; then it filled up with images of Jakia and ole boy from the hotel room. Then images of Jakia taking it from the back like Tiff was now doing made me snap. With my wife gone, that meant I couldn't have my cake and eat it too. And that's all a nigga ever wanted. Running my hand down Tiff's face, my intentions with her got colder. "Take your hands and spread those phat-ass cheeks," I commanded, about to give it to her rough and raw. Since she was already pregnant, there was no need to use a rubber.

"Hmm, you know how I like it, daddy," she purred, then followed my orders like a true freak would.

You might think you know. I wrapped my hand around her flowing ponytail, envisioned she was Jakia, and pounded my meat damn near into her womb. "Is this better? Huh? You want it harder? Fuck you how?" I was dogging her pussy like she was a stretched-out street-walker. The more she moaned, the more I ripped off into her relentlessly until she flooded Jakia's and my bed with an orgasm.

"Get up and clean yo'self up," I ordered her. "And help yourself to whatever's in the closet that's Jakia's. I'm about to roll me up a fat one."

Her eyes lit up like they should have. Jakia's wardrobe was grade-A, top-of-the-line. From all the money we got from setups, she stayed in the latest gear. I walked out of the room and heard movement downstairs. Until I saw it was Rocko, I thought it was those Ramos cats, and I was ready to bust shots.

Rocko

As messed up as it was for Jakia to dip out on Spade right after I helped her nickel-slick ass out of a hard spot, I couldn't blame her. My cousin didn't have the good sense God gave him. Matter of fact, within the last couple of months, I've wondered if he was even blessed with common sense. Yeah, I had my wild-out moments and could bash a nigga's head in with no remorse. But Spade was turning into a lost cause. I didn't know what smoke and mirrors game he thought he was playing with me, but I knew about him snorting. Spade thought his newfound love addiction for the white horse wasn't gonna be his downfall, but I knew better.

A few miles from where Spade and Kia lived, I bent a few more blocks and kept my eyes close to the lit-up buses that rode up and down the street. Since Spade and I pulled back up from a dummy mission to Tiff's, my gut feeling was telling me our search was in vain. Shit was crazy. With these Ramos cats on our head and Jakia blowing in the wind, ain't no telling what was about to hit the fan next.

This whole life I was living was starting to get played out. The thrill of setting fools up was still there, but being twisted up with Spade's messiness was getting to be too big of a risk. Now that Jakia was out in the world with a chip on her shoulder, I couldn't settle 'cause I had a feeling some more trouble was about to come our way. Stopping traffic, I crossed over two lanes, made a Michigan-left, then sped over to Spades. It was time to either tighten up our camp or for me to make a solo move out of Detroit.

I whipped up in his driveway. Spade's car was pulled halfway on the grass with Tiff's put-put parked closely behind his—but my manz wasn't answering any of my calls. This was the exact messiness I was talking about. We hadn't dealt with one situation before he was stepping foot into another one. True enough, Spade never stopped dipping off in Tiff, but this wasn't the time—most certainly not the place—to be getting down. I kept calling his cell but wasn't getting an answer, but when I finally turned the radio down, I heard loud screaming and moaning coming through the cracked window of a room.

"Damn, where's this nigga's spare key at?" I mumbled and rambled through my middle console for the key he'd given me when I was temporarily living at his crib.

Once I finally found it, I casually let myself in—and walked straight into a mess. There was broken glass splattered all across the living room, plus the pungent smells of weed, crack, and sex. It must have been from another drag-down fight between him and Tiff because the glass wasn't there when we first realized Jakia had disappeared.

"What up, cuz?" Spade nonchalantly came down the stairs and stepped over the broken glass to get to where I was standing.

21

Jakia

"Stop! Spade, please, let me go," I yelled.

"I'll kill you even in your sleep, bitch." He stood over me with a pillow.

I woke up screaming at the top of my lungs with sweat pouring from my face. I could barely breathe as my eyes fluttered around the room, trying to figure out where I was.

"Jakia, what's going on in here? Are you good?" Bursting through the door, Xavier had a pistol in his hand and was waving it around the room. "Do I need to peel a cap off into a fucker?"

"I was having a nightmare." I finally sat up clenching the covers. "I don't think I made the right decision. If Spade finds me, he'll kill me—no questions asked."

"Shh," he tried calming me down while lowering his weapon. "I won't let anything happen to you. As long as you're here, you're safe—trust and believe that."

When I woke up a few hours later, the sun was shining in the room, and Xavier was asleep in the chair across the room sitting straight up. I remembered why he was here in the first place and felt bad for having him be uncomfortable for even one second on account of me.

The more I watched him sleep, the more attracted to him I became. His chiseled muscles bulged from inside the wife beater he was wearing, and by the way his Hanes lightweight pajama pants were laying, I saw he was working with a large load. I bit down on my lip and gasped, totally intrigued with his morning hard-on. Whenever I was done bleeding, if he was still around, I was gonna enjoy his dick down, I'm sure.

"Good morning, beautiful." He opened his eyes at me, staring.

"Good morning. I guess I've just been busted," I blushed.

"Indeed you are," he smiled, then moved to the side of my bed. "But that just means I don't have to hide my full-blown interest in you."

Leaning over kissing me on the forehead, the light moans I'd been holding in escaped my mouth, then were trapped again but by his tongue. What seemed like a life-time of happiness but was only a few moments, we kissed like reunited soul mates. When things started getting hot and heavy, I pushed him back and reminded him of why I was in the hospital in the first place.

"Stupid me," he rose up. "It's okay because there'll be plenty of time to make you come after you heal." He shocked me by his bluntness. "But listen, that reminds me of something we need to talk about. The doctor you saw in the emergency was very concerned about you leav-ing. She needs to speak with you about some of the test results. I'm about to call in so I can spend the day with you . . . Maybe you should speak with Dr. Wang."

"Sure, I might as well know all the things hanging over my head." I got up and followed him to his phone.

***

Each second of the time that ticked past was a blur. Xavier called off from the hospital to babysit me, even though he refused to call it that. And I'd left messages for Dr. Wang but had yet to receive a call back. We were playing the waiting game for her to reach back out—and for Spade to make a move. He hadn't called the Obama phone yet, which was odd for him to have not done that.

"Let me give you a massage. I can tell from the way your face is balled up that you're tense." Xavier shook me from my thoughts.

From the time his eyes opened, he's been waiting on me hand and foot, plus putting forth every effort possible to make me smile. I should've been jumping for joy that I'd connected with a kind man who seemed to be interested in me, but my soul couldn't settle. The more flashbacks and nightmares I had, the more I battled with staying. Nothing could take the edge off my fear of Spade finding me or this fairy tale not being mine to claim with Xavier.

Ring-Ring!

Xavier moved from making my burdens melt away to the phone, and then was calling me over to speak with Dr. Wang.

"Hi, is this Jakia Johnson?" she sounded professional, even with her accent.

"Yes, it is," I replied.

"It's against policy for me to deliver results over the phone. Can you come in? Today, if possible." She sounded like the matter was more than urgent.

"Of course. I don't think you've given me a choice since you sound so upset and all," I honestly responded.

By the time we hung up, Xavier was holding me up. I didn't know what results were waiting on me at the hospital, but it didn't take a rocket scientist to figure out they weren't good.

Rocko

Tiff gave me her house key, so I went to her crib and came out with Spade's and my stash. My mind was still twisted around the letter and our follow-up conversation about Juan. I didn't know if Juan was out, if he had snitched already, or if Jakia really did tell someone else about how all three of us have been making a living.

If Jakia was helping Juan, who was snitching to the police, were Spade and I gonna end up facing hard time? Spade might've been the person Juan was serving time for, but I was just as guilty as an accessory, plus I carried plenty of bodies more on my own tab. Wasn't shit looking bright but our move up out of here.

Walking to the car, I jumped in and quickly lit a blunt. The game plan was for me to meet back up with Spade and Tiff at his crib, but I couldn't help but contemplate making a different move. Since I had our entire stash, I didn't need Spade to start off brand new. I'd been loyal to him thus far, but the levels have changed now.

Pulling out of the driveway, I headed in the opposite direction of Spade's house. Fuck family—I was gonna go against the grain. So caught up in my tyrant thinking I was outsmarting my partner in crime . . . I didn't sense someone in the car with me until the hollow tip of their pistol was touching the side of my cranium.

Pop! Pop!
Pop-Pop! Pop!

Jakia

The inside of the small room Dr. Wang had me sitting in while I waited on her made me feel like I was in a psychiatric ward. The walls were cocaine white and bare. Besides the two chairs Xavier and I sat in and the desk, there was no other furniture. And the only window in the room had the shade pulled down so no sun could shine through. If I wasn't about to receive bad news, it sure felt like it.

"Thank you for coming in, Mrs. Johnson," Dr. Wang greeted me. "And hello, Mr. Peterson. I see that you're still working with your client even on your day off." The sarcasm could be heard in her voice as she stared at our interlocked hands.

Xavier shifted nervously in his seat, but I responded, unmoved by her attitude. It might've been frowned upon for him to fraternize so closely with patients—or has-been patients—but I was only there for test results. I had enough confusion and drama in my life, so I didn't need to add her criticisms and judgments to the list. "Um, my stomach has kinda been in twists since our brief conversation earlier, Dr. Wang. Can you just give me my test results?"

With one hand, Xavier rubbed, then braced my back; and with the other, he allowed me to squeeze it tightly. In spite of me holding my breath waiting on Dr. Wang to start talking, when she finally did open her mouth—I felt the same way about her like I did about the judge who sent Juan away. She was sentencing me for more than ten years—for my whole fucking life.

"I'm sorry, Mrs. Johnson, but from the blood work we've pulled, you've tested HIV-positive." Handing over the paperwork so I could look myself, I reached for them and felt Xavier drop my hand.

"Are you sure, Dr. Wang?" Surprised and looking back and forth between her and me, Xavier's expression told his thoughts—he wasn't fuckin' with an infected girl. I couldn't blame him, though. Why should he shorten his life because mine had an expiration date?

"She's more than welcome to get a second opinion. Until then, there are support groups here at Sinai, but treatment shouldn't be delayed." The more Dr. Wang tried making me knowledgeable about the disease, the benefits of a lifestyle change, and how it was my responsibility to inform all sexual partners that I was carrying was a law I better abide by, the more I wanted just to get buried right then.

"Thanks—or no thanks." I snatched the folder of information from Dr. Wang's hands, then stood up. I rushed out of the office as she was still talking, letting Xavier finish the goodbyes.

Two seconds of putting my head down ready to throw a pity party, I took off running down the hallway to the stairwell corridor so I could beat Xavier to his office three flights below. If I was carrying HIV, there were only two people that could've given it to me—Spencer Spade Johnson or Robert Taylor.

Once reaching the office Xavier shared with two other social workers, I slowed down my pace, then got my composure together so they wouldn't expect me of anything suspicious. They acknowledged my presence when I walked in but kept busy at paperwork. Grabbing his keys from his jacket pocket, I clutched them tightly, then walked out just as coolly as I'd crept in. Spade had trained me well in being slick.

When I got outside, I leaped in Xavier's car, then reached in my purse for the blunt I'd rolled to calm my nerves after I heard the news. Doctors didn't call you in for lollipops and flowers, so I knew shit in my life was about to hit the fan. I just didn't expect it would be this bad.

"Jakia, hey, open the door." Xavier had caught up with me and was at the side of his driver's door—now mine.

I didn't give him a chance to dismiss me. I didn't give him a chance to take back all of the things he'd promised me just days before. Instead, I pushed my foot all the way down onto the gas pedal and steered clear of killing anyone until I reached Spade.

22

Juan

The Night I Took the Blame . . .

"A'ight, sis, don't talk me to death. I know you don't like Rocko and Spade, but that's how I've been lining my pockets and throwing you a few dollars." I laced up my shoes tighter, ready to hit the door. I loved my baby sister, but I wasn't trying to hear her yapping.

"You're gonna learn your lesson with them, Spade. They ain't nothing but bad news. The whole hood talks about them."

"Bye, Jakia. I'll see you when I get back." I hugged her, then bounced. I didn't need her killing my vibe before meeting the fellas.

As soon as I hit the block, I greeted everyone, then made my way to where the cousins told me to meet up at. Whenever we robbed someone, we'd meet up right before, and they'd give me the details for the plan. You might as well say I work for them, but I was okay with that. I had to start small in order to get big.

"Where is yo' ass off to?" Coming out of the alleyway, Phoebe cut me off in midstep. "Don't ignore me, boy. Where is yo' ass off to?"

"None of your business, Phoebe, so back up." I pushed her out of the way, but not hard enough for it to be considered a push. Dirty, smelly, and a crackhead, Phoebe was still my mom.

"Everything you do until the day you die is my business, Juan. Now, give me a few dollars." She put her hand out, breathing and heaving in my face.

"You're such a nuisance." I dug in my pocket, putting a ten dollar-bill in her hand. "Now, take yo' ass home and get high in the basement so at least someone will be there with Jakia." Moving to the left to get out of the way and on about my business, she wasn't satisfied with the money, so she jumped back in my path.

"Oh naw, boy, you don't get out of answering me that quickly. Thanks for the ten spot, but where are you going?"

Realizing that she wasn't going to stop pestering me, I chose to answer her so I wouldn't be late. If Rocko and Spade left me out of the robbery, I was gonna be hotter than hell. "Out with the fellas to make a few more of those ten spots you're thankful for. So move." I pushed her again, this time with a little more strength.

Phoebe stumbled, caught her balance, then sprang right back in my space. "You need to stop fucking with that crew 'cause they're nothing but bad news. They ain't doing nothing but using yo' gullible ass," she spat. "If anyone needs to be heading home, it needs to be you."

"Okay, if you feel like that, give me my damn money back," I challenged her opinion. I knew she wasn't getting ready to feel so strongly about what she was speaking when her crack cash was on the line. And I was right.

"You must be a damn fool for real if you think I'm giving any part of this ten dollar-bill back. You just paid for my knowledge and wisdom. Matter of fact, gon' and give your mother every dollar in yo' pocket so I can really take you to school."

I huffed and hung my head low in an attempt to gain some chill. She was testing my patience, and I was two seconds from snapping on her like a stranger and in a bad way. "Look, Ma, I'm going whether or not you like it. I'm tired of listening to whatever you've got to say. And I'm close to giving you two quarters to beg into a dollar. So for the last time, gon' about your merry way and spend that ten. We're done."

"Well, if you want to be a fool, be my guest. I've been on these streets longer than you've been born so going against what I know won't turn out good for you," she spoke behind my back.

"Don't pick today to start giving advice and paving the way. I ain't trying to hear that shit now." I threw the peace sign up, then took off jogging. Since she'd made me late meeting up with Rocko and Spade, I had to make up for lost time.

Not long after that, I learned my mother was right. I learned she knew the streets better than I did. But the ego I had thinking I was a man couldn't allow me to bid out wrong.

Present . . .

Damn, I wish I could go back to then. I'd snatch the ten-dollar bill out of her hand and buy Jakia and me some food or something for the night. But unfortunately, only the rich can turn back the hands of time. I blamed myself constantly. Because of my constant bad decisions, my sister has been suffering like a prisoner too.

However many years I had to serve in this rotten prison would be a cakewalk with my sister safe and sound. Since I knew there was no way in hell I'd be the man to protect her on the outside, I was certain I'd be Gonzalo's punk in here if necessary to ensure Jakia remained okay. It was a sure thing Phoebe wasn't gonna be able to do that. I'd failed my family as a man. It was a good thing I'd met Gonzalo to stand up where I had failed. His family—his soldiers—were the only links I had to the world outside of the barbed wire fence and double-cemented walls.

"Count time! Count tiiimmeeee!"

Jumping up from the bed standing straight up stiff as a board, I'd fallen asleep reading Jakia's letters over and over again and was now replaying them back.

"Yo, bunkie, I've been waiting on you to get up," Gonzalo spoke low. "My crew handled Rocko; left his head bleeding out on the steering wheel. Spade is next. He's as good as gone."

"Damn, say the word on that." I contained my excitement only because of the circumstances.

"If nothing else, bunkie, my word will always be one hundred."

23

Jakia

I had a lot on my mind. A whole lot on my mind. But I wasn't about to sit up with no hospital psychiatrist pouring out my soul or trying to make sense of it. I'd been a battered woman for too long, and it was time to pay a muthafucka back. I was getting ready to serve my husband and his right-hand man up with a round of bullets that would hopefully send them straight to hell. It was gonna be funny to see their heads turn and the quiet girl finally getting one in. Rocko and Spade have used me for too long, and although Rocko didn't put his hands on me, he allowed it and even watched it. I wanted them both to pay in pain.

Well, they say you save the best for last—and this was getting ready to be the farewell of a lifetime. Hearing that I was HIV-positive rocked my world to the core, and it became crystal clear that even though I didn't want to die with Spade, I already had. The loyalty and love I had for his evil, malicious, and devil-hearted ass is the reason I'm supposed to take medication for the rest of my life—you know—*before* I die.

Rick Ross's *No Games* was giving me the right amount of juice to go in as it played through Xavier's factory speakers. Hell, I had nothing to lose. The setups, brutal beatings, gruesome murders, my unborn baby that I was forced to abort and damn near died while doing so—and now my last saving grace in Xavier—Spade had even taken my soul from me. I couldn't believe the amount of deceit, betrayal, and battles I'd lost in the name of love. And I couldn't think of one thing I gained.

I gripped the steering wheel roughly, clearly not giving a fuck. I was doing twenty over the speed limit when I saw the suburban police swerve out of the parking lot they were hiding out in with their lights and sirens on, but I didn't slow down. I turned the music up and drove faster.

"Please, pull your vehicle over. Please, pull your vehicle to the right," one of the officers commanded over the loudspeaker as they began to pursue me.

"Not till I have another dead body under my name, you rat pigs!" I screamed out inside of the window referring to my involvement with the Robert Taylor case.

I was breaking every traffic violation of the Michigan Department of Transportation, but that was nothing compared to the felony I was about to commit.

Cars swerved to avoid a head-on collision with me, horns were blaring from irate drivers who were held up by my reckless driving, and metal-to-metal noises could be heard from other vehicles crashing into one another. I was causing total mayhem. Fuck the law. Their hands hadn't served me any justice.

"Yeah, that's right. I'm taking y'all asses on a ride today."

At this point, I had strength and courage. I was relentless. The feeling was bittersweet, however. With me knowing my time in this world was now on an official countdown, I couldn't live within the celebration of my freedom because I wasn't really free. I couldn't let Spade live with me dying. I couldn't let him beat me to death. If it weren't for him being so evil, so selfish, so manipulative, so hateful, so fucking spiteful—I would at least have pieces of a life to put together. Without this deadly diagnosis, I could at least try my chances at real love with a real man.

After almost a mile more of havoc, I was coming up close to my turn. I only had one more traffic light to get through, while at the same time getting myself some space between the squad cars behind me and me. There were now two, and I'm sure there were probably more within my route to cut me off. I wasn't about to let my moment be short-lived, though, which is why I was refusing to pull over. The bitch that's been embedded within me wants to come out swinging and go down in glory, and I knew they'd arrest me or at least detain me until Xavier got here to get his car and gun.

Hitting replay on Ross's track and turning the volume up to the max, I checked my rearview mirrors and took off up the road on some *Grand Theft Auto* shit. With my back and neck pressed against the seat, my foot pressed all the way down on the gas pedal, and both my hands firmly gripping the wheel, I had damn near did a donut in the middle of traffic when I hopped the curb and flew over the median.

"Oh, muthafuckinggggg shittttttt!" I screamed out, swerving off the median and into the middle of traffic.

The light had just turned, and cars were starting to cross over, unknowing of the high-speed chase that was going on. It was a sea of horns and curse words as they tried not colliding into me as I tried getting control of my vehicle. As soon the car was on all four wheels, I bent the corner and pushed the speedometer back up to the max.

"Yes, yes, yes." I was panting, hoping they hadn't seen me turn or dip off into the alleyway. I'd gained some room in front of them when I hopped the median, and they didn't.

I finally burned rubber and turned on to the usually quiet street I'd been making a home for Spade and me for so long. A feeling of pure hatred came over me as all the memories of our relationship rushed back into my mind. I'd been a fool for so long that waking up was turning into a nightmare. My head was pounding, my heart was racing, and even though I was trying to be hard core—my body was trembling.

The fairy tale I ain't never had with Spade could no longer be denied—not even to myself. I've spent so long trying to make-believe that I was happy that it was hard for me to admit that I was purely miserable. His coward ass was about to feel my wrath, though. I couldn't wait to show him how much of a bitch he'd turned me into.

"Is this a joke? Spade must think my love for the last year has been a game! What is this trick doing at my house? Oh—his ass fa'sho got it coming!"

My heart nearly jumped out of my chest at the company being kept in my house. Spade's car was pulled halfway on the grass with Tiffany's car close behind— almost touching his bumper. I was overcome with rage, although I really shouldn't have given a fuck. I should've been happy that she was willing to take over my problem, and that his attention was focused on her.

They kicked it heavy before I came into the picture. And obviously, they ain't slowed nothing down. "Okay— bet, that bitch must die too." I thought about all the times he paraded her around me. *Dirty dick-ass nigga probably got this HIV shit from her. He fa'sho is about to feel my wrath now.*

I knew I wouldn't be able to successfully get out all I needed to say once I jumped out of the car with my unexpected police escorts on my tail. I was sure they'd be cutting back in on me shortly. Backing all the way up in my neighbor's driveway across the street from my house, I threw the car into park and reached for my phone. My fingers were trembling as I dialed Spade.

"Please let this nigga pick up. Please please please!"

"Hello," he answered like wasn't nothing up.

"Straight-up? It's like that? You've got that bitch boo'ed up in my house?" I was caught up in my feelings ready to explode. I guess deep down inside, my heart still pumped with love for Spencer, even though I wished upon a star it didn't.

"Your first priority shouldn't be worrying about Tiff. It should be that body bag the coroner gonna carry you away in for telling your ho-ass brother all of my business. I got y'all little letters." Trying to get out of Dodge so quickly the other day, I'd left the letters, and obviously, Spade was now in possession of them. "You walked up out of here on your own—so anything that goes down up in here ain't got shit to do with you. I should've never stopped fucking with her to fuck with yo' ole weak ass anyway."

Although sirens were blaring off all around me, I got quiet on my end momentarily, then the courage inside of me detonated. "Yeah, well—I'm calling your bluff. You pulled my bitch card on the wrong day. What I only had for you, let her know I got for her too. Come on outside with y'all *HIV-carrying* asses."

I ended the call without waiting on his reply and set out for complete mass destruction. I opened Xavier's glove compartment, where I'd stashed the gun, pulled it out, and stroked it like it was a dick. I needed the chrome piece to let it go like a muthafucka. I felt justified to kill. Rage was pumping through my veins.

"Forgive me, Father, for I'm about to sin!" I hopped out of the car when I saw Spade and Tiff emerge from the house. They didn't know what car I was in, so I had a few seconds to run toward them before being spotted. I was out of hiding like fuck the world.

It was muthafuckin' Jakia Time!

"Oh, hell naw, bitch!" Spade yelled.

"Yup, say that shit again." I extended my arm and let 'em rip.

Pop! Pop! Pop!

"Detroit Police! Cease-fire." The cops swerved up and started jumping from their squad cars. By this time, there were about five squad cars for little ole me.

I was running on rage and all the vivid memories of me getting my ass beat. My adrenaline was pumping. I was so focused on my mission that I couldn't think or see straight. I wanted to kill him so badly that I kept walking up on him, with my chest pumping up and down, wanting him to see all the agony I'd been holding caged inside of me for years. I finally felt cocky and in control, and even had Tiff backing down. She hadn't even come too far from off the last step of the porch.

"For real, bitch? So you just gonna shoot me and think shit's sweet? You better make sure a nigga takes his last breath." Spade continued to mock and torment me.

I didn't respond. It wasn't that I couldn't. It was that I knew Spade didn't take anything I ever said seriously or to heart and wasn't about to start now. My words weren't going to make me feel better. Just like him beating up on me made him feel like more of man, me getting a few licks in was about to make me feel less like a battered woman.

"I've been down with you for too long," was all I kept saying. Over and over and then louder again. "I've been down with you for *too long*."

Knowing I was just about out of time because the cops were eventually going to detain me, I ran toward Spade like I was going to shoot him but slapped him straight across the face with the pistol instead. Like the piece of shit man he was, he cried out in pain, grabbing his face in agony and disbelief. I hit him with so much strength, built-up anger, resentment, and agony that I felt his bones crack. The feel and taste of his blood on my skin and in my mouth was the best feeling I've felt in my entire life. Lifting Xavier's gun back into the air, I kept pulling the trigger and hoping it would unjam.

Spade was stumbling toward me with his fists balled up, ready to strike me one last time. "I should've killed you when I had the chance to, bitch."

"I've been down for too long." I was crying.

"Drop your weapon, drop your weapon," the cops shouted out, but it was too late.

Pop-Pop! Pop-Pop-Pop!

A firework of gunshots sounded off and lit up the community. There were at least ten rounds shot off before silence fell over the block. Spade's body got filled up with bullets. His entire chest was ripped apart. I smiled as his body hit the ground. But that celebration was short-lived as well.

Pop-Pop!

I heard another two gunshots sound off, then tires screeching off.

"Aaah!" I screamed out in excruciating pain. A pain that I'd never felt before.

Spade's Karma had become my Karma. I hadn't even been the one to kill Spade. Xavier's gun never unjammed. But I'd taken two bullets in the back. My whole body felt like it was on fire as it fell to the ground beside Spade. I didn't deserve for the cops to shoot me.

"Oh my Godddddddd, Spade! Noooooo." Tiff's shrills filled the air, reaching the high heavens. "Help my baby daddy! Do somethingggg!"

Did this trick just say "baby daddy"? Did he have me kill my kid only to breed with her? Tiff's words haunted me as I started drifting out.

I saw flashbacks of Juan and me walking to school together, him bringing us burgers in the middle of the night because Phoebe sold all the food stamps, and me on the abortion table the day I allowed my child to be killed.

"We need the paramedics! Ma'am, shots were fired from a vehicle we have a lead on. Help is on the way. Hold on." A cop kneeled beside me, trying to give me hope, but I wasn't buying into it. The same helpless feeling I've had all my days with Spade, I was having them now. I knew this was it for me.

"Fuck her," Tiff shouted. "Why are you trying to help her? *He's* the victim. *She* hit him. Take her psychotic ass to jail and save him. My baby needs a father." Her shrills sickened me.

The only valuable lesson I've learned from the many ass beatings I've taken from Spade was how to move quickly. And that I did.

Squeezing my eyes shut for strength, I fought through the burning sensation my body was feeling and reached up for the cop's hand. She was a woman, so she sympathized with me, even muttering more words of hope like—she "understood" and "it was gonna be okay." I hated to play into her sympathy, even worse if it was empathy; but my desire to get revenge was too strong for me to ignore. I didn't feel like I had anything to live for.

"It—will—never—be—okay." It hurt to stutter as I grabbed for the officer's weapon and pulled the trigger two quick times.

"Noooo," the lady officer cried out and tried grabbing her weapon, but it was too late.

I'd shot directly into Tiff's pregnant belly, making her body hit the ground as well. If I could have it my way, despite what my destiny was about to be, no seed of Spade's was going to thrive, be born, and walk this earth. However, before I could blink to see what Tiff's fate was, another officer came from the back and rammed my face into the ground, then threw my arms behind my back.

"You have the right to remain silent. Anything you say can and will be held against you in a court of law," his raspy voice spat into my ear.

With the police officer's knee in my back, it was even harder for me to breathe than it was when my back first took the bullets. I can't even say he was unnecessarily rough, because even on the ground and down, I'd still mustered up enough spunk to fight. I've been trained to keep going despite my wounds. Spade wasn't even living to see what he'd made of me. His body was lying lifeless not too far from me.

"Do you understand these rights?" The officer questioned me, starting to handcuff my wrists.

I couldn't answer. I was getting weaker. It seemed like I was drifting further away from all the commotion going on around me. I didn't want my ending to be written like this, but I guess my mother was right.

"Well, fuck you too, Jakia. The same grave you want me in, you'll fall in before I will." I heard Phoebe's voice and words from the day I left her to be with Spade.

The officers were lifting my eyelids and looking for me to give them a response, but I didn't have any control whatsoever over my body. I didn't even have enough strength to beg God to have mercy on my soul before my whole world went black. I loved a man more than he loved me . . . and it sent me straight to the grave.